JILLIAN DAVID

AUTHOR OF *IMMORTAL FLAME*

Crimson Romance

New York   London   Toronto   Sydney   New Delhi

CRIMSON
ROMANCE
Crimson Romance
An Imprint of Simon & Schuster, Inc.
1230 Avenue of the Americas
New York, NY 10020

CRIMSON ROMANCE and colophon are trademarks of Simon & Schuster, Inc.

ISBN 978-1-4405-8940-9
ISBN 978-1-4405-8941-6 (ebook)

Acknowledgments

Thank you again to editor extraordinaire Gwen Hayes for helping take this book from its earliest stages to something so much better. Thanks also to Devin Govaere, Bev Rosenbaum, and Annie Seaton and her mystery editing associate for improving this manuscript. And special thanks to Julie Sturgeon, my editor at Crimson, who will return an email literally at any hour of the day. It's still a mystery when she sleeps.

I appreciate my supportive hubby who is still gunning for a short, bald guy to grace the cover of one of my novels. Next novel, I keep telling him.

Chapter 1

Dante entered his seventh bookstore to case since he'd arrived in Portland, Oregon. Smoothing his Armani slacks, he folded himself into the worn reading chair at Cover to Cover Books and fingered the worn chintz fabric. He relaxed, taking in the clusters of scarred wooden chairs around oddly paired tables, several upright upholstered chairs like the one he occupied, and three threadbare loveseats. The smell of old books and wood polish lulled him into a state of nostalgia for quaint shops from his homeland, Sweden. The images almost distracted him from the mission. Almost.

Of course, he could have telephoned each store, but a strange man asking for Jessica Miller might have driven her to ground. That might not even be her name anymore. With what little he knew about her past, he wouldn't blame her if she tried to disappear.

So he'd been patient and systematic as he performed this different kind of stalk, but a stalk well within his forte. He'd honed his tracking skills over centuries of hunting devious criminals; finding a woman trying to hide in plain sight would take only a fraction of his talent. And time? Who cared how long it took to find her? He had all the time in the world. He was an Indebted—cursed and long-lived. Weeks, months, or years meant nothing to him.

In response to curious glances from customers, he rotated his wrists in his lap to hide the shiny gold cufflinks. He needed to blend into the population, quite a task for such an impossibly sexy man like him, standing at over six and a half feet tall. He didn't even have to be dressed to impress, come to think of it. Thankfully, modesty was one of his many exceptional traits.

Exceptional traits like killing? *Kristus.* He forced himself to relax his hand, lest he splinter the arm of the chair like he'd splintered the limbs and heads of criminals for centuries.

Thankfully, the citizens didn't realize a murderer lounged among them in this genteel business establishment. An Indebted killer. Quite the title to go on a business card. Despite his expertise with his weapon of choice, that godforsaken foot-long knife, truth be told, he'd prefer to have a luscious *flicka*'s legs wrapped around him any day of the week. Thankfully, he was proficient at both activities.

Clenching his hands into fists, Dante fought the urge to stretch his fingers toward the handle. For 300 years, whenever he killed a vile criminal, he supplied the energy needed to feed his boss, Jerahmeel's, soul. He'd have to find a criminal soon and satisfy the blade's hunger, or innocent citizens would begin to attract the weapon's attention.

A few sideways looks from customers of the female persuasion reminded him that he was, as usual, looking spectacular today. He flexed his shoulders, pleased when several sets of eyelashes batted. Not that he doubted his charm. A particularly luscious blonde and long-legged *flicka* had casually dropped her card off at his table at a restaurant yesterday. He licked his lips, anticipating a rendezvous this evening. Par for the fantastic course of his unnaturally long life.

Recently, though, his powers of attraction did not satisfy like before. What was missing? He patted his shirt pocket, reassured to feel a heavy bond paper still stored there.

Too bad the thought of a tryst didn't hold his interest right now. Since when was he indifferent to sex? Since never. Maybe he had fallen ill?

Flipping through the Bedier translation of *Tristan and Iseult*, one of his favorites, Dante glanced around the store. Despite the modest street entrance, the comfortable bookstore sprawled into a labyrinth of stacks, which enticed him to wander and explore. They even used library ladders here, which added to the shop's charm and reminded him of bookstores long gone. But that wasn't why he sat here, near the hissing espresso machine as an aproned worker brewed another cup. It was all about his objective.

Jessica.

And then what?

He'd decide later. Improvisation was one of his strong suits. Well, improvisation, a massive physique, and sexual magnetism, of course.

When a customer entered, the breeze wafted a scent of early fall trees mixed with the coffee and musty books, lulling him into a rare state of calm. He would sit here for hours if necessary.

A diminutive woman appeared at the register and murmured in a low voice to a customer. How had he not seen this worker before? It was as if she'd materialized out of the bookshelves, with a dull, gray sweater that hung off her frame and allowed her to blend into the walls. She kept her movements understated, wary, like a mouse trying to remain undetected. It was this deliberate effort to disappear that caught his attention.

Dante sat up straight when she spoke. Something about her rich intonation that flowed like silk across his face, the smooth sound at odds with her bland appearance, sent a frisson of excitement into his chest. He glanced at her over the top of his book.

Her strawberry blonde hair brushed her shoulders, and freckles dotted a cute button nose. She ducked her head shyly at the customer and bit her lip. When she made eye contact to run the credit card, those soft lips tensed. But then she smiled at a comment from the customer, and her entire face lit up, transforming an average countenance into a radiant one. A jolt of longing froze Dante in place. *Where had that emotion come from?*

Soulful chestnut eyes behind black frame glasses flitted toward the door. That warm gaze slid over him like she didn't acknowledge his presence.

Vad i helvete? What the hell? Since when did a woman not stare at him or resist his beauty? It must be because her glasses weren't calibrated properly. No other explanation made sense.

When the door opened, she startled like a frightened deer and pulled the gray cardigan around her. He tensed, ready to dart over to her. How odd. In his hundreds of years on this Earth, he'd never experienced that strong of an urge to safeguard someone, especially not a woman he hadn't even properly met.

What would she look like beneath that shapeless sweater? The alabaster skin of her neck was cruelly hidden from his view by the sweater's modest neckline. Were her curves lush or subtle? Would her breasts fit easily in his hands or did she hide more bounty? Damn it, he couldn't tell, and that limitation only made him grit his teeth in frustration.

Another customer, a middle-aged man, wandered between Dante and the cashier. No longer able to hide behind the book, Dante craned his neck to continue studying the woman.

Her delicate hands as she worked the register made him wonder how those hands would feel on him. Would they drift like silk against his hard lines and angles? Desire tightened his groin, and he shifted to relieve the unexpected pressure.

How could he be this interested in a woman without her reciprocation? Yet here he sat, responding like a randy schoolboy. Was this the woman he searched for? Or was he just on another of his *kvinna* hunts, led by his overactive libido?

If this twenty-something woman was Jessica, she stood in stark contrast to her stepfather. Raymond Jackson had been large boned and full of burly cruelty. Sharp rage speared Dante. *Ja*, if this were Jessica, she wouldn't have stood a chance against that monster.

When she slipped out from behind the counter, Dante nearly missed the movement. He couldn't resist following her thin frame, clad in a flowing pale pink skirt, as she floated down the aisles.

She sidled around customers, adroitly melting into the bookshelves to avoid contact. When she took several swift steps, her hips swayed unevenly and one foot scuffed against the hardwood floor.

As she stopped and cocked her head to the side, he dove into the next aisle and grabbed a book at random. Opening it, he flipped through the pages, pretending to study the content.

From a row over, her smooth voice rolled over him as she directed a customer. The soft rustle of her skirt brought back unbidden memories of homespun cloth and whispers of parishioners in his village's Lutheran church. So strong was the memory that he smelled tallow candles and wood polish. He blinked.

As he heard her walk away, he inhaled the faint scent of coffee, flowers, and book pages.

When he stepped out of his aisle to follow her, she ran into his leg, squeaked, and stumbled. Dante wrapped his hand around her slim upper arm to keep her from falling. Her head didn't even come to his shoulders, and he fought an overwhelming need to fold her into his arms.

When she tilted her head up, the color drained even more from her pale face, enhancing the delicate freckles over her nose. He devoured the view of her alabaster skin from her cheeks, over her jaw, and down her neck—until that damned sweater impeded his ability to explore further.

She tugged against him again, and when he let go, she darted away like a frightened rabbit, her hands fluttering as though she couldn't decide where to place them.

"Can… can I help you?" Her soft voice, laced with a hint of a quaver, couldn't have shocked him more if she had yelled.

As her warm espresso gaze darted to him and away, her cheeks reddened beneath the freckles. There, that response was more like it. Now that he stood close enough for her to see him properly, she was clearly overwhelmed by his handsomeness, like every other woman.

"Just browsing the *stacks*," he said.

He gave his suave words just enough innuendo and mentally patted himself on the back when the red flush crept down her creamy neck. *Fullstandig*. Perfect.

For someone more than 300 years of age, he still had the goods to impress the ladies.

"Did you find something interesting?" Her voice cracked as she indicated the book he held. She must be overcome with nerves, so great was her attraction to him.

"Oh, yes, I did find something interesting. And some books, too."

Most women batted eyelashes and swooned at this point. In control, in his element, he created a seduction—a work of art. Truly, he was a maestro. She only had to absorb his charm, and then the pump would be primed.

"Hmm, well. You've picked out an interesting topic." The corner of her pink, moist mouth rose, and those impish brown eyes widened. Her tongue darted out to wet those soft lips.

She most likely imagined his masterful kisses and caresses. Her attraction to him was obvious. He had her. Dante straightened to full impressive stature and stood poised to reel her in.

Until he noticed the book in his hands: *The Woman's Guide to Successful Breastfeeding.*

Air whooshed out of him like a rapidly deflating balloon.

He would salvage this one. He was Dante. Women never said no to him.

"I, um, like to be well read."

She quirked one fine eyebrow above her glasses rim and wrinkled her nose.

What? Was she poking fun at him? At *him*? How did his never-fail charm become a train wreck in the space of two breaths? Inconceivable.

"Well, then, any other books I can point out for you? Maybe understanding your body during menopause? Or perhaps getting in touch with your inner Earth goddess?"

When she didn't quite hide another grin behind her hand, his jaw clenched.

That comment hit below the belt, but it was well played. Beneath that shy exterior, she had spunk.

He studied the shapeless sweater that hung from thin shoulders. He considered her twinkling eyes hidden behind rectangular lenses. Flecks of gold swirled within the irises, and he swore that a glimmer of interest, replaced by fear, crossed her features. Then she bit her lip and glanced away.

He had to know more. There was something oh-so-tempting about her but also something broken. A mystery. As he replaced the book that had cruelly betrayed him back onto the shelf, he powered up his never-fail megawatt smile and extended a hand.

"My name's Dante."

"Hi, Dante."

Her hands remained at her side. He groaned. But all was not lost. Time to go to the next level of seduction. He puffed out his massive pectoral muscles and gave her his best rakish grin. This maneuver always succeeded.

"And your name is?" He leaned forward, undoubtedly impressing her with his overwhelming masculinity.

"Not interested."

A bucket of cold water couldn't have shocked him more. Did she truly rebuff his advances? Impossible. Had never happened before. She definitely wore deficient glasses.

She turned away, spine stiff. "I'm sure it's mutual."

Off balance, he stammered. "I'm not... no I just—"

"It's okay, Dante," she said. Her pronouncement of his name left him with a taste of whipped cream in his own mouth, her voice was so soft and sweet. "Please let me know if I can help you with anything else. In the bookstore."

She glanced back and away, but not before he caught the downturn of her mouth. For the space of a split second, he wanted to touch her lips with his, to take away whatever caused that sadness. *Vad i helvete?* Since when did he desire anything besides his base carnal needs?

With a rustle of cloth and a whiff of flowers, she disappeared into the maze of shelves. Fascinating. Unsettling. If this were Jessica, then he understood her fear. If this were Jessica, he'd have to figure out a gentler, subtler approach.

Gentle? Subtle? Those two words had never inhabited his vocabulary, ever.

What if this weren't Jessica? Who cared? His curiosity was still piqued. This woman still intrigued him. Something about that sweet mouth, the shy glances behind those practical glasses, the flit of her hands to brush back orange-gold hair captured his interest with laser-sharp focus. At minimum, she would provide some welcome diversion while Dante completed his work here in Portland.

Game on.

His jaded heart actually skipped a beat in anticipation of their next encounter. At that next meeting, he would use a different tactic to weave his web of seduction. He wouldn't fail.

He'd confirm if this was Jessica Miller and deliver his message. And then what? Once he delivered the message, he'd be persona non grata. *Hi, I killed your stepfather, want to hang out?* A hell of a pickup line, even for him.

But if that *oåkting* was the bastard Dante suspected, maybe Jessica's gratitude would drive her into Dante's arms. Ah, yes, of course she'd want to repay him for ridding the world of the disgusting Raymond Jackson. And Dante could think of numerous ways for a woman to demonstrate gratitude.

First, though, he really needed to take care of that damned knife lust and go kill a criminal before Dante's mind exploded. The blade pulsed in its hidden sheath on his leg, demanding attention, demanding that he kill again. He hadn't fed it in a week because he'd been too focused on finding and delivering his message to Jessica. Damn technology. His boss, Jerahmeel, had finally crawled into the cellular age and used text messages to divvy out special assignments these days. For standard kills, all Dante had to do was find a criminal and drive the blade into him, which typically slaked his need.

Speaking of exploding, it had been far too long since he'd had sex. Time to rectify that situation. And finally, if appropriate, he'd try again with his advances on this woman and, of course, succeed. Of course. He was Dante.

Very well. His foreseeable future included espresso, death, sex, and browsing books. *Spektakulår.*

Chapter 2

In the restroom, Hannah splashed cool water on her heated skin and took a deep breath. Her heart thudded so hard it had to be drilling its way out of her chest. Okay, so the man looked like a windswept, blonde Norse god who moonlighted as a fitness model, and he had attempted some sort of blatant come-on. What was wrong with that?

Everything.

Damn his square jaw and glacier-blue eyes; no man had the right to look that savory. Even his firm lips, meant for sin, which pressed together in frustration when she didn't give in to his obvious pass—those lips made her wonder what she'd been missing all these years.

She had watched several female customers—and one male—sidle past Dante with a touch on his massive arm, a whisper, or a press of paper into his hand. A wink, accidentally brushing into him, licked lips, tossed hair—he had politely ignored all of the advances.

But then he had looked at her with what appeared to be male interest. In her twenty-four years on this Earth, she'd never encountered someone this handsome and persistent.

Seriously?

She examined her shapeless but neat thrift-store clothing—appropriate for work but no one would accuse her of being a fashionista. Heck, no bumps or curves pushed the fabric in any enticing pattern. Her clothes went straight from her shoulders to the floor.

Guys like Dante did not go for her.

No guys went for her. For the past four years, she'd rejected the few men who had showed even the slightest interest. She refused to allow anyone to come close. Not with her stepfather, Ray, still out there. Not with what he'd done and what she had to hide.

Even now, she jumped at shadows and sounds, paralyzed stupid by fear. But her fear was warranted. One day, if she relaxed her vigilance, Ray would again find her and her brother, Scott. It didn't matter that she'd changed their names. Jess—no, Hannah, damn it. Flustered as she was by Dante, she had to make a conscious effort to maintain her identity, even in her own mind. In truth, the woman that stared back at her in the mirror was no longer Jessica Miller. Jessica had disappeared four years ago in Philly, never to be seen again.

Didn't matter that she and Scott had fled from Philly to Portland. Ray was out of jail. And he was pissed.

She reached down to rub the ridge of scar and misshapen bones on her right foot. The sole remained numb, and the top of the foot still ached when the weather changed. Even with surgery, the damage remained. At least bones could be pinned and skin stitched together. Other injuries weren't as obvious.

Geez. Snap out of the pity party already.

But she couldn't help herself. She peered into the mirror, trying to imagine what Dante had seen. Brown eyes behind rectangular glasses looked back at her. Freckles splattered across her pale face. Her dull clothing. The weight she'd lost when… everything happened had never returned to her frame. Four years of fear, of waiting for him to return. She never relaxed her vigilance.

Had it really been four years since she and Scott ran away? How long would it take to have a normal life?

At this rate? Never.

Damn Ray to hell.

Damn her for not being able to move on with her life.

Would she ever have a normal relationship with a man? Logically, she acknowledged that there were good guys out there who could be trusted. Maybe Dante was one of them. Beyond the swagger, she could see… more. And oddly enough, he didn't scare her, which was a first. He made her laugh with his attempts at flirting, but for all his massive bulk and impressive height, her reaction to him wasn't fear. It was interest.

Interest. Now there was a new and terrifying emotion.

What about trusting herself? Problematic. The minefield of her physical wreckage paled in comparison with the emotional damage. Maybe one day she'd get over it, but that wasn't likely to happen anytime soon.

Past traumas aside, how would she explain her fake last name, attempted murder, and larceny? How would she explain withholding her strange power?

She shook her head. She'd never open up that piece of her life to anyone, would never tell what she and Scott had done to get away from Ray. Better to avoid a serious relationship rather than risk rejection or, even worse, discovery.

Oh yeah, I'll be going steady with Mr. Gold's Gym Meets an Archangel by week's end.

Why try to change her life now? Jobs, a few college courses—she and her brother were finally getting back on track, thanks to their hard work and the ability to keep secrets. Slowly and surely, they were clawing their way back toward a normal life. She had no time to spare on a certain tall, handsome man with ice-blue eyes that danced with humor and suggestiveness and made her heart flutter.

Smoothing her hair and running her hands over her cheeks, she nodded, satisfied that the traitorous blush had finally subsided. She blew out another big breath and let the tension in her shoulders relax. This random encounter with Dante was simply an aberration in her otherwise bland life.

She didn't need any man. All she wanted was for Ray, or the specter of Ray, to leave her alone forever and let her rebuild her new, safe existence here in Portland. At some point, she'd have to learn to trust herself again and even figure out how to open herself up to others. Not now, but maybe one day.

• • •

Hannah limped along the sidewalk to her dumpy rental at nine that evening. What kind of brother would she see tonight? The younger brother who had driven her across the country to get away from Ray, the brother who faked sinus infections and foot sprains at urgent care clinics to get antibiotics and braces for her ankle—he'd been replaced by a different person. He'd become more braggadocio here recently, more into hanging out with the guys, more demands for money, more erratic behavior. She wanted her quiet, supportive Scott back. Not this jerk.

The deafening roar of a bus rolling by made her long to be on board. Her foot ached even more as she stumbled on the sidewalk when her foot dragged. No bus rides for her, though. She had to save every penny for college. Besides, exercise had to be good for her foot, right? She wiggled her toes. Still numb. Damn Ray. God, she hated him. She normally didn't wish bad things on people, but she made an exception for her nasty stepfather. Even the thought of him made her neck prickle, and she couldn't help but dart glances over her shoulders, still expecting to see the seething mass of cruelty that was Ray.

Ah yes, the low rent district. While Portland wasn't known for its slums, she and Scott had gotten close when they used their new, fake Social Security numbers and rented a dilapidated house in this borderline neighborhood. The last block or so to their house always gave her the creeps, and the neighbors looked out for no one.

When she wearily turned off the sidewalk toward the front door of her run-down rental, the squeal of tires and pounding bass stopped her. A tricked-out orange Civic's back door opened, and Scott jumped out.

Like Hannah, he had their mother's strawberry blond hair and brown eyes. But unlike Hannah's petite stature, Scott's lanky frame made him look gangly, even in his early twenties.

His friends shouted from the car, "Hey, Hannah! Jump in."

Brandon, the ginger in the front seat with spiked hair and acne, flicked his tongue out in a lewd gesture. "Come on, honey! Just once around the block, huh?"

His soulless stare never failed to creep her out. What Scott found pleasant enough about Brandon to hang out together, she'd never understand.

The other two guys laughed and high-fived each other. Adjusting her glasses, she ducked her head. When these idiots talked to her, she wanted to scrub her skin with bleach. At least with Scott here, she was relatively safe if not disgusted by these guys.

"Back off my sis. Rules, assholes," Scott said from the sidewalk.

"Catch ya later, my man!" Brandon yelled.

Brandon flicked his wrist for the driver to pull out, which was done with a dramatic spinning of wheels as they peeled off down the street.

At the disapproving glare of an older lady peeking through her windows next door, Hannah ducked her head. "Let's go inside and have some dinner."

"I already ate, sis, no worries."

The aroma of cheap beer hung in a stale cloud around him.

"Come on, Scott, eating out costs too much. Drinking out, too."

"I need to live a little, sis." When he smiled endearingly like that, she witnessed a flash of her kid brother from Philly. Then he staggered to one side, and the illusion was gone.

She jiggled the door handle until the key settled in the rusty lock. Entering the house, the vision of the living room, devoid of any furniture, weighed on her like a heavy hand on her shoulder. But for right now, they didn't have a choice. Living here allowed her to stay with Scott. Up until Scott started going out with his newfound friends, it was more economical to live under one roof.

Of course, he wasn't the teen who fled with her from Philly, but she still felt some responsibility to watch out for him, and one day things would change. Maybe it was nearing time for each of them to move on. If only she could get him away from his so-called friends.

Smiling, she sighed and indulged in a vision of her future. She'd have her degree, a job helping people cope with their lives, and a nice house decorated with new matching furniture, like from Ikea. One day.

What about a partner? A family?

The only vision that came to her had a chiseled chin and a twinkling blue gaze.

Yeah, right.

She opened her eyes to ripped linoleum and bare, cracked windows. "Please be careful how much money you're spending."

"I gotta hang with my posse," he said, hiccupping. "You keeping me from my friends?" He swayed, his bloodshot stare unfocused.

"Of course not."

"It's my life, Hannah. You can't tell me what to do."

He stumbled against the spool they used for a table, a lucky salvage from a construction site. But as the main furniture in the living space, it was a pitiful reminder of the shell of their lives.

"I'm not your mother. You make your own decisions," she said.

"You got that right. Besides, I got us out of that crap back in Philly. You owe me. I saved your life."

"We both went through hell, and yes, I might not be alive if you hadn't helped me."

He leaned against the makeshift table and fingered a new gold chain around his neck. "I hope Ray dies and rots."

"Me too. I never want to see him again."

"What that sicko did to you..."

"We're not talking about it." Her foot throbbed like it did the night Ray had thrown her down the basement stairs. Amazing what lengths a maniac would go to exact his warped sense of revenge.

"Our tracks are covered. Only my friend in Philly knows where we live."

Not good enough. "For how long are the tracks covered?"

"As long as we keep looking out for each other, Ray won't be able to hurt us. If he does, I'll call my crew."

She sighed. Back to the stupid crew. A group of boozed up guys with too much testosterone and not enough brains.

"I'll always appreciate what you did, Scott."

She couldn't remember large chunks of their journey from the East Coast to the West. Scott had probably saved her life. Maybe now he was growing up, coming into his own self. The twinge in her chest reminded her that he was all the family she had left.

"Damn straight. We're a team here." He belched.

Hannah sighed.

"Sis, that reminds me, you got some extra bucks? I'm light."

She groaned. "No, I haven't gotten paid yet." Glancing at his new name-brand shoes and jeans, she bit the inside of her cheek to keep from commenting.

"Quit holding out on me."

"I'm not. I don't get paid until later this week, remember?"

"You're hoarding money! I need cash to... to put gas in the truck. How'm I s'posed to make a living if you won't help me?"

"Good grief. Here's all I have left." She dug in her ratty purse and pulled out six dollars. "This'll take care of gas tomorrow."

"That's all you have? Where's the rest of it?" He leaned toward her but staggered again.

"I gave you everything else last week after I got groceries. There won't be any more until Thursday. Make it last."

"You're a piece of shit...," he slurred again.

"We were a 'team' a few minutes ago."

"Until you refused to give me gas money."

The usual pattern for his drunk nights. Shame. She shook her head. There was no arguing with him. So much for both of them trying to build their lives. So much for escaping all the drama with Ray and his insanity. But as frustrating as Scott's behavior had become, at least he'd never been physically abusive. He spouted off insults when he was drunk, sure, but his behavior paled in comparison to the hell they'd endured at Ray's hands back in Philly.

And then there was her attempt to use her gift to heal others, as Ray had demanded. Her gut clenched. That altruism had nearly killed her when Ray snapped. She wouldn't talk about that disaster, either. Hannah had been crucified the one time she wouldn't—couldn't—use her power, and she'd paid for the lapse ever since. Actually, Aunt Linda, God rest her gentle soul, had paid the greater price.

She sighed. "I'll see what I can do tomorrow about an advance."

"'Bout time you did somethin' useful. Shit. My life sucks."

He pocketed the cash and leaned against the wall.

"Good grief, let's get you to bed." She held out hope that Scott would come around and improve, but damn it, she wasn't a doormat. She nudged him toward the only room with a bed on a frame. "Good night, Scott."

He dropped, fully clothed, onto the messy blankets, completely out.

She sighed, closed his bedroom door, and trudged into the kitchen. Her ramen noodle dinner tasted like cardboard.

•••

In the dimly lit club, strobe lights pulsed in time with a pounding techno beat as oiled female bodies writhed in cages and on countertops. In a velvet-upholstered alcove, Dante sipped tepid beer and cringed. Sure, it was alcohol, but this swill paled in comparison with *brännvin*. His kin called it "burn wine," and the fire that seared the gullet lived up to its name. This watered-down American beer would do for now.

At least luscious *flickor*, women, hadn't changed through the ages. He flexed his chest, feeling the heavy bond business card in his pocket. Why hadn't he called that magnificent and leggy woman from the restaurant last night? Totally out of character to pass up an opportunity with a woman like that.

He'd come to this club instead, hoping that something else would pique his interest. When he lifted one finger, he commanded the attention of two bare-breasted dancers. Good. He was the sun. The heavenly bodies of these women? Helpless to resist his pull.

What would it be like to have a woman want him without his magnetism? Notice the nuances of his character? Not care about who or what he was? Fill the hollowness that these brief interludes never quite satisfied? Perhaps a good woman could retrieve the humanity that had been driven from his soul.

Shaking his head to clear the uncharacteristic melancholy, he concentrated on the women standing at the ready. The dancers practically vibrated, their bodies quivering in anticipation of his slightest touch.

He projected his voice over the thumping bass beat. "Ladies."

Something of a misnomer, but the lie didn't matter. When he brushed his thumb against his upper teeth, the dusky dancer licked her full lips in response. One down.

"Oh, honey." The cocoa-colored woman ran a hand over his torso. "Your abs are so hard I could chop coleslaw on them."

He crooked his finger at the other woman, pleased when her pale breasts bobbed in quicker rhythm with her breathing.

He imagined their nimble fingers roving over every inch of his body.

Nothing moved inside of him.

Nothing?

His typical lust didn't rise; his groin didn't tighten in anticipation of the impending ménage à trois. Even imaging all their limbs tangled around each other, satiating his desire—none of it moved him. Literally.

Vad i helvete?

Since when…?

Kristus.

Since this mission. Since meeting a mousy woman who remained immune to his charms. A woman who was nothing like the *flickor* who typically drew his attention.

He pushed up from the table and shrugged off the women's hands. Even their pouts of disappointment didn't sway him. He strode, alone, into the fall night.

Was it the challenge or the woman?

Didn't care. He needed to see her again and deliver his message.

Chapter 3

The next morning, Hannah left Scott at home sleeping off his bender. Hopefully, he'd make it to work today. They couldn't afford for him to lose another job. Despite her working full time at the bookstore, the money only went so far. If he continued to contribute to their joint efforts, with any luck, she'd have her degree in another three semesters and be one step closer to realizing her dream of becoming a psychologist.

When she took a deep breath, the cool morning air gave her a boost, and she pushed her uneasiness about Scott aside. Even her messed up foot didn't slow her down as much today, and she reached the store a few minutes early to open up shop.

Her long skirt swished over the top of her foot with each step. Broomstick skirts were more rustic than her usual, conservative style, but she'd discovered that the skirts hid her deformed foot and minimized the appearance of her limp.

When she unlocked the front door of the bookstore, she stood in the front room and enjoyed a few minutes of peace. As she warmed up the espresso machine, the scent of coffee made her mouth water. It was too expensive a treat, though, and she wouldn't steal, even a cup of coffee.

The door chimed behind her, and the air pressure in the bookstore changed. A light scent of spicy aftershave drifted past as goose bumps rose on her arms.

She whirled, her tan cotton skirt rasping against silk slacks, as she buried her nose into a massive chest. Standing eye to eye with the sheen of fine fabric stretching across a broad torso, she gulped in a whiff of warm, masculine essence. When she stumbled backward on her weak foot, the espresso cup dropped from her nerveless fingers.

In one continuous blur of movement, Dante plucked the cup out of the air and presented it to her. His confident, sardonic lift of the corner of his mouth hadn't changed. Electric-blue eyes glowed as he smiled down at her, and the curve of his sensual lips commanded her attention.

When he returned the cup, their hands brushed, which sent warmth and a strange jolt of energy up her arm to her neck. She jerked her eyes away. The quivering in her chest couldn't have anything to do with him standing this close. The shakiness had nothing to do with the heat somehow radiating off of his muscled chest.

She had to crane her neck to look up at his handsome face punctuated with high, broad cheekbones and a clean-shaven jaw. His light blond hair waved back off his forehead but for an errant piece. An intense need to sweep that lock of hair into place stopped her cold.

Something shifted deep in her belly, pleasant and warm, like watching a sunrise. She wanted more. When his strong mouth curved upward, her heart fluttered.

Wanted more?

Heart fluttering?

Come on. What's wrong with you?

A bucket of ice water couldn't be a more abrupt wake-up.

She moved back another few feet, cheeks burning, and cleared her throat. She tugged at her too-large knit top and smoothed the shabby skirt. In light of her un-model-like appearance, she had to be a huge joke to a colossal man who looked like a bodybuilder dressed in Armani.

Realizing that too much time had passed where she'd stared like an idiot at Dante, she took another step back.

He didn't move, but simply watched her, the corners of his mouth curving upward. In a flash, she wanted to know how the edge of that firm mouth tasted and how it would fit against hers.

Would his lips be as demanding as his appearance, or did he have a tender side that he expressed when he kissed?

Get a grip. Stay cool and collected. Time to return from fantasy world.

"Ah, thank you." She placed the cup next to the espresso machine. "Can I, um, help you?"

"I'm sure you can." He raised an eyebrow.

Seriously? He flirted with *her*?

After the initial wave of disbelief passed, she fought an urge to giggle. *Oh, geez.*

"What would you like?" She cringed as her voice wavered. Not cool. Not collected.

"You." The meaty man swaggered, but he hadn't taken a step. How was that even possible?

Hannah laughed out loud before she covered the inappropriate outburst with her hand. "Pardon?"

"I'd like *you*, madam."

He hadn't moved, but his presence wrapped around her like a warm blanket. If a warm blanket were made of muscled arms and a massive chest, that is.

"I... I'm not. Uh, what?"

Seriously, where were the hidden cameras?

"I'd like you to go to lunch with me. Or dinner. Or... breakfast."

He flexed his shoulders, managing to appear even more self-assured and Herculean. She stifled another giggle. This entire ridiculous situation, while flattering in a surreal way, had no future. If this poor man only knew her baggage, he'd run far away.

But he wasn't running. In fact, he'd planted his large, polished leather-clad feet, spread his legs into a determined stance, and continued to focus all of his attention on her. After all the obvious messages she'd given him, he persisted in this parody of flirtation. Maybe he was a little on the... slow side? Well then, God bless his simple mind, at least he was handsome.

Might as well have some fun with the insanity.

He winked once. When she didn't move, he winked again.

She covered a laugh by clearing her throat. Unable to help herself, she egged him on. "Do you have something in your eye?"

It was his turn to rock back on his heels. He frowned. "In my eye?"

"It seems *irritated.*" She emphasized the last word, hoping he'd get a hint.

"Irritated?"

"Irritated. As in, something is *bothering* it."

Hints apparently didn't work. Or perhaps he had the emotional fortitude of an Abrams tank. He was built like one.

"What does being bothered have to do with the lunch you're going to have with me?" His smile tightened into a grim line and then drooped.

At his hangdog expression, she almost gave in to his request. Almost.

"It doesn't have anything to do with lunch, Mr. Dante."

"Nothing to do with lunch?"

"*Nothing* to do with lunch."

"So what are you saying?"

Hannah blew out an exasperated breath and crossed her arms. "I'm saying thank you but no thank you."

The big guy's shoulders sagged. "What?"

"Thank you. But no. Now, may I brew you an espresso?"

"No, no," he stammered. "I'll just…"

Mouth agape in a stunned expression that marred his chiseled face, he turned on his heel and staggered out of the store, banging his shoulder into the doorjamb on the way out.

Pressing a hand to her warm cheeks, she sighed and turned back to the espresso machine. Maybe this Dante guy was unhinged or liked to be charitable. But surely to heck he got the message now.

Yes, that should take care of Mr. Incredible. A necessary move.

Too bad. Under all the swagger and posturing, he seemed like a nice guy.

• • •

Vad i helvete? What had just happened?

Dante wove his way down the sidewalk. When he bumped a passer-by, the man muttered at him to watch where he was going.

Rejected? Inconceivable. He held the world record for flirting. No woman had ever turned him down. Ever.

Well, his friend Peter's wife, Allie, had acted uninterested, but that was only because Peter had gotten to her first. That was the only rational explanation for why Peter had bested him in the *flicka* department.

Therefore, Allie didn't count as a miss on the long tally of Dante's conquests. She'd married Peter right after their ordeal last year, and despite her obviously inferior choice of a mate, Dante respected her decision.

But what about this waif of a woman with her sweet librarian glasses? What the hell was her name? He had no idea, but he'd bet his left *testikel* this was the woman, Jessica, he needed to find.

Hadn't he fantasized about finding a woman immune to his charisma? Hadn't he longed for a relationship that relied only on his character and not his other... charms?

Well, that idea was clearly garbage.

The idea bordered on insanity. The idea made his gut churn and shoulders straighten with the need to succeed in fabulous fashion now. A challenge. He loved a challenge.

But what if something had gone seriously awry with his constitution? What if this challenge didn't hold the answer?

He stopped dead in his tracks, staring at his hands. Had he lost his touch?

He looked up at the sun. Was it still there? It shone brightly.

Gravity. Did it still work? He jumped. *Ja*, he came back down to Earth.

When he pinched himself hard, it hurt. All right, so he wasn't dreaming.

Well, now he *had* to have this woman. Had to charm her. Had to win.

Time to regroup.

Spying a young woman down the street, Dante sauntered over and flashed his never-fail, superstar smile. "Well, hello. Lovely day, isn't it?"

The woman tucked her long, black hair behind an ear and tilted her head to the side. "Yes, it is." She licked her lips.

Utmarkt. Excellent.

Dante was back in the game. Momentarily unmanned but not undeterred.

• • •

The next morning, Hannah cracked an eyelid against the light filtering in her bedroom window. With a groan, she rolled off the mattress onto the hard floor and pushed herself up to stand, waiting until her ankle loosened up enough to take the first steps. One day, she'd get a normal bed with a normal frame and box spring. Getting up in the morning would be much more pleasant.

A faint snore drifted from the other bedroom. Scott must've come in late last night.

She glanced at her watch. Damn. They couldn't afford for him to lose another job.

She peeked into the bedroom. Scott lay on top of the blankets, in the same clothes from yesterday. Despite being passed out, his legs shifted restlessly, like when a dog dreamed. Twitchy, constantly moving, even in his sleep. She'd never seen him jumpy like that before. Weird.

"Scott, get up." A snore was her only reply. "You're going to be late."

He mumbled. "Sh'up."

He rolled over and put a pillow over his face. It was nearly 8:30. He needed to get moving, and she had to leave soon for her own job. As it was, she'd have to walk quickly to get there on time. Her leg ached as she anticipated the fast pace.

"Come on, let's go."

She pushed him over, and he swatted halfheartedly at her as he swiped his matted brown hair off his forehead. This entire situation—his behavior, the crappy rental, scraping to make ends meet—all of it was getting ridiculous. She didn't want to fight Scott. Why couldn't he just grow up? She blew her bangs off her forehead.

"Oh, shit, my fucking head's killing me. I feel like ass. I'm calling in."

"No way. You're not losing this job."

Pulling his legs around the bed, she tugged him up to a sitting position and ignored his muttered curses. The overwhelming odor of acid, stale beer, and a weird chemical scent like a new shower liner assaulted her nose. A pitiful figure, he moaned and continued to pick at his arms.

He grabbed her hands. "Help me, sis. Come on."

When she tried to pull away, he held tightly with his sweaty hands. She kept her long, navy skirt away from the questionable stains on Scott's clothes.

She shook her head. "I can't. The last time I helped you, it took me days to recover."

"Please, I'd love you forever." His cajoling tone didn't fool her one bit. "You're all I've got."

But man, he really tugged at her heart sometimes. Could she heal him again? Now? She cringed in anticipation.

He let go of one of her hands to scratch his scalp over and over again. Why was he itching so much? He was acting stranger than his usual hangover.

"Scott..."

"I helped you when you needed it."

That statement served as his best go-to blackmail move whenever he wanted her to do anything. And the worst part? He wasn't incorrect. He'd saved her life. So why shouldn't she relieve his pain and keep him employed? It was the least she could do, right?

Years ago, her ability had erupted out of the blue, and unable to control the power, she'd been hurt trying to help the other person. The first time, with Scott's broken arm, she had put her hands on him and the surge of his injury had cracked her own arm in a flash. The second time her gift emerged, her mother had sliced her hand with a paring knife. Hannah still bore an aching arm and a scar on her hand as testament to the efficiency with which her body absorbed other people's injuries.

Since then, though, she had sure as heck figured out how to hold her ability in check. Now, her control acted like a dam, restraining a massive lake at full pool. But the control was worth it. Instead of spontaneously absorbing the ills and injuries of others, now she made the call. She released the power in a conscious burst of will. A mere thought, and her body's hungry desire to suck out pain from another person surged through the connection of skin and shoved the agony back into Hannah. No degrees, no shades of gray. She absorbed everything from the other person. Or she did not.

That's why she had become very picky on selecting beneficiaries of her gift.

Selfish? Maybe.

But she had no idea of the limits of her power. Altruism aside, it would be nice to avoid destroying herself in an effort to help others.

After another minute of debate, she had her decision. Damn it.

Oh man, she didn't want to take on Scott's hangover, but they had run out of choices. He had to work at the gas station. They needed the extra $500 from his part-time work pumping gas. He'd called in too many times to continue the job if he missed another day. Huh. Couldn't even pull off a part-time job.

She swallowed, clenched her teeth together, and mentally released the floodgates as her power exploded from the restraints. Her skin, hungry to grab the illness in Scott's body, adhered to their joined hands as if magnetized. At the point of solid connection, she took one more breath and let go of all resistance. Her blood or cells or something inside of her reached into every pore of his body and scraped out the sickness and pain. Her gift collected every last bit of disease into a spiky ball of hell then yanked it away from his body.

His pain flowed like electrical fire up her arms into her neck and chest, threatening to explode out her head and fingertips. Unfortunately, the pain remained inside her own skin, eating away at every cell in her body like acid etching torment through every organ. Her liver swelled, stomach clenched, and muscles quivered.

Almost done.

As she absorbed everything wrong in his body, her muscles ignited in fire and a relentless throbbing drumbeat pounded in her skull. The toast she had for breakfast threatened a repeat performance. She swallowed down bile and tried to control her breathing.

Today's transfer of symptoms was more than the typical bender recovery. Something strange occurred. She got jumpy.

Was that a figure at the window? A knock at the door? An intruder?

No. Nothing.

She blinked, unable to concentrate for all the inexplicable fear. Panic paralyzed her lungs, her heart pounded, her leg muscles tensed, ready to flee.

But no one was there. No stalker. No danger.

Edgy and irritable, her skin itched like bugs crawled all over her. Twitching an arm, she tried to dislodge invisible ants from her skin. Damn it, she couldn't get them off of her. She pulled one hand away from Scott and scratched her skin, raising angry red lines on her arms. Still, the sensation of a million tiny insect feet marching up her body persisted.

What the heck?

When she'd helped clear his hangovers in the past, the transfer had never felt like this. More than simply alcohol, she sensed… something else in his system. She tried to dislodge her grip, but he hung on, and with Hannah unable to focus and block her ability, the transfer continued its relentless erosion of her body and soul.

She managed to choke out the words, "What the heck did you do?"

As branches outside waved in the slight breeze, she flinched at the shadows thrown onto the walls.

Muscle spasms ripped up her back, each twitch an explosion of agony. The effort to remain standing warred with her desire to curl into the fetal position.

"What?" she yelled.

He averted his gaze, which now shone guilty but free of pain. He shook his head.

Sweat rolled down her face as she started to shake. "Seriously, what else is in your system? What did you do?"

"Nothing, I swear." He didn't look at her.

"You're lying." She yanked her hands away.

He stared at the floor, shoulders hunched. No longer bloodshot, his eyes shone with vigor, like he'd had a fabulous night's sleep. Even his greasy hair wasn't as matted.

Every joint in her body ached. Her stupid, normally numb foot hurt. Muscles burned like someone struck a million matches over every surface of her body, and she couldn't stop rubbing and scratching her arms. Her head pounded. Light and sound were the enemy. Darting glances around the house, she suspected someone was lurking in the shadows, out to get her. Is this how someone with schizophrenia saw the world?

She rubbed her temples. "What did you give me? What?"

"I'm sorry. It was only once."

When another wave of nausea rose in her throat, she forced it back down.

"Scott?" She blinked her watery, burning eyes and squinted against the harsh morning light.

"Meth. I was messing around. It was just a little bit."

"What the heck? Damn it, what's gotten into you?"

She picked at her arms as she continued to tweak off his meth trip. Or was she coming down from it? Who the heck knew? Unable to stop the compulsion to look over her shoulder, at least she understood the source of her paranoia.

"I'm sorry. I messed up." He smiled winningly, smoothing out his wrinkled clothes and squaring his shoulders.

Until this morning at this very moment, she didn't believe it was possible for her life to get any worse.

She had been wrong.

"Forgive me?" He shrugged.

When he squeezed her hand, she startled, hypervigilant, nerves on overdrive.

He brushed his hair off his forehead. "Please?"

"Just go to work. We'll talk tonight."

Staggering into the bathroom, she unloaded the contents of her stomach into the toilet. She was going to be late for her job, but damn it, she wouldn't call in sick. Although she refused to lose the income, today was going to hurt. She washed her mouth out and wiped imaginary cobwebs from her face. Grabbing her purse, she threw her brother a nasty glare and staggered out into the mercilessly bright sunshine.

Chapter 4

Hannah felt like leftovers from hell, reheated.

To make matters worse, that Dante guy had come back.

She had no patience for the man who sat in the corner of the reading area, sipping an espresso, the tiny cup disappearing in his big paw of a hand. Even while taking a sip, he managed to look manly as his mussed blond hair bobbed. He didn't react to the hidden and not-so-hidden glances from several other customers. Disgusting. All that attention, and he just ignored it. How rude.

Didn't the guy ever work? He dressed the part of a well-heeled, young, hip businessman who worked as a sports model on the side. Some people had all the luck. Pushing the glasses back up her nose and wincing as the movement hurt her face and her hand, she gave herself permission to feel sorry for five seconds.

All right, done.

She tried not to grimace, but every movement shredded tight muscles. The effort not to twitch hurt more than letting the muscles quiver. She had to keep working, couldn't mess up, couldn't let on that she ached from her hair to her toenails. It would be beyond devastating if she lost her job. She had no place to go. There was no one who would help her. She either succeeded or failed—there was no middle ground in this scenario.

When she caught Dante observing her over the top of *Esquire* magazine, she rolled her eyes. After browsing the women's health aisle two days ago? Lose the fancy clothes and the espresso cup, and he didn't strike her as someone who read anything without short sentences and colorful pictures. So what was this guy's deal?

To make matters worse, she struggled to avoid picking at the skin on her arms, the compulsion driving her out of her mind.

Normally, remaining calm was one of her better skills, but right now, focusing on anything was a difficult task.

Scott's going to get an earful when I'm home tonight.

Alcohol and meth? What was he thinking? What was she thinking taking on all that crap? She should've let Scott suffer. Maybe he'd learn a lesson. *Doubtful.* She always bailed him out. And for good reason. He had the trump card to guilt her into helping him: Philly and Ray.

Damn Scott and his stupid experiments.

If Scott was going to do stupid stuff like this, she couldn't help him again. Had they reached the breaking point? The point where she needed to leave him to fend for himself? She was close. But he was still her brother. She had to believe that he'd get over whatever was going on with him. How much time should she give him to get over this phase, to handle his bizarre behavior? What about the drug use? Sometimes, she simply hated her life. Hated the rotten hand she'd been dealt. Hated that she couldn't see a way out of this situation.

Just one break, that's all I need to get out of this hole. What if I got a wealthy boyfriend? She glanced over at one prime example sitting in her bookstore and then dumped that thought as fast as it appeared. *No. Not only would he not want her baggage, she was not the kind of person to use someone. No way.*

To make matters worse, she would never stop worrying that a vindictive Ray could still hunt her down. After that hellish evening four years ago, she and Scott had called the cops and gotten Ray thrown in jail. But their reprieve lasted as long as it took for him to post bail. In the space of time between exiting the jail and going to trial, Ray had done more than the unspeakable. His sick retribution had taught Hannah and Scott a valuable lesson. They would never rely on anyone else to stay safe, ever again. To escape Ray, they'd committed lesser crimes in the process, and she and Scott ran, or rather, limped, away.

Even with a new identity, new documents, she never felt safe. At least she still had Scott. Well, sort of.

One day, I don't know how, but I'll be totally free. No more worrying about Ray. I can't wait. She shuddered at a twinge deep in her belly. What a sick bastard.

A tickle of imagined spider's feet on her neck tormented her, and she curled a hand into a fist to keep from scratching. The ghost insect would drive her insane. Hoping no one watched, she ran her hand over her neck. There, no spider.

At a second prickle, she saw Dante staring at her.

Ray.

Dante.

No way. His presence couldn't be related to Ray, could it? Was he luring her in with flirtatiousness and attention for the kill or worse, or had her meth-infused paranoia taken hold of her mind?

In a sick and logical fashion, it made sense, didn't it? Why else would a guy like Dante be interested in someone like her? Oh, God, if he was linked to Ray, then this whole situation had just gone nuclear.

Every muscle tensed, ready to run out of the shop.

Stop. Think. She planted her feet in place.

How could he have anything to do with Ray? If so, then surely Dante would've acted by now. Why continue coming back to the shop? To toy with her? No, that theory made no sense. Ray would have employed a search and destroy method.

Her heart rate calmed down—if Ray were involved in any way, she and Scott would be dead by now. Period.

Dante glanced up again, and Hannah straightened her ankle-length navy skirt and knit top before she could stop herself. His simple presence here rankled. Hell, even the soft fabric of her skirt irritated her today. She tried to brush away the loose threads on the worn fabric as a wave of frustration beat against her. So maybe she didn't have fine clothing like Mr. *GQ*, but this was one of her better Salvation Army finds. Each item for a buck. Bet ol' Fancypants there never shopped at the thrift store. Ever. Probably wiped his hard butt with dollar bills.

Turning to ring up a customer, she forced her protesting muscles to cooperate. Oh man, it hurt to look at the register. She ran the customer's credit card and afterward placed her palms flat on the countertop—anything to anchor her spinning vision and throbbing head.

She startled when the front door jingled. *Geez, calm down.*

Mildred, one of the regular customers, entered the store. Her gnarled hand wrapped around a cane as she shuffled her stooped frame to the front desk.

"Hello, dear, how are you today?"

Mildred's silver hair had been curled and sprayed into a neat nimbus. A sharp acetone and thick rose perfume scent wafted over Hannah. Mildred must've come from her weekly hair appointment.

Hannah forced her lips to turn up. "A little tired. You?"

"You know, my usual aches and pains."

The lady's stiff, swollen fingers deviated away from the thumbs, her knuckles red and puffy. Shame flooded Hannah's chest like a warm, ugly puddle of nasty mud. How dare she feel sorry for herself when folks like Mildred were still struggling to enjoy life on a daily basis?

Mildred reached back and patted herself awkwardly on the shoulder. "And my ol' hump back here is giving me fits today, my dear. Maybe the weather is changing."

"Are you taking the pills to help your pain?"

"Most of the time, but since Ralph died, I don't always remember. He always reminded me." The loose skin on her chin quivered. "And I have trouble opening the bottles myself." She waved her clawed hands. "Ralph used to help me…"

Ashamed to blow off the sweet lady, Hannah simply didn't have the energy to ask for more details, although Mildred looked like she wanted to talk about her beloved husband, deceased now a year. Mildred and Ralph used to come in together, leaning on each other for support as they strolled into the shop. Sadness now creased the woman's lined features.

Hannah wanted to kick herself for being so selfish. "May I get you anything? Coffee? Tea? A magazine?"

"Yes, dear, I would love some Earl Grey if you have it. With sugar."

The lady fished out a few dollars and change and doddered over to a seat near the espresso machine. Thankfully, she sat on the other side of the room from Dante, and she chose a seat a good distance away from the ten or so customers present. When Hannah took the tea over, she furtively snuck a glance. Dante's aristocratic nose was buried in the depths of the *Wall Street Journal.* The *Journal?* Whatever. But good. He was distracted.

"Now let me see your poor hands," Hannah said.

The lady obliged, and Hannah gingerly knelt before her, rubbing her fingertips over the ropey veins and swollen joints. Bones jutted from beneath tissue-thin skin. Mildred made an *oooh* of discomfort when she tried to curl her fingers.

Hannah cringed. Should she do this? *Could* she take more pain on top of what Scott had transferred to her? But how could she not try? Mildred was hurting today. It's not like when Hannah had tried healing her Aunt Linda's terminal illness. Mildred only had arthritis. How bad would it be?

Gingerly, Hannah dropped the mental barrier and opened herself to the connection. Despite her caution, the gift didn't know moderation. She clenched her jaw as Mildred's arthritis pain slammed into her own hands. Hannah's hands contracted into stiff claws as the fingers bent in awkward angles. Shooting pains into the smallest finger joints brought her to tears. Even Hannah's knees, hips, and shoulders began to swell and grind in the sockets. She had to stop. No more for today, or she wouldn't be able to function.

Mildred stretched and wiggled her suddenly nimble fingers. "My dear, my hands are better! How did you…?"

Hannah shot a glance around. No interested stares from the half-filled seating area. No one noticed the transfer. Half of the patrons remained buried in a magazine or a book, and the other half were busy watching Dante. Fine by her.

"Sh. It's just the nice, warm tea. It soothes the joints."

"But I haven't—"

"Let me know if you need anything else."

Hannah stood, stifling a cry when her back and hips popped, and shuffled away. Ducking into an aisle of books, she brushed the tears away with a swollen knuckle. The pain of transfer would last only a few days, but boy, did it hurt now. At least the aches distracted from her suffering from the hangover mixed with meth. Now there was some good news.

When she returned to the counter, Dante awaited her there, his ever-present smile now pissing her off. The man oozed self-assurance, like nothing kept him down for long. Apparently, he hadn't gotten the hint from the failed salvo yesterday.

Hannah groaned. *Come on, not today, Mr. Esquire.*

"Lovely to see you again."

Darn his chiseled jaw, but she had no energy or desire for his advances. "Yes?" she said between gritted teeth. She forced her mouth to relax into a smile. Even hapless meatheads didn't deserve for her to be mean to them.

Another wave of skin ripples hit her. *Don't itch. Resist the urge.*

When he grinned, his white, even teeth were as big and perfect as the rest of him. *Figures.*

"I don't believe I got your name yesterday."

He leaned over the counter. If he weren't so handsome, and her skin weren't crawling with invisible maggots, she might have welcomed intrusion into her personal space. For the love of Pete, he even smelled amazing. A mixture of leather, a hint of expensive cologne, and a hint of wildness like mountains. She inhaled deeply, an olfactory vacation from her daily life.

"Madam? Your name?"

She stopped herself mid-sniff. Busted.

"I didn't give it to you."

His ice-blue eyes appraised her much too closely for her comfort. Could he tell what she'd done? The transfer? No way.

"Perhaps you should reconsider."

What was this guy's deal? She studied his sincere face. Good grief, he was one persistent fellow.

What would it be like to run her fingers over his strong jaw?

Come on, are you serious? Get a grip.

She held her breath. Was he in cahoots with Ray or not?

Crap, his open face gave no hint of deception. Could she trust herself to judge his character?

Apparently so. "Hannah."

"Hannah," he said. "Beautiful name."

His bass voice sent chills up her spine, and she rubbed her arms. He stared at her more intently than was appropriate or comfortable.

"I don't think I properly asked yesterday, but may I take you out sometime?"

"Like on a date?" she blurted out. Dating this man—any man—was beyond a horrible idea.

He smiled.

Her heart thudded, not in excitement but panic. She resisted the need to flee.

"Of course," he said.

What the heck? Had he not gotten the hint from yesterday?

Her reasons for avoiding men were beyond solid. First, who would look twice at her when she worked so hard to be bland and unremarkable? Second, after her twisted initiation into the arts of intimacy by Ray, she didn't plan on dating anyone anytime soon. Sure, she had more confidence now, after having rebuilt her entire life from ashes, but what Ray had done to her had torn out a piece of her soul. A piece that might never return.

"Ah, no thank you again. I'm not... not interested."

"Boyfriend?"

"No."

"Oh, then, maybe you're more into women?"

He drummed his thick, square fingers on the counter. *Da-da-da-dum. Da-da-da-dum.* This situation had moved into awkward territory. Her skull pounded in time to his tapping fingertips.

When he stepped back, she had an unobstructed view of his broad chest and shoulders. She swallowed as her vision split into two parts. Logic saw a handsome man. Sheer, unadulterated terror viewed a snarling Ray looming over her all over again. Damn it, she couldn't breathe.

She forced her mouth to form words over a panic-dried tongue. "No, I'm not—Look, Mr. Dante, is there something *related to the bookstore* I can help you with?"

He cleared his throat, his jaw set. "Yes, well, I need to pay for the paper."

She rang up his order, and when he handed her the money, his finger brushed hers, sending a strange, adherent zing through her hand. She jerked the hand away as a burst of her own healing power shot into her finger.

As though it came from him. *What?*

If he noticed a similar sensation, he gave no indication.

After several attempts with her swollen fingers to pick up the coin that had dropped on the counter, she gave up, and mortified, an embarrassed heat spread up her neck again.

Dante slid the coin into his palm and pocketed the money. He raised a thick, blond eyebrow. "Quick question, if you don't mind."

"Yes." Her eyes widened.

"Are you from back east by any chance?"

"What?" Her vision blurred, and she gripped the counter to remain upright. "Pardon?"

"Just curious. You remind me of someone. Never mind."

She opened and closed her mouth without a sound. Her heart pounded in her chest.

"Well, you have a nice day… Hannah."

"You, too," she whispered to his retreating back.

That pause. Did he know her real name? Did he know about her history? Was he involved with Ray? Had he come for her? Oh God, she needed to leave, but she needed to make a plan. Had to convince Scott to leave as well. Panic constrained her breaths until she saw stars. She stared at her swollen hands resting on the counter.

Breathe. Relax.

She frowned. There was something more.

When she rubbed the finger that had contacted him, it no longer hurt.

Chapter 5

The crippled octogenarian, "Mildred," had motored around the bookstore like a spry fifty-year-old, ever since Hannah held the woman's hands. And what about Hannah's fingers and knuckles when she tried to pick up the coin? She had become positively geriatric in the space of minutes.

Even though she obviously didn't feel well, she had still been polite to all of the customers, including his persistent self. He didn't miss the flashes of pain in those gold-flecked brown eyes that the glasses didn't hide. For a split second when their hands brushed, he'd gotten a brief sensation of pain in his finger. But the feeling was gone before he could examine it. Curious.

At first, he'd figured Hannah to be a meek, demure mouse of a woman, but there was steel beneath her fragile form. She was a walking contradiction. Her appearance said "hands off," but the kindness with her customers revealed a warmer side. She had rebuffed him, but the cracks in her tough façade fascinated him. He wanted to find out more.

Needing some distance from this woman so he could think, Dante strolled to a nearby café. While he wasn't exactly inconspicuous, he could at least watch the entrance of the bookstore without encroaching on Hannah. Had she truly taken away the old lady's arthritis pain? How was that possible? Did she have abilities, too?

Allie, his friend Peter's wife, could see death when she touched people. It stood to reason there would be other people like Allie, maybe with all sorts of different talents.

As an Indebted, Dante healed quickly, his personal self-repair a side effect of his eternal contract, which made sense. Jerahmeel, his boss, wouldn't want his employees to die of mortal causes.

Fragile contracted killers made for bad investments. Dante had found out about the fast-healing ability when he broke his leg during the French Revolution. Fifteen minutes later, he had been back on his feet again, in pain but leg intact, swinging away with his fellow citizens.

The *Sami* people who inhabited the territory above the Arctic Circle in his native Sweden had been renowned for their healing abilities, so he'd heard of mysterious healers as far back as when he was a boy. If the stories were true, the Sami could make it snow on command and bring in the giant herds of reindeer, so what was truth and what was legend? Things happened in this world that no one understood. Hell, Dante was living proof of that fact.

What about that nasty Raymond Jackson guy? Dante gripped the metal café table until the rim bent as rage rumbled up and threatened to break over him like a tidal wave. It would've satisfied Dante more if Jackson's death had lasted much longer than it had. The knife on Dante's lower leg pulsed, as he recalled the satisfaction as the knife entered Jackson's chest cavity, the almost orgasmic relief as that evil soul poured its last drops into the knife until the blade had been sated. Another criminal out of the way.

Knowing that Jackson had apologized for hurting his children, was there any doubt why Hannah was terrified of Dante? Of her own shadow? Dante still needed to tell her about Jackson's demise. This woman had to be Jessica Miller, now called Hannah. The way she reacted hid nothing. Maybe Hannah would be so relieved at the news of Jackson's death that she would run into Dante's open arms. He would be a hero. *Utmarkt*. Excellent.

Mission accomplished.

But unfortunately, killing Jackson did not satisfy the big mission, the Meaningful Kill, as evidenced by the fact that Dante remained an Indebted. Maybe soon, like Peter, Dante might break his contract and be free of the eternal curse.

Didn't he like his eternally powerful life? When had that changed?

Before he examined his change of heart, a new hunger swelled. It had been nearly two weeks since he'd performed his last kill, and the impulse usually built until he couldn't think of anything else. Normally, two weeks was right at the limit of his control before the urge consumed him. With effort, he pushed the desire to kill aside. He needed to focus on Hannah for a while longer.

Now that he'd met Hannah and was prepared to deliver Jackson's deathbed message, so to speak, Dante found he didn't simply want to be a messenger and then leave. If he delayed his announcement, he could spend more time learning more about this intriguing woman.

And then do what? He had nothing to offer, even if his news endeared her to Dante. His entire existence personified the definition of morally corrupt. At this point, though, his interest was more than professional and more than his usual sexual interest.

When was the last time he'd felt so strongly about anyone? Two, three hundred years ago? Why try again? It would only bring pain for all parties involved.

Thoughts churned in his mind until he gave up trying to create order out of chaos. His unhappiness changed nothing. At a loss to raise his spirits, he simply tucked into a delectable multicourse meal.

Just after seven o'clock, the faint jingle of the bookstore door drifted over to him in time for him to see Hannah leave the store and walk up the street. Her hips swayed unevenly under the long skirt. He briefly indulged in envisioning her body beneath her clothes. Would his hands span her tiny waist? What would she feel like, folded into his arms or, even better, lying beneath him?

As if he had the right to think about such things. He did not.

He easily caught up to her slow, limping gait. "Hello, Hannah." He spoke without preamble, pouring on the charm.

She gurgled a cry and jumped back, tears welling in her bespectacled eyes. It was true: He was an idiot. Damn it, he had to consider what she might have endured with Jackson. Time to back off and try a softer approach.

"I'm sorry to scare you," he said, letting his deep voice vibrate the air.

When he reached out to her, she flinched away like a wounded bird desperately trying to fly away. He cursed himself again. *Gently, man. Tone down the machismo.*

"What... what are you doing here?" She flicked glances up and down the street.

He could listen to her low, breathless voice for centuries, and it wouldn't get old.

"I, uh, was walking by when you came out of the store. Would you like a ride home?" He cringed. Still didn't hit the right tone. He needed this encounter to come across as less creepy stalker, more casual happenstance.

"No, no. That's not... no. I'll just walk like I usually do. On my own. Alone."

Okay. Kid gloves, then. "Could I walk with you?"

"No, I don't—no. But thank you."

He enjoyed how the flush crept over her face and neck, and his hands itched with the desire to see if that skin was as baby soft as it appeared. And that pulse jumping at the base of her neck? *Ja,* he wanted his lips there.

"I'd really be more comfortable walking you home. It's getting darker earlier these days. Um, because it's fall," he stammered.

Lame. Where had the smooth operator gone? He'd deserted Dante, pure and simple.

"Yes, but it's more than a mile," she said.

"I think I can manage."

"I'm not sure..."

When she crossed her arms, the barest shadow formed in the fabric nestled between her breasts. It took all of his unnatural strength not to stare at that spot.

He kept his arms close to his body but turned his palms up to her. "Look, we got off on the wrong foot, and I apologize. Sometimes I'm less than... couth. I truly want to walk you home, nothing else. I promise. And I do sincerely believe that it's dangerous for a lady to walk home alone in the dark."

He pretended to consider the twilight sky, drawing her attention upward, then stood still for a full minute. Her silence nearly killed him. He wanted to plead his case, try another round of sure-fire seductiveness, but he now knew those tactics wouldn't work. Quelling the urge to squirm beneath her scrutiny, he tried to come across as nonchalant and nonthreatening, which for someone of his size was an almost impossible task. *Please.*

"Okay. Big streets only. And I have pepper spray."

She stood as tall as possible, which wasn't saying much. Dante tried not to laugh out loud. If only she knew what he was capable of, with his unhuman Indebted strength, his occupation, she would never walk with him. Barehanded, he could destroy any mortal man, to say nothing of this scrap of a female. But her safety was his paramount concern, even if she didn't realize it.

Trying to pour reassurance into his reply, he smiled. "Sounds reasonable. You can pepper spray me at any time. Actually, you can do it once for practice if you will feel more secure."

Forty years ago, he'd been pepper sprayed at an environmental protest in the Redwoods. He so did enjoy participating in citizen revolts over the ages. *Ja*, damn spray hurt like hell, but with his superhuman self-healing, the effect only lasted a minute or two. If Hannah needed to burn out his eyeballs to accept his company, he'd gladly let her do it.

At her hesitation, he added, "Would you like to carry the bottle in your hand? You'll be ready to take action, if needed."

She wrinkled her nose at him, rotated her purse to sling it in front of her, and damned if she didn't fish out the spray can and palm it. Her sweet lips pressed into a thin line. Spectacular *bestämning*. Determination. Grit.

• • •

The walk home flat out hurt. Between her headache, every joint in her body aching—save that one finger—and the blond giant next to her who, bless him, hadn't tried any funny business, Hannah had zero energy left.

Despite her exhaustion, she didn't miss when several women flirted with him on the walk home. Beautiful women with hungry glances that locked onto him; a few women even licked their lips. What hurt more was the way their expressions changed as their eyes slid from Dante to Hannah. She wasn't a threat to these women, just an aberration, a peculiarity, like a puzzle piece that didn't belong. Despite the attention, Dante appeared to ignore it all and concentrated solely on Hannah, and that focus unnerved her.

Why *was* he here with her? As she drifted along with their light conversation, she only half listened. She kept searching for an ulterior motive, a hint of pity, an angle having to do with Ray, anything.

Somewhere a few blocks north of the bookstore, she'd returned the pepper spray to her purse. It hurt her fingers to hold the bottle. Besides, she could scream pretty loudly if he tried anything.

To his credit, Dante had planted his hands at his sides and hadn't moved them for twenty minutes. He walked close enough that his massive frame gave her the perception of safety, but he didn't encroach on her personal space.

Hannah experienced a fleeting illusion of companionship, rapidly replaced by a wave of terror. She was alone with a man.

Never mind Dante's kind, blue eyes and the heat that somehow radiated out from him and wrapped around her like a warm blanket. Despite the fact that he had made no advances, had done nothing improper, she couldn't overcome the quaking inside her body. Her shivers had nothing to do with the handsome man next to her and everything to do with her wrecked state. Even the slight movement of his light hair in the breeze made her flinch.

God, her mind was a disaster zone.

If he noticed her jumpiness, he gave no indication.

Instead, their conversation, or mostly his, centered on weather, things to do in Portland, and one of her favorite topics, books. He'd transformed from a beefy flirt into a perfect, nonthreatening gentleman. He didn't even seem bothered when he had to adjust his long stride to match her ridiculously slow pace.

But he paused a few times during the conversation, as if he wanted to say more but thought better of it. What was he hiding?

As if reading her mind, Dante finally cleared his throat. "May I share something with you?"

"Maybe. Depends on the information."

"Good point." His lips thinned. "Are you Jessica Miller?"

"What?" For the second time today, he rendered her speechless.

And terrified. With her bad foot, maybe she couldn't run, but she could damn well pepper spray him.

She fumbled in her purse.

Dante didn't move.

Relief washed over her like a cool shower when her fingers wrapped around the metal tube, and she raised it in front of her. Damn how her arm shook.

"What do you want?"

He still hadn't so much as twitched a muscle. "I need to deliver a message to you. I'm not here to harm you whatsoever. Please believe me."

"Who sent you here?"

"I met a man in Philadelphia a little while back. I believe you know him. Raymond Jackson."

Nausea churned in her belly. "Oh God."

Her legs went weak, and when he reached for her, she waved him off with a menacing wave of the pepper spray. "Don't touch me."

He dropped his hand. "I met Raymond Jackson at the end of his life in Philadelphia."

"Ray's dead?" Damn it, but sound and light slid from side to side. She had to concentrate on Dante's face to remain upright.

"Yes, he's dead."

"How did he die?" Like it mattered. At least that monster was gone for good.

He couldn't look at her. "Stabbed in an alley. But before he died, he asked me to give you a message."

"Okay." She spared no sad emotion for that sick animal, dying in the streets of Philly. Good riddance.

"He said he had roughed up his children."

That's putting it lightly.

"And?" With her fingers still wrapped around her puny weapon, she dropped her shaking arm to her side.

"He was sorry for everything he had put you and your brother through."

Dante smiled as though he'd delivered her the Ark of the Covenant.

Poor guy had no idea.

A simple apology didn't undo Ray's destruction. A simple apology only ripped open wounds that had started to heal.

But there was a tiny spark inside of her. A tendril of relief surrounded by layers of pain and fear. She'd have to take time to absorb this information. Maybe Ray's death would help her move on with her life. She'd never be normal, but knowing that he couldn't hurt her again gave her a flicker of hope.

Poor Dante stood there with such a hopeful expression on his handsome features.

She swallowed. "How did you know Ray? How did you come to be there when he died?"

He stared at the concrete for a long moment. "Happened to be in the right place. Um, when he gave me the information to deliver, I came to Portland."

"You just picked up and came here to find me and deliver this message?" Something smelled fishy. He wasn't telling her everything.

"I, uh, have a lot of flexibility with my job."

"What exactly do you do?"

"Um, pest control." His expression was more question, less statement.

"Looking like this?"

"I run my own business."

"Hmm."

He cleared his throat. "So isn't that a good message?"

Darned if he didn't look like an overgrown schoolboy, awaiting praise. She hated to burst his bubble.

"Kind of. Well. Thank you for going to all the trouble to tell me."

"So Raymond wasn't a nice guy?"

"I'd rather not discuss him, if you don't mind."

"Of course." He hadn't moved a muscle in the past five minutes.

"Can we just keep walking for a while?"

"Whatever you wish." His stiff stance belied his polite words.

Perhaps she hadn't shown the proper gratitude. He had come all the way from Philadelphia and somehow tracked her down, all to give her this message. That effort had to have taken time and money. Even if he was independently wealthy, he still had taken a lot of initiative on her behalf.

She tried to formulate a statement of appropriate thanks, one that she could say without breaking into pieces. Nope. Couldn't do it.

Deep in thought, they strolled side by side in pensive silence. She'd be sure to thank him by the time they reached her house.

Fewer and fewer cars passed as they passed into the run-down residential area. The pleasant companionship eased the tension in her shoulders. For the time being.

Lulled into a relaxed state, she almost forgot about her disappointing life, almost forgot her aches and pains. Too easily, she imagined all of her days ending like this, walking home with a handsome man, enjoying polite conversation and companionship.

Until she blasted back into reality.

Up the street, Scott and his nasty friend, Brandon, stood at the front door of the house, beer bottles in hands. Their expressions were hidden in backlit shadow from the porch light, but the silhouettes of their heads rose as she approached. *Oh geez, not good.*

"Okay, so I'll go on from here alone, thanks." She smiled in what she hoped was a convincing manner.

Slowing down her pace, she prayed Dante would get the hint.

"I don't mind walking further."

"No, really, it's fine. Thank you and good night."

She had to get him away from here. Shame for her brother and for her life rose up. So much for the gentleman walking her home to her pleasant life. Nice dream while it lasted. Dear lord, Dante wasn't stopping.

Scott raised his bottle in shaky salute. "Hi, sis, who you got there?"

At an encouraging nod and smirk from Brandon, her brother sauntered to the sidewalk, planted his feet, and crossed his arms.

"I'm Scott. Who the fuck are you?"

Mortified, Hannah opened her mouth, but the man next to her spoke up first.

"Dante Blackstone."

She hadn't heard him project his voice before, and the bass tones vibrated through the concrete into the soles of her feet. Wow.

Scott rocked back a half step. "What the hell are you doing fooling around with my sister?"

She wanted to dissolve into the cracked pavement.

Although he remained civil on the surface, Dante's censure was obvious. "There was no fooling around, as you say. It didn't seem right to make your sister walk home in the dark. I'm surprised you don't have more concern for her safety."

Scott sputtered. "Well, I've got my own business to take care of, my man. It's cool. She can take care of herself. She's a big girl."

Her brother didn't look at her but instead glanced at Brandon. After a long draw on the beer, Brandon leered at her and nudged Scott.

What the heck? Her brother had become another person altogether around this guy. How much she'd give to keep Scott permanently away from his so-called friend.

Brandon's narrow face squished into a scowl. "You don't want a random dude sniffing around your sister, do you?" His nostrils flared as he smirked at Dante with open hostility.

Just being in the same zip code as Brandon made Hannah's skin crawl.

Dante reared back and stared at Brandon as if the ginger jerk had given him the worst news of his life. Dante's brows drew together, and his mouth clamped into a hard line. Did these two men know each other? Their reactions were unusual, to say the least. In the silent standoff, she squirmed.

"No way, bro." Scott wiped his mouth on his hand and glared at Dante. "All right, buddy. You did your charity work for my poor sister." She flinched at Scott's sarcasm. "You should head on home now before you try to get your hands on her. Payment for your services and all, right?"

Dante actually growled, and the heat coming off him increased until she started to sweat. How was that possible? It had to be her nerves. Mortified, she half turned to Dante. Although his hands had curled into massive fists, he kept them pressed to his sides. Maybe she could salvage the evening and whatever the heck was going on between these guys before an actual fight broke out. Dante's electric-blue eyes had turned black. Had to be a trick of the streetlight.

"Thank you for walking me home."

When she placed one finger on his arm, his black eyes bore into hers, and she froze. Thankfully, she had secured the transfer instinct, but warmth flowed up her finger into her hand, and she yanked her hand back. Somehow, Dante appeared bigger. Muscles stood out on his neck as rage radiated out from him, like a crazy, blond grizzly about to charge.

Standing stiff against the waves of disapproval behind her and the waves of anger in front of her, she repeated herself with as much force as she could muster. "Thank you again. I appreciate it. Have a good night."

Dante looked like he was about to rip everyone's arms off with his bare hands. Then he blinked down at her. Black eyes lightened to blue.

"I enjoyed the company. Hopefully, your brother will realize it's inappropriate to make a lady walk home." He stared down Scott and Brandon. Through gritted teeth, he said, "And adjust his priorities accordingly."

He nodded curtly to her, spun, and walked off, his heavy tread fading into the night, leaving her empty and alone. And pissed.

She whirled around. "What's wrong with you, Scott? Are you a gangster now, threatening folks?"

"Go in the house. Brandon and I have business to discuss."

"What business?"

"None of your business, that's for sure."

"More drugs?"

"Shut up. Just let me do my work and look out for you. I need to provide for us."

"This?" She motioned at Brandon's thin, sneering leer. "This is looking out for me? I seriously doubt it."

"You gonna let her talk to you like that?" Brandon asked.

"No way, bro. Get in the house, sis. Brandon and I need to talk about things."

"I bet you do." She gave him her meanest glare. "I'm disappointed. That was a nice guy just doing a good deed, and you were rude to him." She poked him in the chest. "Grow. Up."

"You ever wonder what a nice guy would want with you, sis? How about nothing?" He belched. "That guy was slummin'. Once he gets in your pants, he'll throw you away like last night's dinner."

"How about you work on yourself? Would it be so wrong if a stand-up kind of man wanted to pay some attention to me?" She'd never snapped at her brother before, but he had really hit a nerve.

"No. But what would happen if things got more touchy-feely, huh? Not so perfect, then. You going to explain what's wrong with you? To him?"

"You're a total jerk, Scott."

Brushing away tears, she stomped into the house and slammed the door shut. What the hell had gotten into her brother? Her mother would've been horrified. Actually, their mother would never have tolerated Scott's behavior. Some days, Hannah really missed her. Hannah missed the old Scott, too.

The worst part of his assessment? It was true.

She bore visible and invisible scars from Ray that would never fade. No man would be brave enough or dumb enough to take on that mess.

So what about Dante? Well, so much for him. The male attention was nice while it lasted. Scott chasing Dante away saved her from disappointment and embarrassment later, anyway.

With a sigh that bordered on a sob, she dragged herself to the indented mattress on the floor of the tiny second bedroom. She might not be back in Philly with Ray and his sick vices, but right about now, this life here sucked, too.

• • •

Dante doubled back.

Alarms blared in his mind.

He circled the block, sneaking through a neighboring yard to get next to Hannah's house. Something wasn't right, and it had nothing to do with her moron brother. It was his annoying friend. He seemed… off. Really off. Like… Dante.

Damn it. Anger had caught him off guard. He didn't have a chance to study the orange-haired man, let alone question him, but Dante had caught a whiff of… something familiar. Couldn't put his finger on it, but chances were this guy was bad news.

Hannah around that guy? *Kristus*. Dante fought the need to break down the door and get her out of there.

His leg pulsed. The cursed knife knew his mood and his desire to fill the blade with a criminal soul. Was it seeking his attention because he hadn't killed in a while? Or because of Scott's friend? What did the knife know that Dante didn't?

Scott's friend. Pinched face, shifty. Total bastard with secrets.

Someone like Dante.

He could've sworn he knew most of the Indebted. Unless Jerahmeel had created a new employee in the past year or so. But Dante would've heard about it, right?

Cold dread hit him like a sucker punch to the gut. *Jävlar*. Shit.

The asshole was just like Dante. But not. That explained the similarity.

A minion.

Maintaining his stealthy footsteps, he picked up the pace, desperate to get closer to the house. A minion. *Herre Gud*, this was bad, bad, bad. The last minion, Anton, almost killed Peter and Allie. Nearly as evil as Jerahmeel, minions were exceedingly hard to kill—harder, even than killing an Indebted like Dante, and that was difficult enough.

If the guess was correct, then this minion already knew that Dante was an Indebted. Like called to like.

Why did Jerahmeel need a minion now? Normally, he used them to extend his reach and prevent Indebteds from completing their contracts, but why a minion here? Why with these people? Something didn't add up.

He needed to get advice from his old friend, Barnaby. This entire situation was very wrong. Dante's kind didn't casually run into a minion. Come to think of it, few mortals met a minion over the millennia and lived to tell about it.

Hannah and her brother didn't stand a chance.

Dante's heart began to jackhammer its way out of his chest.

Hopping the six-foot chainlink fence behind Hannah's house, Dante alighted on the balls of his feet, turned, and slid into the shadows. He might be big, but his ability to stalk counted as an art form. He was a master. As he slunk through the darkness, he placed his feet deliberately and silenced his movements.

Using peripheral nighttime vision to better navigate, he sidled up to the house. He crouched in a shadow and stilled his breathing into noiselessness. Hidden, he could see the front of the house but would not be easily seen himself.

Scott and his friend stood in the porch light on the sidewalk. Straining to hear, Dante picked up their conversation.

"... don't you think it's weird, your ugly sister bringing home a hot guy all of a sudden?"

Dante almost rounded the house, with fists cocked and ready. Ugly? Hannah? What *oåkting* would say that about such a sweet woman?

"Yeah, that is weird, Brandon," Scott said.

Her brother accepted a fresh beer from this... Brandon. The asshole was getting the kid *druken*. What a good friend.

Scott's speech slurred. "I don't like this guy one bit. Hannah's my sister, and it's my job to watch out for her, not some mook with fancy clothes."

"He's probably a pimp," Brandon whispered.

Persuasion oozed off the *røvhål*, the asshole. Dante would break his own hands if he didn't relax his fists. Strategy. He couldn't take this guy in a one-on-one fight. Not that he wouldn't try if this Brandon guy put her in danger, but Dante had to consider all of his options right now.

Damn it, he didn't have many.

Brandon sneered. "That moron wants to steal away your sister, even after everything you did for her."

"Yeah, he's bad news. She's just going along for the male attention. God knows she doesn't get any."

Not flying across the yard to punch those two guys took all of Dante's willpower.

"Even more reason to keep her away from that asshole. Come on. You're the man of the house, right?" The minion leaned in close and clapped Scott on the back.

Dante froze as he surveyed the scene. Something was totally wrong about the way the minion acted and how he manipulated Scott when they made contact.

"Keep her away. You bet I will." Scott upended the bottle and threw it into the street with a harsh crash. "I'll lay down the law. For her own safety, of course."

"Dude, you're such a good brother."

"Yeah, you got that right." He staggered toward the house. "Give me another beer."

"Whoa, hold on there. What're you going to do about the hangover tomorrow, dude?"

"Hannah will take care of it. She always does."

"What the fuck are you talking about?"

"She cures me."

Radar on overdrive, Dante strained to listen. He wanted to know what the fuck Scott was talking about, too.

"Bullshit," Brandon said.

"Dude, it's sweet. When I'm sick or hurt, she fixes it."

The minion grabbed him by the shirt as Scott staggered backward.

"What do you mean, fixes?"

"She's got mad skills, my man. Yeah, when there's something wrong with people, she can make it better."

"Explain." No longer playing the solicitous friend, the minion shook Scott. "Explain!"

"Chill, dude. She puts her hands on me, and whatever's wrong goes away. Like when I broke my arm, she healed it. Course, it broke her arm in the process but not quite as bad." He slurred his words more. "She'll take away my hangover tomorrow. I'll be as good as new."

Dante's regard for her brother's character dropped another notch. She'd be sick as a dog, absorbing the pain from Scott's bad decision. So, the elderly lady in the shop, Hannah's limp, how ill she acted this morning? All from taking away sickness?

Kristus. And the minion knew.

The downspout he gripped crumpled with a raw squeak.

Brandon jerked his narrow head toward the side of the house where Dante crouched. The minion stood motionless, staring into the shadows.

Dante held dead still as the hungry knife heated up. *Jävlar.* Shit. The damn knife would give him away. He unwrapped his fingers from the crushed metal and folded them into a lethal fist. If Brandon approached, Dante'd be ready. At least he had the element of surprise.

Thankfully, Scott took this moment to vomit all over the pavement, much to the disgust of the minion. But it distracted Brandon.

Dante crept back behind the house, leapt over the fence, and sprinted inhumanly fast for a few blocks to get some distance between his knife and Brandon. If the minion knew who Dante was, or *what* he was, this could spell horrible news for Dante. But the minion definitely knew about Hannah, and she was in the most danger now.

The knife pulsed.

He needed a kill.

Not now, damn it.

He needed to get Hannah away from Brandon.

And do what? Hide her away forever? She wouldn't want to be in the same country as Dante when she learned what kind of creature he was.

What a disaster. All he had to do was deliver a message and leave well enough alone, and now he'd gotten tangled up with a minion, an asshole, and a woman who held his attention like no other woman ever had. And Dante's mere presence had put her life in danger.

He had to figure this mess out before an innocent got hurt.

As if on hellish cue, his phone vibrated. When he thumbed it on, the command displayed on the text message took his evening from bad to disastrous.

Chapter 6

Dante stifled an impatient groan as the man across from him steadied the shell with elegant silver tongs and, using a two-tined fork, slid the slick, gray-brown meat from its coiled depths. After an elaborate dip into the garlic-herb butter, the man popped the *escargot* into his mouth, fluttered his eyelids, and chewed. At the ostentatious dab of linen against his too-red lips, Dante wondered if the guy shouldn't get a room. Alone.

Although as an Indebted Dante didn't require food, he still enjoyed the occasional indulgence in a fine meal. Jerahmeel appeared to be indulging, all right, but why did his boss command Dante to meet him here? It was so… public.

He'd have to tread carefully with Jerahmeel, the being who had deployed the minion. Dante prayed he could avoid making a move that jeopardized Hannah. *Stay sharp, damn it.*

"Ah, my dear Mr. Blackstone. Tonight my mind and palate travel back to my native France, the France of *Empereur* Napoleon. He was such an admirable and odious little man. Not the France of my youth in Carcassonne, where my family…"

Dante remained motionless as his boss's scowl pulled his groomed black brows together over ember-cruel eyes.

When Jerahmeel set down the snail fork, it had melted and glowed a faint red. He blew on spidery fingers until tendrils of smoke and sulfur dissipated in the dim light of this corner booth in the luxurious wood-paneled restaurant.

The tuxedoed waiter wheeled over a mahogany cart, bowed, and deftly prepared the Chateaubriand; Jerahmeel's mood cooled as the food simmered. Cooked mushrooms and garlic coated the tenderloin. The waiter poured wine into the pan, and the entire dish briefly flashed in blue-yellow flame. Dante swallowed. Even sitting across from the creature who disgusted him most in the entire world, Dante could still appreciate a well-cooked meal.

The saliva in Dante's watering mouth turned to dust when Jerahmeel cut away a piece of pink meat that still wept bloody juices. Unable to watch the grotesque food consumption further, Dante cleared his throat.

"My lord, I don't want to keep you from your meal. If you would share why you've called me here…"

A wave of volcanic heat buffeted Dante. The piece of meat still speared on the fork charred in seconds until Jerahmeel dropped the utensil and burnt food to the plate.

"*Merde!* You imbecile."

Uh oh. Not the right tactic. Dante balled a fist on his thigh and pressed his leg to hold it still.

"What information do you have?"

Dante gripped the seat with his other hand until his fingers ripped the fine leather. "About what, my lord?"

"You'd better not be insubordinate. I've killed people for less."

Draw no attention to Hannah.

"Well, I have plans to procure another kill for you soon. Unless you have a criminal selection in mind for me to stalk?"

"I question your ability to focus."

"That's never been an issue in the past, my lord."

"Have you met anyone new recently?"

Protect Hannah. "I meet people all of the time. So many, I cannot recall."

"Any new ladies?"

Dante gave his best hearty chuckle and leaned back in the booth. "You know me, boss. I meet ladies constantly."

The eyes burning across the table had narrowed to two red glints in an abyss of blackness. Smoke, like from a volcano, drifted from Jerahmeel's fingertips. "Don't play games with me, my pawn. You're distracted because of a special lady." Before Dante denied the words, Jerahmeel continued. "She's special all right, more than you realize."

"How do you mean?"

"This Hannah you're after, leave her be. Look for your entertainment elsewhere. Pay attention to your work."

Dante's blood congealed in his veins. "Why should you trouble yourself with a mere mortal, lord Jerahmeel?"

"My minion reports some interesting abilities with this one. Healing, I believe."

How could he have known that so quickly? "Who cares if she can heal? You're more powerful than any mortal. Why bother with this woman?"

"She reminds me of someone I know. Someone I want."

Damn that minion, Brandon. Hannah had attracted Jerahmeel's attention. No human withstood Jerahmeel's… attention for long. It took every ounce of Indebted strength Dante possessed to remained seated across from his boss, his jailor, his deceiver.

"Surely she is no threat to you. Simply ignore her." Unfortunately, his powers of persuasion had little effect on his boss.

Jerahmeel waggled manicured fingertips in the air, then inspected his unmarred cuticles. "You are to stay away from her so I may do with her powers as I wish."

The hell you will.

"Why?"

"It's not for you to question but to obey. Perform your Indebted duties in a timely and efficient manner. Understand?"

"Sure, but what can she mean to you?"

"I'm not certain yet, but I want to claim her for my future purposes. I will consider the possibilities and make a decision soon."

Kristus. Sand had started to slip out of the hourglass for Hannah.

"Ignore her, and I will maintain the possibility of releasing you from the contract."

"The Meaningful Kill?"

Jerahmeel took a sip of wine, his thin lips glistening with the darker red of the merlot. His red tongue darted out to trap a droplet.

Dante's stomach wrenched. That mouth, those spidery fingers weren't going anywhere near Hannah.

His boss nodded. "You have to stay in my good graces to have a chance of escaping the contract."

"Then I will do exactly as you ask." Except not. He'd do anything necessary to protect her from this nightmarish creature.

"Reject her and she lives."

In the hell of your creating? No way.

"Of course, my lord."

He waggled his fingers. "Now leave me. I fancy a crème brûlée tonight."

Any hunger Dante might have experienced was obliterated by the image of this disgusting creature eating dessert. Dante slid out of the booth, dipped his head, and beat a hasty retreat from the fine dining establishment.

What the hell was he going to do?

Could he simply walk away from Hannah and leave her fate in the hands of Jerahmeel?

• • •

In the morning light, cracked paint on the walls of the living room emphasized Hannah's broken life. Hah. Living room. Not a lot of "living" going on here.

"Sis, I feel awful. You've got to help me." Scott's whining voice drifted out of his bedroom.

Not again. She hadn't recovered from yesterday's transfer of his hangover and Mildred's arthritis pain. And what about the revelation about Ray? The suffering that news brought on wasn't physical, but it hurt just the same. Every piece of her body throbbed with a deep, bone-grinding ache. Except that one finger felt completely fine where she had touched Dante. How strange.

"Hannah!"

She ran into the bedroom. Scott had passed out on the floor this time, urine staining his clothes. Her eyes watered at the stench, and she tried not to inhale too deeply. At least he didn't appear injured, only hung over, or still mildly inebriated, she couldn't tell which.

"Please. I've got to get to work." He moaned.

She stood a few feet away from him, out of his sloppy grasp. "I'm sorry, I can't take more right now. Yesterday about ruined me."

"Bitch." The word stung, even though she knew her brother was still impaired. "You're the only one who can make this go away. Why won't you help me?"

"I can't, Scott."

"You're so selfish."

"I love you, but I can't do it this time."

Her tears welled up at the pitiful picture her brother made on the floor. It hurt, leaving him there. But she couldn't take on more pain and hope to function today.

How much *could* her body take? What would happen if she went past the limits of her healing power? She'd gotten a glimpse of those limits when she put her hands all those years ago on Aunt Linda's cancer-riddled body.

Hannah's heart still beat wildly as she recalled her terror at Ray's demand. But just like always, Hannah had agreed to try. She had placed her hands on the basketball-sized rock-hard tumor in Aunt Linda's abdomen, expecting to encounter the pebbles of cancer, and released the dam holding back her power. The gift should have exchanged Aunt Linda's illness for Hannah's wellness, but instead the voracious cancer overwhelmed Hannah, consuming all her healthy cells. Her senses failed until she couldn't sort out any specific sensation in the melee. Before Hannah had absorbed a measure of the disease, her aunt had pulled away with an expression of horror and sadness that Hannah had never forgotten.

Aunt Linda might have saved Hannah, but the failed healing sent Ray's fury into orbit. Hannah only remembered bits and pieces of the rest of that devastating evening. It was probably for the best. Thankfully, Scott hadn't been there that night.

"I should've left you in Philly."

Coming back to the present, she blinked. "What?"

"You're ungrateful." He groaned. "Look, if you can't help me, then at least do one useful thing."

He hit her where it hurt, right in the guilt complex.

"Sure, Scott." Tears burned her eyelids.

"Just stay away from the giant asshole you brought home last night."

"What?"

"You heard me; he's bad news. I'm laying down the law on this one, sis. You might be older than me, but I'm the man of the house. Don't hang around with him anymore."

"Why?"

"Because I said so." He moaned and held his arm over his forehead. "God, can't you follow one simple direction? For me?"

"Um, sure. But you should know he gave me some news yesterday."

"Like what?"

"Like that Ray was dead."

"Bullshit."

"He saw Ray die."

"He's lying."

"What?"

"To get into your pants. He's lying."

"That makes zero sense. Why should he go to the trouble to come all the way across the country just to lie to me?"

"He didn't travel that far. He's making up the story so you'll do him. Look, just steer clear of that ass clown."

"Um, sure." Totally a moot point. After the warm welcome Dante had received last night, she doubted he'd want to be in her company anytime soon. But it still didn't make sense that he'd make up the story about Ray. No one here knew her old name and her past. Except Scott.

Oh no, had Scott talked? If he blabbed, they were in deep trouble, regardless of whether Ray had died or not. Once the police figured it out, Hannah and Scott were busted.

"Get outta here before you're late. And bring back money. Ughhh."

He rolled over on the floor. After a few moments of silence, he snored again, his breathing deep and even.

Her chest hurt. This entire situation was so completely wrong.

Scott's behavior was deteriorating and unlikely to improve anytime soon, and she didn't know how to fix it. Time to reexamine the option of leaving. Would Scott be safe on his own? Who knew?

And Dante? Such a pleasant evening had ended so badly.

Could I catch a break here? Just one?

With aches in her heart and in her joints, she walked to work, dreading the day. But she dreaded the time after work even more. Although she loved her brother, she needed to be free of this depressing existence.

• • •

Dante had driven all over Portland and the surrounding area for hours after he left the disturbing meeting with Jerahmeel last night.

So, what had he learned?

He still had the possibility of getting out of his contract. Damned stupid hope lit up in his chest. He tamped it down as fast as possible. The Meaningful Kill and an end to his murderous career were in reach.

If.

If he continued to perform his duties to the letter and kill criminals for Jerahmeel.

If he left Hannah alone.

And what? Let Brandon interfere? Let Jerahmeel get his nasty fingers around her?

Abandoning her to Jerahmeel's whim didn't bode well for her future. Dante could only imagine what they'd do to her. She'd end up chained, in pain, and forced to heal. Or worse, she would die. But those two creatures wouldn't kill anyone quickly. *Kristus*, she'd live a life of nothing but torture.

This morning, Jerahmeel's command ate at his insides like acid.

Since when did he care about someone's future other than his own?

Jåvlar. *I have to walk away from this situation.*

Hannah enslaved to Jerahmeel or destroyed by him. Not a viable solution.

But why should Dante care? It had to be the concept of Jerahmeel hurting an innocent being. Dante's caring had nothing to do with this one particular woman.

No wonder that he wanted to punch the steering wheel even now, after driving around all night. Instead, he tried to calm down as he navigated the steep drive into the Forest Park neighborhood.

He barely registered the million-dollar mansions and meticulous landscaping as he drove past.

He had to figure out a plan.

Eight a.m. was as good a time as any time to wake up the old man.

Dante parked his Hummer in front of an immaculate stone Tudor home. Checking himself before he slammed the black metal door, he inhaled the loamy, damp scent of the woods and the Columbia River flowing at the bottom of the bluff. For a moment, every muscle relaxed as the scene transported him home to *Värmland* in central Sweden with its fresh-scented spruce trees and the mossy undergrowth softening the forest floor. He could still taste the crystal clear water of any of a hundred springs burbling through the wooded landscape.

He jammed a hand through his hair, as if the act would push back the rest of that rogue nostalgia.

Enough. There was work to do.

He knocked on the massive walnut door. A tall woman he'd never seen before answered.

"Yes?" No emotion. But there was dissatisfaction on her impassive face. Disappointment with… him? But she'd only met him.

Dante plowed ahead, bringing the charismatic sizzle as he rose to his full, impressive height. "Ah, is Barnaby home?"

"Whom may I say is calling?"

No-nonsense, with auburn hair pulled back into a severe bun, this woman was clearly not going to let him enter without appropriate clearance. Oddly enough, though, she had an air that she knew exactly who he was.

"Dante Blackstone."

She blinked gold-flecked hazel eyes once, the only evidence of any emotion on her sculpted features.

His knife heated, not with the desire to take a soul, but pulsed almost… in greeting.

"Please come into the foyer, Mr. Blackstone. I'll make sure Sir Emerson is able to receive visitors this early."

Her disapproval dripped off that last word. Eight in the morning might be early for some people, but Barnaby was elderly. Didn't all old people get up before first light? Dante struggled to think of Barnaby as human now, with typical weaknesses and bodily needs like sleep.

All of the Indebted shared the same last name, a convention adopted thousands of years ago, even before Jerahmeel came into existence. Apparently Barnaby had gotten himself knighted back in the Elizabethan times when he'd lived. Or his friend had taken the affectation of "sir" simply because he could.

Barnaby's house retained the Tudor motif on the inside. Exposed beams of dark wood outlined the white drywall ceiling. Rich, oiled wood paneling ran the length of the foyer and the hallway. When he peeked into a front room, he smiled. Yes, even the front windows had the typical crosshatched iron over the glass.

Hearing the dull tap of loafers on the walnut floor, Dante looked over as the gatekeeper returned. A handsome woman indeed, solid, probably close to six feet tall. Built like… he searched for the appropriate modern slang… a brick shithouse.

"He'll meet you in the patio room. Come with me."

She didn't wait for his answer but spun and walked away. Normally, Dante would've salivated at such amazing curves packed into those bland, serviceable khakis, but apparently his overactive libido was still on the fritz. He could only work up a mild interest in the woman.

Peter entered a sunny room where banks of floor-to-ceiling windows overlooked the Columbia River with views of the Cascade Mountains beyond. He crossed the tiled floor and, with a groan of contentment, dropped into the plush lounge chair the statuesque woman indicated. Tea service steamed on the table next to him.

You've done well for yourself, old man. This is the life.

Moments later, he heard a cough, and then his friend shuffled into the room, the woman hovering next to him. When Dante jumped up, the glare she shot him could've frozen lava.

"Dante, my boy!"

The strength in that handshake had diminished since last Dante saw his former colleague a little over a year ago. Barnaby patted him on the shoulder.

"Hi, Barnaby. You're looking…"

Dante searched for something polite to say. Miss Starched Pants scowled.

"Elderly? Decrepit?" Barnaby's grin creased millions of lines in his face. The man's chuckle disintegrated into wheezes and coughs as the woman guided him to a chair.

Dante cleared his throat. "How about, you're looking 'wise'?"

His friend had rubbed elbows with The Virgin Queen Elizabeth, although knowing Barnaby's proclivities back in the day, the sly fox might have singlehandedly made that queen's nickname a misnomer. Calling Barnaby wise barely scratched the surface of the man's vast knowledge and experience. He had already walked this Earth for more than a hundred years before meeting Dante. And they had lived some amazing adventures for the 300 years since making each other's acquaintance.

Dante never considered that Barnaby would age and leave this world. He'd never known him as anything but an unhuman Indebted. Until the past few decades.

"Oh my. Wise. That's the nice way to say it, my friend. You do know I'm older than dirt. Literally. You can say it. I'm not offended."

He waved the woman away, and she exited, silent save for the light footsteps.

"What's with the bouncer?"

The lines around Barnaby's pale blue eyes crinkled. "Oh, Ruth? She's taking care of me."

"You need help?"

"I'm getting on in years, my boy. Any family I had died hundreds of years ago. I've got no one left. My beautiful Jane and I didn't have children. But I've got money, so I might as well hire good help."

"Nurse Ratched? She's got the personality of a lump of rock."

"Ruth is exactly what I need right now."

"Is she here all the time?"

"Of course. My needs are not overwhelming, but as an advantage, she doesn't require sleep."

"What?" He glanced back at the closed door. "She's like... us?"

"Like *you*, son. I'm retired, remember?"

"Interesting. Explains why my blade responded when I met her. What's her story?"

"She came from the American Civil War. She was a Union nurse. The rest of the story, I'll not share. It's her history, not mine."

"I thought I knew most everyone in our line of work."

"Yours."

"Okay, mine."

"Ruth's managed to keep an exceptionally low profile over the years."

"I'll say. But Jerahmeel's aware of her, *ja*?"

"Of course. He transformed her years ago." He scratched at a few scaly, sun-damaged areas on his bald head. "He seems to have an unusual interest in her, so she tries to remain inconspicuous."

"Interest? That's bizarre."

"Yes, we don't know what to make it of. So she performs her assignments for Jerahmeel in a prompt and efficient manner and returns to help me. She tries to attract no attention. And no drama." He scowled at Dante.

"Unlike Peter? And me?"

"You and Peter have done exactly the opposite. Ruth does her job and doesn't make a fuss."

He glanced toward the closed door. "Is she happy?"

"I can't answer that question, but she seems content to help me for now, and I do appreciate her aid."

Dante sipped tea from a perfect china teacup and took in the mountain view before him. "Pretty nice digs here, Barnaby."

"My dream home with Jane, God rest her lovely soul. She didn't get to enjoy it for as many years as we would have liked. Shame. But I figure I might as well spend all my money on making this as pleasant of a haven as possible. There's no one to inherit. Why, do you need money?"

"No, man. I have tons of it, trust me. Compounded interest is an amazing thing when spread over hundreds of years."

He nodded and sipped at the tea. "So, then. What brings you up here so early in the morning? I fancied you more of a night owl."

"I always thought you old codgers were up at the crack of dawn. Something about not being able to sleep with the prostate acting up?"

Barnaby chuckled and added a lump of sugar to his tea. "Oh, my boy, the prostate is the least of the parts not working right now. And yes, I'm normally stirring before this hour, so you didn't bother me. Ruth's just very protective." He paused, watery gaze thoughtful. "But you're not here for a social call, are you?"

"No, I need advice. I wasn't sure who else to ask."

"What about Peter?"

"I don't want to intrude. Not with everything he went through. He's got his own mortal life to live now." Dante missed his friend, but Peter had broken his Indebted contract to be with Allie. Dante tried his best to respect his friend's choice and give him and his wife space to try to live normal human lives.

"Then how may I help you?" Barnaby asked.

"First of all, I think I've got a minion to deal with."

The elderly man sat up ramrod straight, his quick movements belying his age. "What do you mean think? Another one?"

Dante told him the whole story: the kill in Philadelphia, Raymond Jackson's request for Dante to find Hannah, her ability to heal others, the confrontation with her brother and the minion. And now, because of the minion, Jerahmeel had knowledge of what Hannah could do.

Barnaby took a long time considering the information. Dante squirmed at the delay.

"Oh my, son. That's something."

Dante gritted his teeth. "What do you mean, 'something'? Something good? Bad? Life altering? What, Barnaby? What am I supposed to do about this? What's it all mean?"

"Well, this Hannah will certainly interest Jerahmeel. Like Allie did. Hmm." He scratched his sagging jowl. "Maybe there's a connection between the two women? Who knows? All I do know for certain is that Jerahmeel's attention is deadly for any special mortal."

"I don't understand. Why would healing abilities be useful to him? He's immortal."

"Not exactly immortal, but he's close. If what you say about Hannah's abilities is true, then people like her can put Jerahmeel out of business. He doesn't like anyone meddling in his schemes. If he wants a human to die, that person needs to die. He wants that particular soul to feast upon and be done with it. Someone cannot come behind and magically heal that person."

When Barnaby paused and paled, Dante's stomach dropped out from under him.

"What?"

Barnaby faced him squarely. "I had another terrible thought. What if she's forced to heal a savory near-kill, over and over again? Quite a useful tool for Jerahmeel's never-ending appetite."

Hannah under the control of Jerahmeel. Forced to heal. How could she survive so much pain, day in and day out? All because of Dante's actions that had thrust Hannah onto Jerahmeel's radar.

No. Not going to happen.

"So have you met anyone like Hannah before?"

It was Barnaby's turn to stare out the windows. "Yes, two people who could heal. The woman was hung as a witch around 1700. I didn't know her very well, other than to say she wasn't a witch. But the man I met during World War I, a medic in the British army. Interesting thing about him, he had the ability to reverse the healing."

"Reverse? How?"

"Not certain, but he said instead of pulling the sickness to him, he pushed it back into the person. I suppose if he took on too much of the illness it might kill him, so he'd learned how to avoid that."

"So Hannah might not have to suffer?"

"The potential exists for her to give back any injury she might absorb. I daresay she doesn't even know about this other aspect to her ability. Unfortunately, I wager Jerahmeel knows by now that it's possible for the healing to go both ways. He has to have met someone with similar gifts over his vast centuries walking this Earth."

"So he's going to be interested in her, regardless?"

"I believe so, my boy."

"What if Hannah doesn't heal anyone again?"

"Doesn't matter. It's like with Peter's wife, Allie, and her abilities. The potential exists that her power can be used against Jerahmeel. Peter managed to convince Jerahmeel that Allie wouldn't use her power anymore. But there's always the risk of Jerahmeel's renewed interest hanging over them." He coughed into a cloth napkin for a few moments. "And Jerahmeel's probably more vigilant for aberrations in his employees as well now, with what Peter managed to pull off last year."

"Getting out of his contract?"

"Mmm hmm."

"How'd he do it?"

"You know I cannot speak of it. Why, are you considering it yourself?" Barnaby propped his slipper-clad feet up on the ottoman and laced his wrinkled hands together over his still-flat abdomen.

"Might be nice one day. Maybe. I guess."

"You guess? Oh, ho, that's a new tune you're singing. For hundreds of years, all you've talked about is how you have the world at your feet. Methinks you've discovered a reason to be a different man."

Dante opened his hands, palms up. "I'm no man, Barnaby. Sure, I can have anything I want—anyone I want. But here recently, it's like a cosmic joke. Don't get me wrong. I love the power, the control, the ability to be faster and stronger than any human." He rubbed his neck. "It doesn't matter that it's bad guys who are dying. I can't abide the creature I've become—an enslaved murderer."

"I understand completely, my boy. Your observations about your life are interesting, as is the minion's appearance. Makes me wonder if you're nearing the end of your contract."

"How's that possible?"

"No idea, but the pattern holds with Peter and with me. First, you acknowledge your disillusionment. Then, find someone to give you a reason to be human. Then, get tangled up with a minion who will do anything to keep you from succeeding."

"But you succeeded."

"There's always the chance that they'll let you succeed but destroy your reason to live. Remember Allie?"

How could Dante forget the sight of Allie bleeding in Peter's arms? She had nearly died, and still bore the scars of the minion's attack from that day. Dante swallowed and nodded.

"You like your lady, Hannah?"

He rubbed his hand against his pants leg. "Well, sure, I guess. I only met her three days ago. I don't really know her."

"I imagine she might mean much more to you, on the whole."

"If you say so. I don't know. Maybe I just need to get laid."

Barnaby smiled. "You can do that anytime. With any woman."

He didn't meet the old man's eyes. "Good point."

"I'd wager if Jerahmeel or the minion realizes that she can inspire you to break the contract, they'll try to prevent that from happening."

"Jerahmeel did say that if I stayed away from Hannah, I still have the chance to attain the Meaningful Kill."

"He's nervous. Fascinating."

"So if I walk away from the situation now, I might be free of the contract. But Hannah will suffer." He raked his hands through his hair. "If I try to help Hannah, I'll never be free of the contract. But she might be safe."

Barnaby sipped on the tea and leaned his head back on the cushions. "That's the first time I've heard you thinking of the consequences to others, my boy." He set the cup down with a clink. "I believe Jerahmeel is trying to manipulate you to stay away from Hannah. There are other ways to get out of the contract, however."

"Really? I'm not sure where to start with breaking the contract."

"When it's time, you'll figure it out."

"How can you be sure?"

The corners of Barnaby's lined mouth curled downward. "It doesn't matter, my boy."

"What doesn't matter?"

"Never mind." He honked into a handkerchief. "Your friend, she may be a target because of her abilities or because of your desire to break the contract. I can't say which for certain. Be very careful, my friend. Something is mightily amiss about this situation. She's in grave danger."

Urgency gripped Dante. He needed to watch over Hannah, protect her. As in, right now.

"Um, Barnaby?"

"It appears you have made a decision. You'd like to leave immediately, I imagine. Find this Hannah and make sure she's still safe?" He smiled broadly, pale blue eyes twinkling, his skin creasing again into numerous wrinkles.

"Yes, old man, I would like to leave." Dante's mind whirled. Contract. Minion. Hannah? How was he going to remove her safely from this situation without her getting hurt?

"You have my number; please call if there's anything I can do for you."

"Thank you."

He bent down to give the old man an awkward shoulder hug but had to be careful not to injure the man's frail bones. Ruth silently escorted him to the front door. His knife pulsed again in proximity to another Indebted.

He grinned. "Thank you for the hospitality, my *compadre*."

The color in her cheeks betrayed her. At least he could change that poker face.

Chapter 7

Hannah had sorting and shelving duty today, which suited her fine, despite the residual aches and pains. Not only did she enjoy arranging books on the stacks, but she often would read passages as she worked. The words transported her to another world, if only for a few minutes.

But today, it wasn't the treat of quiet time with the books that tempted her. Rather, in the depths of the store, she would be less likely to see Dante. That is, if he came back. Maybe Scott was right, and Dante truly angled to have some fun and then toss her away. But why would he go to all the trouble? She tried to look at the situation objectively but couldn't visualize the malicious intent her brother saw. In fact, part of her wanted to see Dante again, if only to be close to him, to smile at his obvious passes.

Huh. She'd avoided men for the past four years. Since when did she want to be around a man?

Since Dante had been a perfect gentleman on the walk home. Since he had teased her but not pressured her. Since he had treated her like a normal woman. For the first time since well before she left Philly, she had a glimmer of what it would be like to feel safe. What woman wouldn't want more?

The news of Ray dying had gutted her. Still, she should have tried to thank Dante for the information. Poor guy—his smiling expression had frozen and then fell when her reaction wasn't what he expected. He seemed to really care how she felt, and she couldn't remember the last time someone gave a flip about her. Scott did, of course, but he had to—he was her brother.

Perhaps she had fallen for a handsome guy and missed the real jerk inside, although that was unlikely. She was normally a good judge of character. Well, except with Ray. She hadn't predicted the depth of his sickness, so maybe she'd missed the mark with Dante as well.

Ray. Dead. Wow. If Dante spoke the truth, then she and Scott might be free of the unending fear of retribution that had hung over their heads for years. Unless Dante had lied to her about Ray.

No, that answer didn't feel accurate. But how could she find out for certain?

Not today—too many people around—but maybe tomorrow, she could get on the bookstore computer when she opened the store and glean some information about Ray's death. She could always call the number to her old house, too.

Or not. What if Dante was wrong about Ray being dead? No way would she risk hearing Ray's thin, disgusting voice, even if it was a thousand miles away.

She pulled wisps of hair out from under the arms of her glasses and readjusted the frames. Now that Dante had been chased off, she might never know the details about Ray's death.

"Here's another batch for you, Hannah."

Her manager rolled over another cart.

Hannah ran her hands over the spines of the books. "No problem. I'll take care of it."

Ignoring the soreness in her joints, she pushed the cart to the back of the store into the literature section. She tugged at a library ladder, the squeak on the rails shrill in the quiet store. Careful not to step on her brown patterned skirt, she lifted the hem to climb up the ladder. Always cautious with her numb foot, Hannah centered it on the rung. The pressure sensation on the sole of her foot registered faintly, even through the sandal, but there was zero sensation on the top of the foot. It made her foot feel odd, like it was round or incomplete.

When she leaned out to push the ladder over a few inches, it bumped against something solid, stopping her abruptly. A book fell as she clung to the ladder.

Dante. His sky-blue eyes shone brightly. She forgot to breathe.

As he reached down to pick up the book, the fabric of his tailored navy slacks stretched over his thick, muscled thighs. Her mouth went dry. She gripped the rails.

When he stood up, Hannah found herself a few inches above his chiseled features. His sensual lips curled into a sardonic smile.

"Here you go. *Tristan and Iseult*. One of my favorites."

"You've read this?"

Although they had discussed books yesterday, she didn't envision him with this particular classic.

"Don't act so surprised." He laughed. "Of course. True love. Eternal love. Tragic love." He gave her a rakish grin. Her heart flipped over. "My favorite line is 'Apart the lovers could neither live nor die for it was life and death together.' They don't write stories like this nowadays."

She blinked hard, took the book from him, and placed it in the stacks, all the while aware of his intense perusal. Why had he come back? After she'd sent him away and after Scott had been so rude to him.

He maintained a casual stance, not approaching her but not retreating. The swagger from yesterday had dropped a notch today, but he still radiated masculine assurance with his feet set shoulder-width apart. And why not? The tailored shirt fit his broad shoulders perfectly.

He didn't seem like a bad person. If he were someone she was supposed to avoid, she struggled to find a reason why.

"So can I help you?" he asked.

Although he stood loose-limbed and spoke in a nonchalant manner, she didn't buy the act for a second, especially compared with his Don Juan demeanor from the last few days. What did he want?

"Isn't that my line? I'm the one working here." Unbidden, a smile pushed the corners of her mouth upward. *A smile? What in the world?*

He passed another book to her. "I do enjoy being helpful."

The double-entendre was subtle, but she heard it. A shiver went up her spine.

"Well, good," she said.

She stood on tiptoes to shelve the book.

"What happened to your ankle?"

Panic short-circuited her brain.

Frantic, Hannah leaned over to smooth the skirt over her sandals and stepped down one rung but didn't detect the step with her numb foot. She lost her grip on the ladder and flew backward, only to land in very solid arms. Instinctively, she grabbed Dante's shirt, wrinkling the expensive gray fabric.

"My apologies." His voice rumbled through their connected chests, sending unfamiliar swirls down to her toes. "I'm not always the most tactful."

His words tickled her hair. He smelled like mocha latte and cologne today.

Inches away, he pinned her with his clear, blue gaze. His strong arms surrounded her as he held her securely. Amazing heat radiated from his body. She'd heard of people running warm, but this couldn't be normal.

His Adam's apple bobbed. "I'm, uh, very glad to see you again."

That deep voice did strange things to her equilibrium, or maybe it was because she rested firmly in the arms of a giant.

"Me too." She swallowed. "Dante, I'm sorry about my brother and his stupid—"

"Don't worry about it; those guys don't bother me. I only wanted to make sure you were okay."

What the hell? Since when did a hot guy want to see to her welfare? Apparently, since now.

Her heart rate sped up, and her voice came out light and breathy. "They're just hotheads. I'm fine."

She bit her lower lip, and Dante's gaze fixated there. His eyes darkened. *What in the world?*

"Your eyes. They're changing."

"It's nothing. Um, they just do that sometimes."

He shifted her in his arms as he watched her. Maybe her glasses looked funny? Hannah froze, locked in Dante's arms.

His inscrutable stare unsettled her.

"Perfect," he whispered. His voice rolled through her bones.

He lowered his head another few inches until his breath fanned her face. Pressed up to him, Hannah enjoyed the chiseled planes of his chest and belly, the tight muscles that clenched as he widened his stance. Trapping her in his arms. She couldn't escape—

Oh, God. No. That night. Images of the basement and Ray flooded her mind.

She pushed, ineffectively, against Dante's corded arms. Desperate to get away, she twisted her head away from his mouth. What Ray did… she'd been trapped. She couldn't move. She had to escape. Ray. Dante. She was going to be sick.

Struggling against the arm that snaked behind her back, she shoved against his chest.

"Dante, please." Her voice cracked.

Dark spots danced on the edges of her vision. When he lowered her to her feet, Dante's arousal jutted solid and insistent against her stomach. Her stomach lurched, and she swallowed bitter acid. The inability to get away squeezed her ribs until she couldn't breathe. Tears pricked then the damp warmth trailed down her cheeks.

Like a man waking up from a dream, Dante blinked his nearly black eyes a few times.

He released his grip but rested his hands on her upper arms.

"Please let go." She backed up against the end of a stack, gasping, as stars in her vision heralded impending unconsciousness. She fought to slow her thudding heart, to slow her shallow breaths.

That night in the basement. Oh, no, not again. The vice around her chest tightened again. Damn Ray to hell.

"I'm sorry, I shouldn't have. You're just so…" He dropped his big arms.

"It's me. I'm not, I can't—"

She wanted Dante, wanted his arms around her. But when he held her, all she could think about was being in that basement prison with Ray. Dark. Her chest burned when she tried to inhale.

"Can you sit down?"

Dante guided her to sit on the hardwood floor and eased her head forward between her knees. "I've heard this helps. Take a few deep breaths."

When his warm hand rested on her shoulder, she clutched it, like a damned lifeline. She took a breath and tried to loosen all her muscles. The barrier in her mind dropped.

Transfer started.

Transfer? What the heck?

But there it was, the connection between their skins, her cells' primal desire to blend, to enter, to trade substance for substance. This time the transfer worked differently. It didn't hurt, didn't try to consume injuries or illnesses. It flowed both ways, less painful, more curious. Searching.

Too easily, her skin accepted contact with Dante. Her body found nothing to heal, but her essence flowed through the contact nevertheless. And then it happened: Her soul, her physical and emotional pain, flowed from her into Dante. Aches and pains that had lingered from yesterday's healings faded, like rubbing away a smudge on the cheek, a light sense of a soft wave lapping away at her pain. Nothing dramatic, but only physical relief remained in her connection to him. And it was good.

When she dug her nails into his hand, he didn't move. Somehow she had unleashed her healing ability. Backward.

She was the beneficiary.

She snatched her hand away from his arm.

He cleared his throat. "Um, can I hold your glasses for you?"

"No," she mumbled against her knees. "I can't see anything without them."

"Okay. Ah, okay." He hovered nearby, not exactly retreating but not moving.

Hannah found that a funny concept: Dante unsure. All because she had a meltdown. Great. She glanced up at him, expecting to see revulsion from... everything. From her panic, from the healing reversal, from the ludicrous scene here in this bookstore.

But nothing in his grim expression indicated that he sensed the reversal of her healing. He simply knelt nearby, as she attempted to salvage something positive from her emotional meltdown.

Salvage? What a joke.

She was a mess, and Dante had no idea to do with a hyperventilating woman. What a pair they made. She took a few deep gulps of air and blew them out. Fine. She'd be fine. Of course she'd be fine, but she wasn't convincing herself.

It's Dante. He's here right now. Not Ray. His warm hands on her arms brought her back to reality, as did his now perfectly normal, electric-blue eyes.

"I must apologize. It was inappropriate of me to take advantage," he said.

Worry and disappointment etched lines on his chiseled features. Hot shame warmed her cheeks.

"No, it's my fault. It's complicated." She waved her hand. "This has nothing to do with you."

She braced her legs to get up; he steadied her. Once she stood on her own, he let go and stepped back. Without the contact, her skin cooled and her knees went weak. Despite the fact that she craved his warm touch, she grasped the stark reality of her circumstances. What future did she have with any man?

Dante cleared his throat. "So, maybe I can help you organize books for a little while?"

The uncertainty his wrinkled forehead conveyed struck her as odd. He usually oozed self-assurance.

"Unless you'd rather me leave, which I will immediately do, upon your request."

Her cheeks and neck heated up. *He's throwing you a line. Carry on like nothing happened. Pretend. It'll be fine.*

"All right, then. Since you're offering. Let's make a junior bookstore worker out of you."

"I'm yours to command. Tell me what to shelve."

He straightened up, but his grin didn't quite make it to his wary eyes as he continued to study her. Dante had decided to stick around, although God knew why. She didn't know whether to be thankful or feel sorry for herself or for him.

• • •

Hannah moved efficiently, her fingers trailing over spines until, finding the book she sought, she briskly pulled it out and handed it to Dante. He fixated on those delicate hands, wanted them trailing over his spine. He couldn't focus.

What the hell had happened just minutes ago? He'd never seen a woman so terrified of anything or anyone, much less himself. Her stiff shoulders and mouth pressed into a thin line painted quite a picture of a person fighting to maintain control—and succeeding only by the barest of margins.

Whatever demons haunted her, he'd like nothing better than to destroy them and take the grim weight of fear from her thin frame. Curiosity pricked at his tongue, but he resisted asking questions. The last thing he wanted was to scare her further.

For now, he'd concentrate on the job of shelving. The questions would wait until later, but he was determined to find answers.

Except for the top shelves, they no longer needed the ladder thanks to his height. At least he could be useful. He certainly didn't want to leave her alone for one moment, what with the minion running around. Truth be told, he didn't want to leave her alone for one moment for no reason resembling altruism.

Other than the occasional brush of fingers, which zinged dangerous sensations straight to his groin and stole his breath, they worked smoothly through the afternoon. Dante tried to keep conversation light, but he continued to watch Hannah. Behind those rectangular glasses were two orbs of deep chocolate, flecked with sparks of gold. While the long skirt and loose top hid her curves, he knew better. He recalled the indentation of her tiny waist, the flare of her hips, her firm breasts pressed against him. Her fragile frame made him want to wrap his arms tightly around her and keep her safe. Not usually what he went for. He liked the taller, buxom women. The curvy, willing women. But Hannah had something indefinable that he couldn't resist.

He wanted more.

Tread carefully.

At times, she acted like a deer about to bolt. He wanted to avoid scaring her away more than anything he'd wanted in a long time. He frowned. *Vad i helvete?* What happened to keeping his options open? To more conquests? To women throwing themselves at his feet?

He'd succeeded, right? He had delivered the news of Ray's death. Although, it rankled that she didn't appreciate his efforts more. Had to be the shock of hearing the news. Or did her reaction have anything to do with the stark fear minutes ago?

No matter. Despite all her earlier rejections and protestations, here she stood, finally accepting his presence. Her eyes had fluttered at him and her soft cheeks turned pink at his attention.

So why did this victory feel empty?

"You missed the spot. Over a few more books, please."

Her smooth, low voice brought him out of his thoughts as he searched for the right location for the book in question. Although he wanted to cast his mind toward more pleasurable concepts, he had to concentrate to follow her directions to the fourth shelf space and correctly place the volume of poetry.

How the mighty have fallen.

And the scariest part? He couldn't care less that he'd been relegated to shelving duty, as long as it meant remaining close to her.

"No problem, boss, your wish is my command." He winked, hoping she enjoyed looking at his physique as much as he enjoyed flexing it in front of her.

Her cheeks turned red beneath the freckles, and she ducked her head and smiled, releasing the tension in her lips and jaw. Desire to make her blush forever shocked him with its intensity.

What's wrong with you, dude? Since when did you get all squishy over a woman like this?

Since Marguerite in 1830, come to think of it.

He'd heard about a revolution in France, and never one to miss a citizen uprising in his immortal form, he traveled there to lend a hand with whichever side seemed most oppressed. Besides, he'd been bored and needed something to do. When he met the Paris cloth merchant's daughter, Marguerite, he fell in love. One bloody revolution and thirty years later, it had nearly destroyed him when she died a natural death at age fifty-two, leaving him alone again. Since his French wife's death, he'd only gone for brief, no-strings-attached interludes. Anything else hurt too much. Human life was so transient. So fragile.

And now?

He was an idiot. Hannah would eventually leave him just like Marguerite did, even if she survived the minion's desire to harm her.

She was mortal. Dante was accursed. Not much to discuss. Then why not enjoy her while he could? He had needs; he was still a hot-blooded male. He wouldn't have trouble getting her in bed—all women succumbed to his charm eventually, right? But the mere thought left him cold. He wouldn't toy with her and then leave her as was his usual routine. She was a forever kind of woman. Which made for a big problem. His forever lasted a hell of a lot longer than hers, and he couldn't go through another loss like with Marguerite.

Maybe he should ask Peter again how he got out of his contract. Last time Dante tried to get the information, his previously undead friend wouldn't tell him. Maybe Peter could be coerced into giving up the information for a curious buddy.

But what would Dante do if he escaped his Indebted existence? At this moment, he had everything: unlimited women, riches, and virtual immortality.

Besides, Peter's and Barnaby's Meaningful Kills were flukes, right? Two men returned to mortal form out of how many Indebted over how many centuries? Dante would likely be here doing Jerahmeel's bidding for hundreds more years. Which reminded him, he'd fallen behind on his quota for the month. He had to go hunting soon.

The throb of the warm blade strapped to his lower leg had been increasing its insistence over the last few days. Desire to plunge the blade into a criminal consumed Dante's mind. He needed the sweet release of some sick bastard's soul bleeding into the knife, then the knife's siren call would quiet down for a time.

"... Dante?"

He blinked and focused on the lovely bespectacled face before him.

"Daydreaming?"

"Guilty."

He couldn't stop smiling around her. Not good.

She glanced at her watch. "Well, um, I'm done for the day. We're done."

"Excellent. I think we should reward our hard work with a nice meal."

"Oh, no, I can't. I need to get home."

The fear that flickered over her created a surge of protective instinct in Dante's chest. How disturbing.

"How about a quick snack and I walk you home?"

"No, thank you."

"Look, are you still upset about the news about Ray?"

"It's more complicated than that. And, um, I have to thank you for the effort you made to deliver that information."

"So why can't you go out to eat with me?"

"We can't."

"We?"

"Scott doesn't—"

"Doesn't what? Like me?"

She dropped her gaze to the empty cart. "Kind of. I'm sorry."

"Don't be. Unless, of course, you also don't like me?"

Her cheeks blazed red; she looked everywhere but directly at him. "No, I don't… No. I wouldn't say that."

He touched her shoulder and cursed himself again when she flinched. "Why don't I walk you partway home and call it good? You don't have to tell Scott."

When her eyes lit up with hope, his big, burly heart melted.

She tugged at a strand of her hair. "Are you sure?"

"Of course. There's a nice café nearby where we can get a bite to eat and then go on home. 'Hope in the heart of men lives on lean pasture.'"

"More *Tristan and Iseult*?"

"Of course. It's surprisingly appropriate."

"I'm not sure."

"About the quote?"

"About the snack."

"Please."

She thought for several long moments. "Okay."

When she smiled up at him, his world narrowed down to her lovely face. Hell, he'd only offered her a sandwich; she acted as though he'd presented her the world. And damn him if he didn't want to give her the world, if only to watch her beam like that over and over.

Herre Gud. He'd found the one woman he shouldn't have. The one woman mixed up with Jerahmeel's minion. The one woman who made him consider ending his endless contract. He envisioned no happy ending here. Only pain and eternal torment.

And he was taking her out on a dinner date.

Du är an idiot.

Chapter 8

Night falling, and her belly full of panini, Hannah strolled next to Dante, north toward the rental. Over the light dinner, he'd even coerced a cell phone number out of her.

Bless him, he didn't mention their hot and heavy interlude in the bookstore or her weenie meltdown. Just like yesterday's walk home, he kept the conversation breezy, asking her questions that weren't too personal. Questions she could answer. Although he avoided serious topics, she glimpsed moments of intensity where he focused on her and nothing else. Like he was hungry. For her.

Yeah, right. He's only completing his civic duty, and then it'll be over.

Truth be told, she wanted to get rid of him long before they arrived at the rental. He shouldn't have to deal with someone as rude as her brother and his creepy friend. Dante had been kind and patient. She could at least return the favor by shielding him from a nasty confrontation.

"I'll, ah, go on home from here." She fidgeted with the purse strap slung across her chest and glanced up the street. Not many people around. Good.

"I can walk with you a bit farther."

His deep voice made her insides tingle. Hannah wanted to drown in that warm baritone.

Stop enjoying it. He needs to stay away. For his sake and for mine.

"No, Scott will be mad. I'm so sorry. It's really not you. I have no idea what's gotten into my brother."

"Well, I wouldn't want to put you in an uncomfortable position," he said.

How he remained civil despite her brother's rudeness and her own weirdness amazed her.

Dante cleared his throat. "Um, I would like to give you a kiss goodnight. With your permission, of course."

Her heart fluttered wildly against her ribcage. Seriously? Well, sure. What would be the harm?

Darting a glance around the residential street in the growing twilight, she nodded. And shivered.

Thankfully, she had a moment to hold the transfer block in place before he touched her skin.

He lifted her chin with one large, warm finger and exhaled slowly as he bent down. The scent of their dinner and his cologne surrounded her. His firm lips, soft but insistent, felt like paradise. Bolts of happiness shot from her lips straight down her legs.

Dante didn't move. He only kissed her, one hand caressing her neck and jaw. He kept the other hand at his side. Hannah's head swam, and she grabbed the front of his shirt, using it as leverage to rise higher and press against his mouth.

This time, she experienced no fear, but only delicate, growing pleasure at his light touch. His warm breath mingled with hers, and warmth, like holding her hands to a welcoming fireplace, flowed through her entire body. Cold panic had been fully replaced by toasty happiness.

The heat radiating from him rose a notch, and she relaxed into him, hoping he would put his arms around her. But he didn't move except to slant his mouth in lovely new angles. She wanted more. More contact, more of the warmth.

Freedom felt like kissing a handsome man without freaking out.

She sighed into his mouth, not wanting the kiss to end, wanting to stay like this forever…

The blare of a car horn startled her. The orange Civic squealed up to the curb. Dante tensed, spun around, and tucked her into his side, encircling her with his large arm.

The crystalline happiness shattered.

"Oh, no," she whispered. She peeked into the shadows. No one was on this quiet residential sidewalk at this hour.

"It'll be okay," he said.

His grip around her shoulders tightened as Scott, Brandon, and two of their friends poured out of the car. Dante pivoted so that she stood partially behind him.

Brandon whispered in her brother's ear and winked at Dante.

Scott called out, "Sis, I thought I told you to stay away from this ass clown."

"It's fine. He's only walking me home."

Her brother's expression wavered from anger to sympathy until Brandon nudged him again. Hannah hated that redheaded jerk.

"Looked like he wasn't doing a lot of walking."

"Grow up, Scott. It's nothing." Damn her quivering voice. And damn Scott for ruining the evening.

"Yeah. I gave an order for your own protection. Why can't you listen to me for once? After all I've done for you, this is my thanks?"

The sickly sweet scent of alcohol drifted over to her. *Not again.*

"It's okay, Dante's leaving." She willed her shaking muscles to calm down.

Brandon again murmured something into Scott's ear. Her brother scratched at a sore on his neck as a muscle twitched in his jaw.

"The hell he's leaving." Scott stepped closer.

Like the drop on a rollercoaster, her stomach fell out from under her.

"Scott, let's go home. We're done," she said.

"You bet you're done."

Scott's arms jumped with more energy than normal, and he kept picking at his neck.

Brandon sneered behind her brother and said, "She'd better learn to listen to you when you give an order, don'tcha think?"

"Stay out of this, *røvhål*," Dante growled.

"Why? I'm just doing my job, same as you." Brandon snickered.

"What does he mean?" Hannah looked up at Dante's shadowed face.

"Nothing."

His fingers dug into her upper arm until she let out a whimper. But she'd rather have his arms clamped around her than face these guys on her own.

Brandon tipped an imaginary hat to Dante. "Now, boys, how about let's get busy?"

Scott and the other two guys nodded.

The cords of muscle in Dante's arm bunched, rock hard. Waves of heat radiated from his tense frame.

"You should leave here. Please." She ducked from under his arm and tried to give him a gentle push. He didn't move.

"And leave you with these *oåkting*? I think not."

"You gonna take lip from this meathead, Scott?" Brandon egged him on.

"No way, man. Get your hands off my sister, asshole."

The guys fanned out in a loose semicircle around them. Hannah shivered in earnest now.

"Dante, get away from here," she whispered.

"I've managed far worse than four morons at a time."

Jaw set, he let go and stepped in front of her.

The guys approached Dante who, to his credit, held his ground with his arms swinging loose and knees bent. Her throat tightened. She couldn't swallow.

Four against one? Not good.

Scott's two nameless friends jumped in first, landing a few blows. Dante leveled one guy with a punch to the guy's jaw and swept a leg around to send the other one sprawling. Scott shot a worried look at Brandon, who sneered in his thin, pinched way, produced a tire iron from the car, and sauntered toward Dante.

"How about you pick on someone like yourself, shit-for-brains?" Brandon said.

Before she could intervene, Scott grabbed her, holding on tightly.

"Don't want you getting hurt, sis."

Scott exhaled a disgusting cloud of stale alcohol and a strange chemical smell. Like cleaning solution, fresh shower curtain, and... cat urine? He smelled like this yesterday morning.

Meth.

"Let me go!"

She struggled, unable to escape her brother's freakishly strong grip.

Brandon circled Dante, grinning. "My turn."

A few test swings of the iron whistled through the evening air, but Dante held his ground and kept Brandon squarely in front of him.

Hannah's blood ran ice cold, leaving her lightheaded.

"This is all your fault, sis. If you would've listened to me, this never would have happened. Brandon's going to teach you and your pimp a lesson."

Scott wrenched her arm behind her back. She couldn't move an inch. He had way too much energy tonight.

Faster than she could follow, Brandon swung the iron into Dante's raised arm with a crack. He then clanged the iron into Dante's lower leg, rocking the big man, but Dante didn't fall. As more blows rained down, he grunted against each one but somehow remained upright.

Dante then countered with a blur of meaty punches, pushing Brandon back. But the jerk kept attacking, a nasty snarl pasted on his thin face. It didn't make sense. One of the men should be dead with as many blows as they were taking.

One harsh strike impacted Dante's ribcage, the snap loud in the evening air. Hannah screamed and pulled against Scott.

Dante spun around, his black eyes locking on to hers, blood running down his temple. He pressed a hand against his ribcage and wheezed. With an expression of murderous rage, he took a step toward Hannah and Scott.

Brandon took advantage of the distraction and smashed the back of Dante's head. Dante went down like he weighed a ton, hitting the ground with a stomach-turning thud. The blond giant didn't move. *Oh God, Dante's dead.* She kicked against Scott, desperate to get to the man who'd stood up for her.

Scott's remaining conscious friend kicked Dante while Brandon's relentless shots with the tire iron pummeled unmoving bone and muscle. The thick weapon had actually bent. Dante tried to get up once, groaning. Brandon hit the back of Dante's skull again, dropping Dante to the pavement. Blood stained his fair hair dark red and ran onto the cement.

He no longer moved.

Bile burned its way up Hannah's throat.

She stomped on Scott's instep with everything she had, freeing herself when he yelped and jumped back in pain. Throwing herself on Dante, she absorbed a glancing blow to her back when Brandon didn't check himself in time. Her muscles knotted in fiery agony.

Beneath her, Dante didn't move.

Sirens wailed in the distance.

"Let's get outta here. This guy's learned his lesson," said the other attacker. "That is, if he survives."

"Help him up." Brandon ordered Scott's friend to pull the semiconscious buddy to his feet.

Scott yanked on her arm as she lay draped over Dante's inert form. "Come on, Hannah."

"Get away from me!" she screamed, pulling away. "You can go to hell."

Her wet tears dampened the back of Dante's bloody and torn shirt. The sirens were getting louder. Police. She couldn't be discovered here. They'd figure out who she was and what she and Scott had done to Ray. She wanted to run. But Dante—

"Come on, man. Just leave her. She's shit." Brandon yelled from the driver's seat.

Scott froze, torn between Hannah and the car for a long moment. She saw a flash of her old brother, and then it was gone, replaced by a paranoid tweaker.

"Bro, come on!"

Her brother flipped her the middle finger, jumped in the car, and the guys sped off.

With extreme effort, Hannah rolled Dante's massive body over onto his back, his strong face bruised and bloodied. Was he still alive?

His chest rose and fell.

Blue and red shadows flashed on the trees and houses as the police turned onto the street. She couldn't drag him anywhere. His limp bulk wouldn't budge.

She wouldn't leave him. If he died, it would be her fault. She should've left him after dinner. Should've made him leave. Damn.

There was only one thing to do, and it was going to really hurt. Could she control her gift enough to wake Dante? And do it without killing herself? She had to try.

Hannah pressed her hands to the side of his warm face, her grip slippery from the blood pouring from all of the cuts.

Come on.

Nothing happened.

Come on, Dante. Please.

The transfer, fast and intense, nearly blew her off him. She held on, taking it all in, like drinking water through a fire hose. No time to prepare.

Bones shattered in her cheekbones, skull, and hands. Muscles tore. Her brain swelled. Skin on her forehead and knuckles burst open.

Dante's black eyes shot open.

"No!" he roared.

She smiled down at him. He leapt to his feet and crouched over her. Their connection broken, the transferred injuries took over and she collapsed onto the pavement.

Chapter 9

"No!"

Dante bolted upright. What the hell happened? The last thing he remembered was the minion getting in a good shot when he'd been distracted. By Hannah. *Herre Gud.*

She lay crumpled on the pavement, blood oozing from the injuries on her face and the back of her head. He touched his own scalp in the same areas, found sticky blood in the exact same places. But no cuts or bruises.

She healed him, but why? His body would've gotten around to it eventually. But of course, she wouldn't have known about his own rapid healing abilities.

She had given him one chance to help them both.

Blaring sirens and flashing lights intruded on his thoughts. Dante rose from the pavement in time to see a police cruiser roll up. He slid his hands beneath Hannah's limp frame, careful of her injuries.

Jävlar. He had to get out of here. Too many questions.

The first officer rushed out of the car, pulling his gun. "Stop! Hands up!"

In one smooth movement, Dante pulled Hannah to him, curled around her, and sprinted lightning fast around a nearby house into the backyard.

"What the...?"

As Dante heard the officer call into the walkie-talkie for backup, quick footsteps drew closer around the side of the house.

Dante shifted Hannah to his shoulder, holding her inert body to his chest. When broken bones ground together in her ribcage, his stomach churned. He had to get her to help. With his free arm, he grabbed the top of a fence and swung himself over, landing lightly. He ended up in a kennel run. With a barking dog.

Kristus. Dante crouched and growled until the dog submitted. The canine lay on the ground, whining.

Yelling for backup, the officer began climbing the same fence, flashlight beams piercing the slats and bouncing shadows over Dante and Hannah.

Dante sprinted across the yard, vaulted another fence, landed in yet another backyard, cursed, and spun ninety degrees. Leaping over another fence, he raced around to the front of a property and followed the driveway to the street.

He sprinted for two blocks and ducked behind an unlit home.

What to do? Hannah needed medical attention. He couldn't go to the hospital with her—it would raise way too many unanswerable questions. Create a trail. His kind avoided places requiring an insurance card, places with security cameras.

But he'd reveal his secret if it meant she would live.

She moaned, her pitiful cries torpedoing into his chest. Adjusting so she rested in front of him but still in his arms, he studied her grotesquely bruised and swollen face. Sick rage almost incapacitated him at such destruction of her smooth skin. He needed to kill something, someone. He wanted to track down Brandon. The knife pulsed, eager to participate. Gritting his teeth, he pushed back the killing urge and focused on the broken body in his arms.

"Dante?"

Her soft voice tethered him to reality but barely.

"Yes, *älskling?*" Sweetheart. He hadn't called anyone that for 150 years.

"Are you okay?" she whispered.

He blinked. She was asking about *him?*

When she tried to reach for him, her arm dropped away. Dante removed her smudged glasses and slid them into his pants pocket. He knew she couldn't see without them, so he'd try to keep them from breaking.

"Am I okay? Of course. I have a hard head. What about you?"

He swept her matted hair back from her bruised forehead. His normally steady fingers shook.

"Not so good."

She winced when she moved, and he tucked her into his arms, holding her steady as he surveyed the damage.

"Why did you heal me back there?"

"... thought you might die."

If only she knew.

"I'm pretty tough to kill."

"They hurt you. Badly. Especially Brandon. He's... bad."

"I agree." At least she'd woken up and could talk to him. "But you took on the injuries yourself."

"It's just something... I can do."

"You're hurt now." A lump formed in his throat.

"Yes, but it's never quite as bad as the original injury."

Really? Because she looked like she'd gone five rounds in an MMA bout and should've tapped out four and a half rounds ago.

"How bad is it now?"

"Well, I thought they had killed you, and I took on all of your injuries." She moaned. "So, not great."

"Can you reverse it? The healing?"

He couldn't handle her being in this much pain.

"I don't know if it's possible." She wheezed.

"My friend Barnaby thinks the healing can be reversed back into the original person who was hurt. Can you try, please?"

When she closed her eyes, it took too long for her to open them again. "I can try. But it makes more sense for you to be healthy than me," she rasped.

He couldn't argue the logic. She knew he'd protect her. He'd challenge the hounds of hell to keep her safe.

"Well, I'm just fine now, so put the injuries back into me, please."

Sirens rang out in the distance, and he tensed. She coughed and cried out, holding her ribs.

He wanted to kill Brandon. Needed to. Now. The knife was hungry. He dragged his gaze back to her face.

"Can you get us out of here?" she gasped.

He thought through his options and made a decision. "*Ja*, but you have to get to a hospital."

"No!" Tears shone. "Please, no."

"You're hurt."

"No hospitals. I don't want... anyone to know where I am."

Of course. She didn't want Scott or Brandon to discover their whereabouts. That made sense. Damn it. Dante would try to take care of her as best he could.

The sirens drew closer again. The police were likely canvassing the area. He had to get her away from here.

"I'm going to run. I'll try to be easy, but it might hurt."

"I trust you."

The glazed pain on her face would've driven him to his knees if he weren't already crouched over her. His heart twisted. She trusted him, a killer, to keep her safe.

Biting off a curse, he cradled her against his chest, trying not to jostle her too much. She pressed her lips together into a thin, white line.

Bending down to brush her forehead with his lips, he said, "I'm sorry, *älskling*." And took off at an inhumanly fast sprint.

He would've moved even faster if he weren't concentrating on smoothing out his gait and sticking to as many shadows as possible. It was harder to stay hidden with the light from a full moon. They were sure to attract some attention, but thankfully at this evening hour, fewer people were out.

Taking a circuitous path through the area of town south of the bookstore, Dante tried to mask their direction. Every so often, he'd leap into backyards, through driveways, creating paths that would confuse anyone following them. A police dog would never catch them, but it might be able to follow a scent. When a small drainage ditch presented itself, he slogged through it for a quarter mile before jumping out and continuing on his way.

At every jolt, he cringed. She suffered for him, taking all those injuries, but she never complained, just pressed her swollen cheek to his chest.

After a period of silence, he tried to rouse her, but it took effort. He needed to get to the car and have her reverse the healing. Now.

Finally arriving at his Hummer, he eased Hannah into the passenger seat and reclined it.

"*Älskling*? Wake up, please."

She groaned, her cheeks glistening with tears and oozing blood. He hated himself. She'd endured more pain than she let on. Brushing her skin dry with his thumbs, he rocked her shoulder.

"We need to leave, Hannah. Can you reverse the healing?"

"Yes, but you'll be sick immediately."

"I don't care."

"Do I look like I can drive this vehicle like this?"

"Well, no."

"What makes you think you'll be able to drive if you're in this state?"

"Ah, I do heal very quickly."

"Not fast enough."

She coughed. Flecks of blood dotted her pale lips. He grabbed her cold hands and squeezed, willing whatever it was she did to send the pain back to him.

"Give it to me. Let me have it."

"No. Get us away to a safe place where we can heal. Then I'll reverse it."

She wheezed, head lolling against the back of the seat. He opened his mouth to argue. She silenced him.

"Hurry, please."

Balling his hands into fists, Dante struggled to keep from yelling in frustration. He hadn't experienced such helplessness since his brother almost died those many years ago.

He removed her glasses from his pants pocket and stored them in the center console. Slipping her purse from around her body, he laid it at her feet. Throwing open the trunk, he searched for extra clothes he kept stashed there. He retrieved one of his shirts and draped it over her, hoping to keep her as warm and comfortable as possible.

No seatbelt. It would hurt her ribs too much. *So drive carefully.*

Concentrating, he wove through town. He tensed at every stoplight, scanning the other cars and cross streets. He wanted to race out of here, but he didn't want to draw attention.

Keeping to the interminably slow speed limits, he obeyed all traffic rules, a perfect vehicle operator, until he got on I-84. He blew out air. They were finally out of town.

Hannah coughed, a strangled, gurgling sound. He put a hand on her shoulder and she moaned, resting her cheek on his hand. Blood trickled down her chin.

Black terror clawed its way down his throat.

He pressed the pedal down.

When they reached the next interstate exit, he pulled off on a dirt road near Sandy River Delta Park. They weren't nearly far enough away from the frontage road and from Portland, but this would have to do. Her suffering had to end before it killed her.

Shutting off the vehicle, he ran around the car, wrenched open the passenger door, and cupped her face in his hands. She startled, eyes flying open, mere ghostly shadows beneath the slanting dome light.

"Hannah, reverse it, please. Something bad is happening to you. Give it back to me, now, *älskling*."

She wrapped a clammy hand around Dante's wrist, and he rotated his own hand to secure his grip. When her eyes closed, he thought she'd passed out again, until the tsunami wave of agony slammed into him. Inhuman pain, fiery torture riddled his body. But it was his pain. His injuries. This was what she'd been holding on to so he could get them to safety. *Herre Gud.* They made a grisly tag team.

His brain throbbed like a mad drummer pounded on his skull. Cuts bled anew, though not as briskly as they had originally. They stung, but he continued the connection. He wanted all of the damage back.

How had she lived through that hell?

He bit off a curse as she continued to push the injuries back into him. His ribs cracked again in deep, sickening pops. Blood pooled in his lungs, and he wheezed as ice pick-sharp pain pierced his side with every shallow draw of air.

Knots of bruised muscle tore through his back and shoulders. His abdomen ached like a bitch. Probing his belly, he perceived tense pressure building up inside, a rapidly expanding knot deep in his gut. *Kristus.* A spleen maybe? And she kept this from him? She might've died if he hadn't taken it back when he did.

As the tension in her hand relaxed, Hannah's weary sigh did his soul wonders. Relief softened the tension on her lips; the bruises and bleeding had receded. When she blinked, the connection ceased, and he staggered back, clutching the doorframe to remain upright.

"Why did you hold on to the injuries so long?" he ground out, his jaw clenched against the searing pain.

"We'd never have gotten far enough away to be safe." Her low voice soothed him. "You're going to feel awful for quite a while." She yawned. "If I can sleep for a bit, I'll drive.

"No need. I just need an hour or so to get better."

"An hour? Who are you kidding? I know how hurt you are."

"Like I said, I heal quickly."

"Are you some kind of freak of nature?"

"You could say that. Can we discuss this later? I need to rest."

He coughed, doubling over. He remained vertical only by virtue of will.

A frown furrowed her brow.

He pointed to the center console next to her. "If you would push those two buttons…" She complied, and the back seat of the Hummer rotated, slid forward, and flattened. "Aftermarket upgrade. Totally worth it."

Dante groaned as he opened the back door and eased onto the seat, lying diagonally and bending to accommodate his large frame. Sleeping in his car wasn't perfect, but it worked in a pinch. Wouldn't be the first time.

"Your glasses are in there." He pointed at the console. "And if you need anything, there are water and snacks, too."

"You keep food in your car?"

"I like to eat." He panted through the pain until he could talk again. "But I stocked it this morning, hoping I might be able to eventually drive you around. Like, on a date. This is not what I had in mind." He pressed a hand against his creaking ribcage.

He watched as she found napkins, wetted them, and scrubbed her face clean. After gulping some water, she sighed. Satisfied that she had recovered, Dante relaxed into the cool, quiet night air that drifted through the vehicle.

"Please?" He raised his hand to Hannah.

He had to have her next to him. She was like a human salve on his scarred and raw soul. She was the good to his evil. The light to his dark. He had to be in contact with her and pretend that he could keep her safe, even in his battered state. Thankfully, his injuries had already begun to knit. The broken ribs had nearly sealed back together, and he moved more easily now.

Hesitating, she stood outside the car near his feet, her expression obscured by the shadows from the harsh dome light. Finally, she stepped in and closed the back passenger door, sealing them in a cocoon of warmth and silence. When she paused again, he gently tugged her arm so she rested on her side in front of him, her head pillowed on his arm, the backs of her knees resting against his kneecaps. With a contented sigh, he wrapped his other arm around her, briefly enjoyed the sensation of her tiny frame tucked into his body, and fell into a rare deep sleep.

• • •

Darkness. She couldn't move. Panic welled up. Another time, another cold, dark space. Another man.

But… warmth?

The scent of latte and maleness and leather. And blood.

Dante. His car.

She let out a breath and allowed the tension to seep away.

He shifted in his sleep and pulled her closer. She snuggled back against the ridges of his abdomen and anvil-hard chest. For all of his strength, he hadn't once hurt or threatened her. He'd used all of that power to keep her safe.

She hadn't felt safe for years.

She wanted to stay here forever, in this car, in his arms, away from all the bad things in her world. What if he wanted more? Didn't matter. Wouldn't happen. She was damaged goods, not fit for anyone in a long-term, forever kind of way. Someone with a messed up leg. A messed up life. The creepy healing thing. Her fear of… closeness. What a bargain.

Dante tensed, grunted, and relaxed back onto the flat seat. He brushed his firm lips over her temple, sending shivers down her spine.

"How are you?" he said. "Is all of the damage gone?"

She loved the way his deep voice rumbled through her bones, and how he kept her tucked against his frame, surrounding her with his body. Safe.

"Almost all of the injuries are gone. I'm a little tired and sore but fine." Twisting toward him in the near darkness, she asked, "What about you?"

"*Ja*, told you, I'm a fast healer."

"People can't recover that quickly. Breathe." She put her ear to his chest while he obediently complied. Sounded okay. "I know what was going on in those lungs an hour ago. How's that possible?"

"It's a long story. How's it possible for you to heal people when they're injured?"

"Good point." She understood how a person would want to keep secrets. She burrowed her cheek into his shoulder. "You're really warm."

"Are you saying I'm a hot guy?" He chuckled.

"Not if it'll go to your head."

"Then best not say anything." When he shifted, the leather seats creaked under his weight. "I have a high thermostat."

As if demonstrating, he rested his rather warm lips on her cheek and moved down to her mouth. Swirls of pleasure coiled down her body as he kissed her gently. When he added a nip with his teeth, she jumped.

He pulled away, half chuckling, half groaning. "Hannah, even with aching bones from getting my ass handed to me by Scott's friends, we should really be working out a plan for what to do next."

"But?"

"But nothing. I'm happy cramped in a car with you right here. I can't concentrate on the next step in our plan."

He brushed his lips over her forehead once more and sat up, helping her to do the same. Opening the passenger door, he muttered something foreign and unpleasant sounding when the garish dome light flashed on. He reached up and shut off the interior light. Now only the light from the full moon illuminated the vehicle.

She pulled out her glasses from the center console and popped them on. As she stepped out of the vehicle in front of him, he swung his long legs out of the car and sat on the edge of the seat. With his big hands, he scrubbed at his jaw. The bruises and cuts had almost healed. Just a little dried blood. Amazing.

"May I?"

She pointed at the crusty blood on his face and in his matted hair. When he nodded, she wet some napkins and stood on the running board between his long legs. She dabbed at the blood, removing most of the crusts and wiping clean the remaining shallow cuts. Dante sighed deeply and leaned forward, thick forearms resting on his knees.

Relaxed, he appeared younger, like the weight of the world had lifted off his shoulders. She swiped the napkin over his forehead, moving a bit of hair from his brow. Over his chin, his cheekbones. Over his lips that were not too full but sensual. Over the thick jaw muscles.

Rested, she easily maintained the block against another transfer. So she gave over to the simple pleasure of touching his skin.

He had stood up to those guys to keep her safe. Didn't run. Didn't abandon her. Tears pricked her eyes, but she kept on washing his injuries.

She bit her lower lip, concentrating to get the last bit of blood off a nasty gash on his temple. It had healed into a puckered pink line already. She pulled the damp napkin through his matted hair, tugging at the dried blood. His hair, a bit longer than most guys wore it, glinted in the light. She drew each strand through, cleaning it.

When her breathing sped up, she met his gaze.

Black, intense eyes in the shadows.

How long had he been staring at her?

Stark hunger etched his features with hard lines from the slash of his eyebrows to his clenched jaw. The warmth radiating from him rose several degrees, yet she shivered.

"Come here."

He snaked his muscled arm around her waist and pulled her close, capturing her lips in a kiss. His other hand cupped the back of her neck. Now at equal height, he held her to him, kissing her lips, cheeks, and temples. She shivered when his lips slid down to her collarbone.

The water and napkin dropped onto the ground as Hannah wrapped her arms around his neck. His shoulder muscles bunched when he buried his hand in her hair and tugged her head back. He arched her to him and nipped at her neck, tickling her with his rough stubble. When her knees threatened to buckle, he clamped his corded thighs onto her hips.

Sliding his rough palms up under her shirt, he grazed the sensitive skin on her lower back, making her shiver even more. With both hands encircling her waist, he slowly rubbed his hands up and down while kissing her. His hot palms heated her core as he traced her belly.

Every muscle in her body tensed, and not with pleasure but with damned fear again.

No more.

No more of Ray's past actions controlling her life now. Dante wasn't Ray. Dante hadn't hurt her. She deserved more than the shadow of a life she'd been living for the past several years. She deserved happiness, and if it came in the form of an overly protective giant of a man, so much the better.

When he entered her mouth with his tongue, warmth flooded her body, and she met his kisses. He smoothed his hands up to cup her shoulders, raising her shirt. The cool air on her back warred with his toasty legs locked around her hips and his heated mouth relentlessly opening her to him. It couldn't be real. Not for her. It was a heck of a dream, though, and she didn't want to wake up.

Headlights and the crunch of gravel plunged them back into reality. A car engine revved.

Had the police found them? Brandon?

When Dante shoved her top down and leapt in front of her, she grabbed the back of his shirt for support. The ropey muscles of his back tensed beneath her hands as he leaned forward. The tremors incapacitating her had nothing to do with the cool night air. Her tight breaths speared through her chest. There wasn't enough air.

Who was out there?

Chapter 10

"Who's there?" Dante yelled, holding his arm up against the glare of headlights.

"Aw, crap. I thought we had the place to ourselves." The lights abruptly shut off, leaving Hannah blind for a moment. "Taylor, get back in the car, baby, we've gotta leave. My bad, man."

The door slammed, lights flashed on, and the car spun backward and away.

Hannah dropped her forehead into Dante's back, let out a sigh, and laughed.

"I agree." He drew her in front of him to rest his chin on the crown of her head. "Well, that pretty much cements it; we should concentrate on what to do next. Staying out here isn't an option."

Warmth seeped from his arms encircling her, and she pressed her cheek to his chest before stepping back.

"You're right, but I'm not sure what to do. I don't want to go back to the rental and Scott and his... friends. I'd rather you leave me here instead."

"Well, that's not going to happen. I am not driving away without you in the car with me."

She had no right to ask him for more help. He'd done far more for her than anyone ever had. "Yes, but—"

He growled. "I won't take you back there."

"But I don't have any place *to* go." Tears burned behind her lids. "No one's left."

"I'm here."

Her heart twisted, and she averted her gaze to collect herself. Although she wanted him to fold her into his arms, thankfully he held back. If he so much as touched her now, she'd fall to pieces.

Another few shaky breaths later, she'd pulled her emotions back from the breaking point.

Opening the front passenger door, he helped her in, came around to the driver's side, and started the car. The dashboard lights illuminated his face in an eerie blue glow. He gripped the leather steering wheel and stared into the night for a full minute.

He banged his fist on the dashboard, and then after a moment, he said, "Okay. We're going to La Grande," and put the vehicle into reverse.

"Pardon?"

"La Grande, Oregon. An old friend of mine lives there with his wife. She's a doctor. She can check out your injuries as well."

"I'm fine."

"Sure you are. But she can double-check. Besides, Peter will have an idea about what we should do."

"We can't just drop in."

"It'll be okay. Besides, ol' Petey owes me." He grinned at Hannah, and her heart flopped over. "He wouldn't have a wife if it weren't for me!"

Humming, as though he hadn't been almost dead an hour ago, he pulled back onto the frontage road and then onto I-84. In the warm car, exhaustion claimed her, and she drifted into a pleasant, dreamless sleep.

• • •

The morning sun broke over the Wallowa Mountains right as Dante turned onto a familiar county road east of La Grande, Oregon. He'd driven this rural route every day for two weeks to check on Allie after Peter's disappearance a year ago, when she'd been recovering from horrific injuries she'd sustained from an attack by Jerahmeel's former minion.

When Peter had returned, he had been human. Somehow, he had broken the eternal contract, gotten the Meaningful Kill. Then Peter had asked Allie to stay with him until the end of his mortal life, and she had agreed.

Just like that, Dante had become unnecessary as a watchman—and a colossal third wheel. So he'd done the only reasonable thing he knew to stay busy. He'd taken off on vicious quota runs, killing hundreds of criminals, providing needed distraction. Things were fine. Until Philadelphia.

He rubbed his chin and glanced at a sleeping Hannah, her head turned toward him as it rested on her shoulder. Fading bruises still stood out in cruel blotches against her fair skin. He squeezed the steering wheel to keep from touching her soft face.

Who would've thought? Raymond Jackson. The kill that changed everything. The kill that led Dante to Hannah.

Speaking of whom, she stirred and stretched, freezing as her eyes flew open.

"What?" His heart thudded as he scanned for new injuries.

"Sore! Everything hurts."

His heart melted as she scrunched her button nose.

"Wow, what a bad night." She pressed the knob to raise the back of the seat.

Dante cleared his throat. "Maybe not all of it was bad."

He treated himself to the vision of her cheeks glowing pink as she intently studied the morning scenery out the front windshield. He'd rather study the scenery inside the vehicle.

"It's pretty here," she said.

"Sure is. Nice mountains. Quiet town. They even have a university here."

"Really? I'd love to go to college in a place like this."

He wanted to know more. "What degree would you get?"

"I've always been interested in psychology. Maybe counseling. I like helping people." She ducked her head.

Unable to help himself, he rested his hand on her shoulder for a second. "You'd be great at it."

"I need to get back on track. I was taking courses at the community college until, um, we moved." Swallowing, she turned her head away.

Cold dread lodged in his throat. At some point, he'd have to tell her the whole story about killing Ray and why, but Dante couldn't do it yet. Not now. Not when every tenuous support had been pulled out from under her.

What an excuse.

"Ah, here we go." He steered the Hummer onto the lane, the pleasant crunch of gravel coming from beneath the tires. Allie's and now Peter's house, a welcoming craftsman ranch, backed up to the base of a low ridge.

"What a nice place."

"I agree. You'll like my friends, too."

As Dante parked, a dark-haired man clad in jeans and a polo shirt emerged from the house. If their unexpected arrival surprised Peter, his old friend didn't show it.

Dante groaned as he unfolded his stiff limbs from the driver's seat.

"What the hell happened to you?" Peter rubbed his chin and studied Dante.

Dante had forgotten about the bloodstained clothing and the cuts and bruises.

"I feel much better than I look," he said, getting out of the car.

"You always did have a hard head." Peter walked to the side of the vehicle.

Dante clapped his friend on the shoulder. "Peter, bro, how's it going?" He pulled back. "Hey, you're finally getting gray hair!"

"Don't remind me." Peter smiled. "I've got new aches and pains, too. The price I had to pay was worth it." He shrugged. "If you look past those bruises ruining your pretty face, you're still the picture of health."

"What did you expect? I'm a specimen." Damn, it hurt when he flexed and postured.

At a small noise, Dante turned to Hannah. She hovered near the front of the car, shoulders hunched.

Before Dante could open his mouth, Peter stepped up with an amiable grin and shook her hand.

"I'm Peter Blackstone. Nice to meet you."

"Hannah Banks." She frowned and glanced between them. "You two have the same last name. Are you… related?"

Peter glanced at Dante with a silent question.

Dante gave a small shake of his head, praying his friend would get the hint.

Peter smiled. "Related in a manner of speaking. Would you like to come in?"

As they approached the door, a giant mass of light brown, barking joy careened through the entrance, its hindquarters hitting the doorframe with a loud *thwack*. Dante sped around behind Hannah as the Great Dane mix launched at her. He caught her as she staggered backward with a cry.

"Ivy! Down!" Peter yelled.

The dog immediately dropped, her tail beating a tattoo into the walkway. Her tongue lolled in a big doggie grin.

"Bad Ivy," Peter said.

Ivy pressed her lower jaw to her paws and gazed dolefully at Hannah, tail still wagging. After setting Hannah back on her feet, Dante released his hands from around her thin shoulders.

"Your dog seems nice," she said.

"She's a giant nightmare." Peter grimaced.

When Hannah offered her hand, Ivy sat up and sniffed until satisfied. Then the dog licked her hand, stood, and leaned her jowls against Hannah's hip with a sigh. Ivy's eyes rolled back as Hannah petted the dog's massive head.

Peter groaned. "Hedonistic dog."

"Hey, do I smell bacon?" Dante said.

"Speaking of hedonist."

"Epicurean, Petey. I'm a connoisseur of fine food."

"Of all food. In large quantities."

"Point taken. So …?" He patted his muscled belly.

"Come on in. Ivy, come here." The big dog trotted after Peter.

The aroma of fresh bacon, eggs, and coffee made Dante weak in the knees. Allie, beautiful as ever, her long, brown hair pulled into a clip, was fixing breakfast, with an expression of concentration and anxiety. She took a few steps toward him, awkward with her large belly.

Allie, pregnant?

"Hi, Dante!"

Allie gave him a sideways hug.

"What the heck happened?" Dante pointed at her very pregnant stomach.

Peter cleared his throat while Allie blushed. Peter draped one arm around her shoulders, beamed down at his wife, and then pinned Dante with a wry grin.

"I would've thought you knew how these things work," Peter said dryly. "With your background growing up on a farm and so forth."

Hannah hid a smile behind her hand.

Dante started to sweat in earnest. "Yes, well, I know how it works, of course, yes. But with…I didn't realize it was possible."

"My friend, why don't you sit down and have breakfast?"

Peter laughed as Dante slumped, defeated, into a kitchen chair.

Allie stepped up, her physician's gaze assessing Hannah. All in the space of a second. Then she offered her hand.

"Hi, I'm Al."

When their hands touched, Allie winced and shot a glance at Peter, who also cringed. *Jävlar.* Allie, the woman who saw death, had sensed something from the contact with Hannah, and since her mind still linked to Peter's, of course he felt it, too.

Not good. Dante would have to find out what she saw. Later.

Hannah appeared unaffected and took a big breath. "I'm Hannah." She gave Allie a shy smile. "Smells great. You must be a good cook."

Allie laughed. "Well, not really, but I need to learn before this baby starts to eat solid foods, or she'll starve. Please make yourself at home. Um, need me to examine anything? You look like you might… have had an accident."

Hannah stared down at the floor. "I'm fine."

Simultaneously, Dante said, "Yes, check her over."

Allie studied Hannah. "Hmm. Can it wait until after breakfast, or should I take a peek now?"

Hannah shook her head. "Later."

"Now," Dante interjected.

After a pause, Allie shrugged. "I'll go with the patient on this one."

When Hannah excused herself to wash up in the restroom, Dante went to his car for a change of clothes. Just getting the torn, bloody shirt off made him feel better. He selected a pair of designer jeans and a black T-shirt and changed, lightning fast, in the open air.

When he reentered the house, Allie shot him another nebulous glare but said nothing.

Face damp but at least clean of dried blood, Hannah returned and settled in a cushioned kitchen chair with a sigh. The breathy sound set his nerves on edge as he imagined her lips making that sound near his ear.

Vad i helvete. Focus, man.

And focus he did as he crunched crispy bacon and toast. He relaxed as Allie talked about her upcoming time off work. The baby would be here in a few short weeks. Peter's besotted expression spoke volumes. As she talked, he maintained contact with his wife—a touch on her hand, a surreptitious caress of her swollen belly.

Dante averted his eyes when a strange burst of nasty emotion hit him out of the blue.

Jealousy. Damn.

Peter had done it. Broken the contract, made a life together with a mortal, created new life. Hell, Peter had gotten a job as a freaking history professor, lucky bastard. What an easy job when you'd lived the past hundred years.

The wife, a kid on the way, the family pet, and a proverbial white picket fence. Nice work if you could get it, but that wasn't Dante's gig. He liked options.

Didn't he?

At the end of the table, Hannah pushed the food around the plate. Her thin shoulders slumped, and those glasses didn't hide the circles beneath her eyes. Faded bruises yellowed her fair skin. He'd bet she still had residual internal injuries. What did she say last night when he asked how she was doing?

Almost all of the injuries are gone.

She smiled vaguely but remained quiet.

With one eye on Hannah, Dante listened to his friends catch him up on their lives since he'd seen them a year ago. The pleasant company and good food lulled him into a state of relaxation.

But as he began his second helping of breakfast, Dante froze.

"Allie? Why'd you make this much food? You two didn't seem surprised to see us."

"Barnaby called yesterday. He thought you might show up," Peter said.

"A feeling?"

"Sometimes people sense things. Don't they?" Allie added in a too-sharp tone as she inclined her head toward Hannah.

She glared at Dante until he withered under her glare. Allie's "feelings" were often accurate. And deadly.

"True."

Allie sighed. "Besides, if you hadn't arrived, I would've eaten everything. This kid likes breakfast. And lunch. And dinner." She grinned at Dante's overflowing second helping. "Though a healthy appetite might... run in the family."

After breakfast, Peter refused to let his wife clean up. He fussed over Allie and insisted she sit and rest.

Something twisted like a knife in Dante's chest, like he couldn't take a deep breath. He was witnessing another item in a long list of life experiences he would never have.

Speaking of which, Hannah's strawberry blonde head nodded over her half-eaten plate. Her lips curved in an endearing smile.

"Peter? Any chance we can crash for a bit?" He motioned toward his sleepy companion.

"Absolutely. We have a guest room."

Allie heaved up from the chair. "Come on, I'll get you both taken care of." She paused. "Hannah, did you want a fresh change of clothes? I have a few things that might fit."

"I'd appreciate it."

At Hannah's soft voice, Dante's world tilted off-balance for a split second. It had to be his fatigue. Only he didn't get tired, did he?

Ivy jumped up from her position near Allie's feet, ears perked, tail wagging eagerly.

"No, Ivy. Stay," Allie said sternly.

Peter shrugged. "She's gotten more protective of Allie since the pregnancy. Unfortunately, all she'd do to an intruder is lick him to death."

Dante grinned and followed Allie, Hannah, and a not-staying Ivy to the guest room. His gaze was drawn to Hannah's slim hips, swaying beneath her skirt.

Allie pointed out the bathroom, set a change of clothes for Hannah on the bed, and then quietly withdrew.

The room smelled faintly of cinnamon and breakfast and... home. Dante gave a deep, contented sigh.

Standing in the middle of the room, Hannah rubbed her arms.

Dante would've loved nothing more than to curl up with her and rest. Or not rest. But he needed to talk to Peter first.

He lightly touched her slim arm.

"You can have the shower first. Take your time. I'm going to catch up with Peter. Get a nap if you like, too. You're safe here. With friends."

"Okay." She pivoted back. "Dante?"

Her mellow, vulnerable voice sliced through him.

"*Ja*," he answered hoarsely. His shoulders ached, so badly did he want to hold her.

"Thank you. For everything. For..." Tears shimmered.

He fisted his hands at his side to keep from yanking her into his arms. She looked so fragile, hugging the towel to her chest.

"No one's ever done anything like that..." She cleared her throat.

He kept his tone light. "Of course. My pleasure. And even better, all of that mess led us to a fresh breakfast, a hot shower, and a nap. Everyone wins. Enjoy."

He backed out of the room, closing the door. Anything more said, and he'd never leave the room, which would be dangerous on every level imaginable.

As he entered the cozy living room, he paused. Allie rested her head on Peter's shoulder as they sat on the couch, murmuring to each other.

Never in Dante's 300 years did he consider himself lacking as a man, a protector. But right now, this—what his friend had found—was what Dante never truly had. This connection. This partnership. Even though he had loved Marguerite all those years ago, their relationship still never had the binding and lasting strength of what Peter and Allie had. Apparently, Dante required an additional 200 years of personal growth to get to the same maturity level as his friends. Late bloomer and all.

With a wave of longing, he wanted to achieve what Peter had, to attain the Meaningful Kill, to be free of the knife, to live a life as a human. Just thinking about the damn knife, it throbbed again. It had been much too long since he'd fed the weapon. The longest he'd gone between kills had been two weeks, and he was pushing that limit right now. The sick siren song of the blade heated his leg with its undeniable hunger as the red desire to kill blinded him. With immense effort, he forced his base compulsions under control.

Peter stroked Allie's hair as they talked quietly.

Dante cleared his throat. They pulled apart as though it took effort.

"Come on in, Dante. Grab a chair," Peter said.

"Hey, professor, push me up." Allie laughed as Peter helped propel her off the couch. "I'll be resting if anyone needs me. Dante, when you two are done catching up, I should probably speak with you."

Not good. Had Allie's unnatural ability picked up ever-present death from Dante? Or from Hannah? *Herre Gud.*

Allie's visions *always* predicted death.

"Sure thing, Allie."

Peter watched Allie with a stark hunger until she left the room.

Dante leaned back on the chair and crossed an ankle over his knee. "Pregnant, huh? So your boys can swim?"

Peter's smirk mixed chagrin and pride. "Apparently so. Ultrasound shows my girl has two arms, two legs, and only one normal-appearing head, so she's not a freak of nature. Yes. My 'boys' must still be good after 70-plus years of Indebted service. Not bad for a 100-year-old guy, huh?"

"I'm impressed."

"It sure shocked us. Didn't think it was possible, so we never tried to prevent anything."

When Peter smiled, creases Dante hadn't noticed before lined his friend's face. The gray at the temples suited Peter, gave him a less harsh, more relaxed appearance. Finally. Time had begun to march on for his friend.

"A pleasant mistake."

"We thought so." Peter stretched his arm along the back of the couch. "So, what's this about trouble in Portland?"

Dante scrubbed his grimy forehead.

"Peter, my man, it's complicated. How much beta did Barnaby give you?"

"He mentioned you'd killed some guy in Philadelphia. And the guy you killed asked you to find the person he'd hurt. Hannah, I presume. And now you've managed to unearth a minion in the process, one who now has knowledge that Hannah can... heal people? Is that about right?"

"You've got the bare bones of it. What I haven't told you is that last night her brother, two other men, and the minion attacked me."

"I wondered why you both looked like hell. But they only attacked you, right? So what happened to Hannah?"

"You know how I'm normally pretty good in a fight, right?"

"You're understating things, my friend."

"Just making sure your mind hasn't slipped as you approach senility. Yes, I managed two men and the minion quite handily. But when Hannah's brother grabbed her, I got distracted, and the minion took the opportunity to deal me quite a blow on the ol' bucket."

"How did that even hurt you? Your skull's really thick."

"Thanks, bro. But yes, I went down. The minion got in a lucky shot. According to Hannah, they kept beating me even after I was unconscious. Right before the police arrived, they ran away. And Hannah healed me."

Peter sat up straight. "So explain how she heals people."

"She's got the ability to take whatever injury or illness someone has and absorb it into her body. Obviously, she didn't realize I'd recover on my own."

"You can take more of a beating than any human. What happened when she absorbed your injuries?"

"She nearly died."

"I bet."

"It was sick."

"All because of a minion?" Peter's eyes no longer turned black like Dante's, but the fury shone clearly nevertheless. Peter knew all too well the damage a minion could do to a mortal.

Dante leaned forward. "Yeah. All of a sudden, I was completely healthy and she was unconscious from my concussion and sporting all of my injuries. So I grabbed her, ran away before the police caught us, drove out of town, and begged her to reverse whatever she did."

"And?"

"Damned if it didn't work. If I hadn't taken my injuries back, she would've died from internal bleeding or the punctured lung."

"She still looks rough."

"I've seen her after she's healed other people. She stays sick for a while."

"So now what?"

"I'm not sure. Jerahmeel knows about the situation, about her. He may have inserted the minion after what I did in Philly. I'm guessing. Maybe he figured I would try to find my kill's victims."

"Plural?"

"Hannah's brother. He didn't get the worst abuse, though. He's quite the piece of work. Easily molded and manipulated, I think."

"By a certain minion."

"Yeah."

"Dante, you think Jerahmeel views Hannah's healing ability as a threat? Like how Allie was a threat to him with her radar for all things death?"

"*Ja,* possible. The question is, what's the priority? Does the minion want to hurt Hannah to punish me? Or get Hannah for himself?"

"You're not popular, that's for certain. But Hannah can potentially block Jerahmeel's desire for someone to die."

"One human can't make that much of a dent in his supply of souls, right?"

Peter reclined back and rubbed his jaw. "Depends on how many of her kind exist and how many Indebted remain to feed Jerahmeel. Barnaby thinks our numbers are dwindling. That's bad for Jerahmeel. Fewer killers, fewer souls, less power."

"Can't he just make more Indebted?"

"Takes too much drain of his power. It's easier for him to make minions. They're already evil. Not as much effort to create."

"So he needs every single kill."

Peter scrubbed at his temples. "A person like Hannah would be viewed as a direct threat to his power sources."

Dante's gut twisted. "I'll keep her hidden."

"Until you have to kill. Then he'll know where you are." He pointed to Dante's leg. "You're fighting the urge right now, aren't you?"

"*Ja,* but I can keep it under control." Dante yanked his hand away from extending toward the knife.

"For how long?"

His forehead had gone damp with sweat. "As long as it takes, Petey."

"At some point, you won't be able to resist."

Dante tried to ignore the eager, poker-hot knife pulsing on his leg. "I'll do what I have to."

"She'll be in danger."

"No, Peter, she will not," he bit out.

"Hmm." His friend leaned back on the couch, breaking the tension. "So how does this involve you? And after your kill in Philadelphia? I wonder if Jerahmeel has become extra vigilant after Barnaby and I broke our contracts. If he's watching you more closely."

"Barnaby mentioned Hannah's healing abilities might make her either an asset or a liability to Jerahmeel," Dante said.

"An asset. Interesting. I hadn't thought of it that way."

Peter rubbed his chin, lost in thought.

"Jerahmeel knows about Hannah's powers, and he hasn't forgotten about Allie's abilities… and now two of his Indebted are out of the business. He's intrigued and pissed. And you killed his other minion last year. Jerahmeel could be feeling vulnerable."

"Jerahmeel vulnerable? You're kidding."

"I'm not. He needs a constant supply of souls to maintain his strength. He needs creatures like us, you, to keep him going. And he might think you're planning to get out of your contract, too."

"I wish."

"Thought you loved being immortal, had the world at your feet. Nothing stopped you, right?" Peter raised his hands, palms up.

"Oh, sure."

"Maybe something's changed?"

"No idea what—"

A ringing cell phone interrupted them. Peter answered on the first ring.

"Hello? Yes." His knuckles blanched as he glanced toward the bedroom. "Hell. Was he harmed? Okay, then. Thank you for the information, we'll make plans."

Dante nearly jumped on him before Peter thumbed off the phone.

"What is it, bro?"

"Barnaby just got a visit from a minion named Brandon."

Chapter 11

"Who was that?" An icy wave of dread flowed through Dante's veins.

Peter nodded. "Some lady named Ruth."

"*Ja*, Nurse Ratched." At Peter's unspoken question, he added, "She's Barnaby's attendant. Also like us."

"Interesting. But I don't have time to care right now. She believes the minion is heading this way." A muscle worked in Peter's jaw as he glanced again toward the closed bedroom door. "We have to get out of here. Now."

"When did he leave Barnaby's?"

"Right before Ruth called. Even speeding, it'll take him over two hours to make it here." Peter jumped up. "Ok. Time to go on a vacation for a week or so. May I recommend you do the same?"

"*Jävlar*. I'm getting tired of this insanity."

"No argument here, my friend."

"Where should we go, Petey?"

"Let me give you a suggestion." He pulled out a map and flattened it on the coffee table. Tracing a route south and then west, he tapped the map. "You'll have cell phone coverage there."

"Then what?"

"No idea. Call Barnaby and ask him. I'll talk with him if I can. But there's not much else I can do, Dante. I'm only mortal now, and I've got to get my wife to safety."

Shame flooded Dante. What evil had he aimed at his friends by coming here?

"Bro, I'm truly sorry to bring all this down on you."

"Comes with the territory. Frankly, I wondered when things would catch up to us."

"Absolutely. Where are you going?"

"Well, seems I finally have to take that shopping trip to Spokane. Baby supplies." He smirked. "The things I do for you, Dante."

"Likewise."

The previous minion had tried to kill Allie. Dante still relished the memory of crunching the minion's spinal column beneath his foot just before he dealt the deathblow. Now an even more disgusting minion was coming, with no compunction about going through a pregnant woman and her mortal husband to reach his goal. Damn.

Peter paused. "Fair enough. You did take care of that last minion so I could help Allie. Let's call us even, then?"

"Deal."

Peter ran back into the bedroom. Allie's alarmed voice traveled through the house as dressers and drawers banged closed.

Dante needed to get Hannah the hell out of here. *Kristus*, bad shit kept following him these days.

· · ·

Warm, relaxed, and clean, Hannah snuggled into the comfortable duvet. Her body rocked, and she tried to roll over to escape the annoying movement.

"Hannah?"

The deep voice soothed her, as welcoming as the covers on this bed. "Wake up, *älskling*. We have to leave."

Hannah tried to pull the covers up, but they didn't budge. With a sigh, she opened one eye. Dante knelt next to the bed, tensed like he was about to bolt. Alarmed, she sat straight up, fully awake. Panic gripped her until she took a deep breath and blew it out.

"What?"

"We've got to go."

"Why?"

Dante studied the duvet cover. "Brandon's headed this way. We can't be here when he arrives."

Heart pounding, Hannah froze under a wave of nausea. "I don't understand. Why would that loser come here?"

"He's a bad guy, worse than you think. And he wants to hurt us. I'll keep you safe, but we need to leave now."

"Okay, okay," she whispered, stifling the questions he obviously didn't want to answer.

She hadn't seen fear on Dante's face before, even when he'd stood up to the guys on the street yesterday. So what did it take for a man like him to be this afraid?

She slipped on her sandals and hitched up the borrowed jeans. Cramming on her glasses, she dashed after Dante into the kitchen.

Allie and Peter shoved supplies and food into two overnight bags. Ivy danced around, tail wagging. At least someone was having fun.

Allie called over her shoulder, puffing as she bent to pack a bag. "Pull the covers off the guest bed. You'll need it for the park in John Day."

"No, Brandon might figure out that we intentionally left. He can't know for sure that you two were here. Best to confuse him as long as possible," Peter said. "Stop by the Walmart in Caldwell, Idaho, and pick up the bedding you'll need there."

Hannah's cheeks warmed. Bedding? With Dante? Never mind. She'd worry about that later; they needed to get out of here first.

"Dante? I need to speak with you." Allie motioned him into the living room.

Hannah tried not to eavesdrop, but their murmurs filtered back into the kitchen, punctuated by one emphatic "No!" from Dante.

When they returned, Dante didn't look directly at Hannah. His brows drew together in anger, but in his eyes, there was only sadness. When he cupped her elbow with extreme care, the alarm bells sounded in her mind. This was a different kind of touch, almost like pity, and she didn't like it.

"Good luck, you two," Peter said, hefting both bags and a satchel of food onto his shoulders. "Honey, did you call work?"

"Sure did. I've got tomorrow's shift covered, so we're good for a few days."

Hannah cleared her throat. "Um, thank you, for breakfast and a place to stay. I'm sorry about you, us, having to leave. And that jerk coming here—"

Allie hugged her. "It's nothing we can't handle. Besides, you're in good hands." She punched Dante on his meaty arm as they all exited the house.

The smile didn't reach Allie's eyes.

• • •

What was wrong with Dante?

He hadn't said a word for the past two hours while he continued to stare straight ahead. His grip on the steering wheel shifted between strangle and throttle, and the muscle in his jaw jumped every few minutes as he kept glancing in the rearview mirror.

After announcing loudly to the gas station attendant that he was traveling to Boise, Dante proceeded to not travel to Boise. About twenty miles outside of the city, he veered off the interstate and doubled back on frontage roads and county roads until they drove through the mountains south and west of La Grande.

When he took a curve too quickly, he grumbled, "Sorry."

She attempted conversation, but his curt, albeit polite, responses involved one syllable or a grunt. The few times he smiled, the curve of his mouth was cruel and grim against the tension in his neck.

The one time he initiated a conversation, he only asked her to shut off her cell phone and not turn it on again. In silence, she dropped the phone into her blood-stained purse.

What the heck happened? Yesterday, she was holding down a job and rebuilding her life in Portland. Last night, the attack by Brandon, assisted by her drug-using brother, destroyed everything she'd worked so hard to build. And now she was on the run with Dante. True, he might be a gentle giant with her, but she'd seen his brutal temper. She didn't know anything about him.

So why then did she blithely go with Dante?

Right now, this virtual stranger was the only thing keeping her out of Brandon's cruel hands. What choice did she have? Sit around and wait for Brandon to arrive? No thanks.

What about Scott? Had she written him off so quickly? No. She loved her brother. They had suffered together in Philly and escaped together. But he was an adult now. He'd been making his own choices and rejecting her input for years. Aside from wallowing in her guilt, there was nothing left to do.

Speaking of guilt, what about her job? Her life in Portland? She'd torpedoed all of it. Now she had nothing and no place to go. She couldn't have done a better job of destroying her life if she'd doused it with gas and lit a match.

What if she could go back and pick up her life?

No. Too much baggage with Scott's crap. Too dangerous back there if this Brandon guy was as bad as he seemed.

As they passed through forested hills on winding chip-seal roads, she, too, stared out the window. They hadn't passed any other vehicles in the past half hour.

The silence in the vehicle amplified the emptiness echoing in her aching head. She glanced over at Dante and cringed at the black scowl. Waves of heat rolled off of him. A bead of sweat trickled between her breasts, but she wasn't about to ask him to adjust the temperature. She concentrated on remaining inconspicuous.

Maybe he was worried about their situation. Made sense. But she'd seen worried Dante. This emotion was different. This Dante appeared ready to rip the steering wheel off the column.

He was probably mad that she dragged his friends and him into her mess. Understandable. She blinked hard and tried to focus on the scenery.

By early evening, they descended west from the mountains into John Day, Oregon. The town itself was a dusty collection of buildings, nestled into a wide spot in a river valley. Along the river, swaths of trees, their green leaves tipped with early fall gold, contrasted with the terra cotta hills rising on either side of the river. Inhaling the dry, pungent scent of pine and juniper mixed with the wet, green river, she sighed. A far cry from Philadelphia. And from Portland.

She couldn't relax. Was she safe with this man who looked about to erupt?

The way she saw it, there weren't many other options.

"We're here."

Her heart skidded at his rough voice, too loud in the vehicle.

"Where's here?" she asked.

"Where we're going to stay hidden for a while."

She flinched at his icy tone but kept her hands folded in her lap and held still while he pulled up to the ranger station. The sign read "Clyde Holliday State Park."

"Stay here." He slammed the door shut.

The state park, nestled between a bend in the river and the main highway, provided a relaxing backdrop for the setting sun. Any other time, this place would make a perfect rustic vacation. Any other time but now.

When the driver's door whooshed open, she flinched and grabbed the handle of her door.

"Just me," Dante said between gritted teeth. "We're checked in as the Pages, in case anyone asks."

"Pages?"

"Best I could come up with on short notice. All I could think of was the bookstore." One corner of his mouth quirked upward before settling back in a firm line.

Lies and a fake identity. Familiar territory.

"Are we…?"

"On a cheap honeymoon? Yes."

Warmth flooded her cheeks. "Oh."

He pulled into the gravel parking area. Hefting the bags of groceries and supplies he'd obtained earlier, he kicked the Hummer door closed and lifted his chin.

"Come on."

She limped behind him from the vehicle to a small cabin a few hundred feet away. The river rushed by the front of the cabin, replacing highway sounds with the murmuring rapids. Inside the cabin, knotted floor creaked beneath her feet, and she inhaled the rich aroma of past fires in the grate.

Cozy cabin.

Handsome man.

Too bad he looked like a man whose life had been ruined.

By her.

"Hannah?"

The weight of his voice dropped like an anchor into her stomach.

Breath caught midway up her throat as she slowly turned back toward him. Dread, like a lead apron, made her movements sluggish.

"Um, you look tired," she said.

"I guess. It's fine. I don't really get tired."

She flinched at the flat tone.

He stepped once toward her then stopped.

"Have I done something wrong?" she asked.

"Of course not."

Although the corners of his mouth rose up, his ice-blue eyes remained hard.

"Then why are you treating me like a burden you'd rather be rid of?"

"What?"

"I realize it's been a pain helping me. Geez, you got beat to a pulp for your kindness."

"I wasn't beaten up that badly."

"You were almost dead there for a minute. Look, if you can drop me off somewhere or help me get a rental car, I'll be out of your hair."

"You're kidding."

Hot shame burned a path up her neck. Why had she thought this man felt anything more for her than pity and compassion? Inflated sense of duty motivated Dante. She wouldn't blame him for wanting to be rid of her after everything he'd withstood.

"I'm serious. You've got better things to do than go on the run from…"

"From what?"

He stepped closer, and intense heat radiated again.

How'd he do that?

"Stuff catching up with me, I guess."

"What stuff?"

Brandon must have something to do with Ray, fulfilling Ray's desire for revenge. It was the only logical explanation. "I'd rather not say. I'm only sorry you're mixed up in my mess."

"I'm mixed up in your mess?"

"Well, sure." She motioned to the bags of groceries, his still blood-tinged clumps of hair, and the foreign, if not pleasant, rustic surroundings. And can't forget about the maniac tracking her down.

He loomed over her. "There's nothing else I'd rather do."

Temper flared from a place buried deep down inside, an emotion she hadn't experienced in a long time. "Excuse me, are you making fun of me?"

He lifted her chin, his warm finger an immutable force. The compassion in his kind expression hurt more than an accusation.

"I would never tease you."

He brushed her lips with his thumb. At the tingling transfer sensation, she slid the block into place and relaxed into his hand.

Chuckling, he added, "Well, not in this predicament. I might find other reasons to tease you, but not about this situation."

"Like what?"

"Like the fact that I have to work very hard to kiss you when we're standing toe to toe." He bent down.

She forgot to breathe.

He tilted her head up to him and kissed her deeply. The angle of his mouth changed, nudging her mouth open. Encouraging. Demanding. For a moment, she stood there, stiff, uncertain if this was still part of a joke. Then she answered in kind, pouring her fears, her pain, her regrets, and her past, all into the kiss. Dante pulled back, wiping her cheeks with the pads of his thumbs.

"Tears?"

She hadn't realized. His touch drew out long-suppressed emotion. Emotion she couldn't explain. Wouldn't explore.

"Just stressed with everything going on."

He folded her into a bear hug, wrapping her in his heat, his strength. For a moment, she relaxed in the cocoon of his body. As she melted into his chest, she slid her arms around his back, enjoying the long, firm muscles there. A girl could get used to moments like this.

"Well," he rumbled against her ear. "Maybe we should think about dinner."

"Good idea."

She stepped back, bereft of his touch.

His eyes had darkened to a blue-gray slate, his expression hungry, but not for food. Until he blinked and the color returned to ice blue. "Any chance you can put some food together while I clean up? I never got to it earlier today."

Because Brandon was tracking her down, and Dante had continued to help her while she slept earlier. Shame rushed through her. How much more would Dante sacrifice for a near stranger until he walked away? He had to be nearing the point where normal folks would throw in the towel. If he did leave, she wouldn't blame him.

In the meantime, at least she could feed the guy.

"How about canned soup and sandwiches? Not exactly gourmet."

"Sounds perfect."

After a long, inscrutable stare, he left her alone in the cabin.

She turned the lock on the door.

Chapter 12

Two cold showers and a dose of dread later, Dante emerged from the bathhouse, clean, but without any ideas for how to resolve their situation. At least a fresh T-shirt and jeans had helped relax his tense muscles.

He had to tell Hannah what he'd done to Ray and why, but doing so required full disclosure of Dante's true nature. Assuming she didn't run away from that information, then he'd have to explain why Brandon, that sick bastard, hunted her. It was Dante's fault. Jerahmeel was pissed about Dante killing the minion who'd tortured Allie last year. While Jerahmeel hated to interfere directly in Indebted affairs, he hated to be interfered *with* even more.

Peter was right. If Jerahmeel thought his power supply was threatened, he would lash out. He'd throw everything at the offender and anyone the offender treasured.

Allie was Peter's reason to complete his contract. So, when Dante had killed the minion who tried to destroy her, Dante had fallen from the top of Jerahmeel's most-popular list. It'd take years of good, solid, nutritious kills for Dante to make up for his misstep. He might never get out of the contract at this rate.

Neck muscles tensing anew as he exited the bathhouse, he scanned the park on his way back to the cabin. He hated leaving Hannah alone but was reasonably confident that no one could find them here.

Yet.

If Brandon still tracked them, the trail should go cold in Caldwell, Idaho, where Dante had abruptly backtracked into the forests and isolated high desert of central Oregon.

The knife blade pulsed, reminding him that it hadn't been fed in far too long. His hands itched to wrap around the handle and plunge it into a criminal heart. But if Dante used the knife to kill, it would act like a homing beacon. Jerahmeel would send Brandon here.

To Hannah.

A twisting sensation in Dante's chest made him stagger as he stepped onto the cabin porch.

To Hannah.

When he turned the doorknob, it was locked.

His imagination imposed horrible images on his mind's eye. Hannah laying on the cabin floor, broken and bleeding. What kind of protector was he to leave his charge alone?

Clinging to a vestige of control, he knocked on the door and fidgeted until he heard a light step inside. The deadbolt snicked open, harsh and loud in the twilight.

Gold-flecked chestnut eyes and a cute, freckled nose greeted him. It was a vision he'd be happy to see for many years to come.

Dåre. Idiot. After she learned about his past and what kind of monster he really was, there would be no future, at least not together. His only goal: give Hannah a future. Nothing more.

Resisting the need to haul her back into his arms, he pasted a bland smile on his face, stepped into the cabin, and relocked the door. Not that a locked door would make much difference if Brandon found them.

The aroma of beef stew and grilled cheese sandwiches distracted him from the maudlin thoughts. Dante's belly growled. When was the last time his stomach had actually rumbled?

He took a quick glance around the cabin; nothing appeared amiss. He sat down in front of a steaming bowl of soup and a fresh sandwich.

He could get used to this kind of companionship—a dangerous thought.

Happily sated after the meal, he washed and dried the dishes, enjoying the mundane domestic activity. The incandescent light overhead cast the wood interior of the cabin in a warm, yellow glow. The tension in his neck seeped away. He glanced over his shoulder.

Hannah sat on the futon, head bowed.

"Would you like a fire?" he asked.

"That sounds great."

He had the fire crackling in no time, bathing the cabin walls with flickering shadows. Maybe for tonight, they could pretend that no one hunted them, that her life wasn't in jeopardy. Maybe for tonight, he could give her comfort without scaring her.

Normally, he'd swagger, flirt, suggest erotic activities, and then sit back and wait for the woman to come to him, but Hannah wasn't any woman. He wanted to give her pleasure, but do it safely. For her.

He was massive, powerful, wealthy, and long-lived. He could have anything he wanted. Except tonight. It went against everything he'd ever done before, but it was time for a change in approach.

He cleared his throat. "Mind if I sit with you?"

A pause.

"Sure."

She scooted over and bent her knees under her chin, watching the fire. The shifting light emphasized the dark circles under her eyes.

"Do you still feel it?" he asked quietly, not wanting to startle her.

"Pardon?" She turned halfway toward him.

"The injuries you took from me yesterday."

"Yes, a little. It always takes a few days for the injuries to completely go away."

"Where did your ability come from?"

She leaned back against the futon and scrubbed at her face. Dante wanted so badly to take her into his arms that his fingers tingled.

Patience.

"No one in the family understood my little gift."

"I'd hardly call it little."

"I'd hardly call it a gift. It's caused nothing but trouble."

"Trouble how?"

"Um, various ways."

She clamped her mouth shut, and Dante did the same. He wanted to tell her about killing Ray, but not right now. Maybe later.

Coward.

"So when did you first realize you could heal people?"

Sighing, Hannah laid her cheek on her bent knees. The fire flickering made her features appear half animated and half corpse.

"I healed a cut on Mom once. She and I were so shocked, we chalked it up to weird happenstance and tried to ignore it."

"Did you ever heal anything major like you did with me?" he asked.

She shook her head. "The biggest healing before that was when I was a teenager. Scott was doing something stupid on his skateboard. I heard him scream and ran outside.

"His arm was bent all wrong. When I touched his skin, a sensation like a vacuum sucked all of his pain into my body. Then my arm cracked."

"It broke?"

"Loudly. It didn't bend like his arm did, but I felt the pop. Boy, did it hurt."

"What happened after that?"

"We were totally shocked of course. All of a sudden, he was better, and I had a broken arm."

She studied the fire and rubbed her shirtsleeve. Dante stretched his arm over the back of the futon, fingering her fine hair.

"So did you go to the hospital?"

"Well, yes, but by then Mom was freaked out about what happened. She made up a story for the doctor."

"Did she know where your power came from?"

"Not exactly. There was a rumor about a grandmother with strange talents, but Mom didn't know details. Apparently, no one in our family talked about it."

"Did anyone else find out about what you could do?"

She bit her lip and then pressed her lips together. "My stepfather. He wanted to use my powers on other people."

At her tight, closed expression, he held very still. He would not scare her. No surprises, no sudden movements.

"What happened with these other people?"

"I failed." She raised a finger when he opened his mouth. "End of story."

Moving slowly to give her time to protest, he ran his fingers over her cheek, careful to avoid the bruises. Such soft skin hiding the tough woman inside. After a few minutes, she dropped her head onto her bent knees again.

She yawned.

"You're exhausted," he said.

Her shadowed gaze darted around the cabin. "Yeah, but I don't want to sleep."

"Why?"

"Isn't it obvious, with everything that's happened in the past few days?" She put her head in her hands. "At least if I'm awake, I can see what's coming."

As her voice cracked, something cracked inside of Dante.

"Come here," he said. "Please."

Jävlar. Her fear was unacceptable. Maybe he had nothing to offer in the long term, but he could make her feel safe this evening. He turned sideways on the futon and pulled her into his lap.

Those delicate hands resting on his thighs branded him through the denim, and he gritted his teeth. He wrapped his arms around her shoulders and tucked her head under his chin. When she turned her face toward the fire and sighed, the sound melted his soul.

"Sleep. I'll stay up."

"You need rest, too."

Hardly a chance with the growing interest her petite derrière tucked into his groin generated. At least his desire for her distracted him from the knife's call. For now.

"I don't need sleep."

She looked up at him and lifted an eyebrow. "A quirk? Like you run warm and heal quickly?"

Damn it, he wasn't ready to explain.

He squeezed her upper arms in his hands. "I will keep you safe tonight."

"You promise no one will find us?"

"No one will hurt you tonight. I swear it." *Including you,* oåkting.

She snuggled in closer, challenging his self-control and his promise.

"Nice." She rubbed her cheek against his T-shirt-clad chest.

"What's that, *ålskling*?"

"Your voice. It's wonderful." She yawned again, bent her arms up at the elbows and grasped his encircling forearms that rested over her chest. "Please keep talking to me."

If that's what it would take to comfort her, then he'd do it until the world ended. "What would you like me to say?"

"How about that *Tristan and Iseult* you like to quote?"

"Anything you want."

He recited as many lines as he could remember from the old story of love found, love lost, and love eternal. Even after her slow breaths stirred the hair on his arms, he continued. He didn't care if he repeated lines.

Brushing his lips over her silky hair, a delicate floral cloud drifted up, mixing with the smells from dinner and the wood of the cabin. He inhaled her scent—if he ended every night like this in a cozy home, snuggled up with Hannah, they'd make love—sometimes tender, sometimes wild—until her belly swelled with a child beneath his palm.

Although her tiny frame disappeared in his arms, he sensed every inch of her soft body nestled against his. She'd relaxed, trusted him to keep her safe. As long as she needed him, he'd watch over her. He ignored the knife-lust eating at his mind. He didn't care about all of the other elements of his surreal life right now.

Didn't care about the minion out there.

He cared only about the woman in his arms.

• • •

Daylight blinded her when she rolled over. For a split second, she panicked, disoriented until she got a good look at the room. The cabin. She lay on the double bed, wrapped in a cocoon of blankets.

The smell of fresh, hot food awakened her stomach with a vengeance. As she stretched sore muscles, Hannah tried to recall how she got into the bed. Recalling nothing more than the memory of falling asleep on the futon in Dante's arms, she gave up.

After stopping in the bathroom, she shuffled into the kitchen area where Dante industriously flipped more grilled cheese sandwiches and stirred a soup pot. Her heart flopped at the sight of his biceps flexing as he moved from fry pan to pot. He hummed quietly, stopping when he saw her standing there.

"It's about time you got up."

"Why? What time is it?"

"Three. In the afternoon." His wide grin sent a frisson of happiness all the way down to her toes.

"I've never slept in that late."

"You needed the rest."

At an ominous hiss, he whirled back to the pot, which threatened to boil over. Laughing, Hannah scooted him over with her hip and rescued the soup before it scorched. She brushed her arm against his, enjoying the heat that flowed between them.

See? She could touch him without freaking out. Taking a calming breath, she nudged him with a shoulder.

He didn't move, but when she glanced up, the intense expression on his face stole her breath away.

Maybe there was hope for more between them. What would he look like without that shirt on? How would those ridges on his chest feel to her bare fingertips? Would his skin be hot to the touch, or would goose bumps pebble his skin when she touched him?

When the typical wave of panic rose up, she held her breath and tamped down the fear until she allowed herself to ponder Dante's abs again.

One tiny victory.

Clearing her throat, she pretended to care about the food in front of her as she stirred. "Thanks for tucking me in last night."

"It was my pleasure. Anytime." He winked.

Now that was back to the old Dante, with the suggestive undertone. Her heart fluttered beneath his avid gaze. He grinned, took his plate and bowl, and followed her to the table.

"Sorry that the meal isn't very original." He gestured toward the food.

"If you cook it, I'll eat the same thing for every meal and be perfectly satisfied."

She crunched a charred bite of sandwich and washed it down with a swig of water.

He grimaced. "A chef I am not."

"Then we're a good fit, as I'm not a picky foodie."

Chuckling, they tucked back into the meal. After lunch, or dinner, or whatever meal this was, Hannah washed the dishes and Dante dried. The comfortable teamwork soothed her frayed nerves, like they'd done this together a hundred times.

In any other situation, this would be the jackpot. Now? Not so much.

Oh well, she would at least enjoy the companionship while it lasted.

• • •

Dread settled in his gut as he stacked the last dish. No more stalling. He had to tell Hannah the truth about Raymond. Had to tell her the truth about himself.

A half dozen times last night, he nearly woke her up to confess everything. But watching her sleep so peacefully in his arms, her expression finally relaxed, he couldn't bring himself to disturb her rest. It was well past midnight when he had carried her to bed. Her exhaustion was so profound, she didn't stir when he had wrapped the fresh blankets around her.

Last night he'd also gotten a good look at her ankle. Whatever happened had ripped skin and shattered bone. The irregular lumps told a tale of excruciating trauma. How did that happen? Who did this to her? Raymond? Someone else?

Several times he'd circled the cabin's perimeter, checking for anything unusual, listening to the night sounds and smelling for any hint of the minion. Each time Dante had left the cabin, the desire to see Hannah compelled him back into the bedroom to make sure she was safe. For hours, he simply watched her sleep.

Something he'd never done with a woman in the bedroom.

But as much as he wanted to preserve this idyllic situation, he couldn't do it. Wouldn't continue pretending that he didn't know about Raymond. Couldn't hide the reason they were on the run.

Once she found out that he was cold-blooded killer, that would be the end of the interlude. No more fireside chats. No more domestic bliss. No more Hannah.

But she deserved the truth.

Even now, with Hannah in the bathhouse, he paced like a caged animal, fighting to stay here in the cabin and not watch over her. Truth be told, he'd dashed over there and back several times to make sure he heard her milling around in the shower. He monitored to ensure no one lurked nearby as well.

His hypervigilant behavior had increased, and it wasn't due to lack of sleep. His kind didn't require sleep, although he'd never gone more than three or four days without indulging in at least a period of rest. Just because he didn't need to sleep didn't mean he didn't enjoy it.

When she entered the cabin, he couldn't help himself. He flew to the door, yanking the doorknob from her hands.

"You're quick," she said, frowning.

"Uh, I happened to be right at the door," he hedged.

He inhaled her clean, flowery scent and appreciated how the ends of her damp hair curled at her shoulders. She'd changed into a long-sleeved T-shirt and jeans he'd bought when they stopped in Caldwell to stock up. He approved of his selection; the denim gave her curves she never had in those shapeless skirts.

But her glasses didn't hide the circles remaining beneath her eyes.

Time to fess up.

"You still look tired," he said.

She studied him until he squirmed. "And you look like you've got a lot on your mind."

If she only knew. "I need to talk with you about some things."

"Uh oh, that doesn't sound great." She dropped the toiletry bag on the kitchen table, faced him, and took a big breath. "If you need to leave, I'll understand completely."

"What?" His mood went from somber to foul in a split second. Leave her? Alone to wait for... *Kristus*, he didn't want to contemplate her fate if she had no protection.

Maybe she wanted to be rid of him? Conceivable, given the minion he'd helped to attract.

She pushed her hair behind an ear. "This ridiculous situation. You're in danger. Brandon's coming for me. What a rotten babysitting gig you've gotten."

Frustration strangled him until he sputtered, "Are you kidding me?"

As he leaned forward, she took a step back. "Of course not. Isn't that what you wanted to tell me? That you've got better things to do than wait around for something bad to happen? That's what I'd say, if I were in your shoes."

Her spine was ramrod stiff, but the shimmer of tears belied her matter-of-fact tone.

"No. No, I'm not leaving, and I'm not dumping you off anywhere. I swear."

He grabbed her and folded her into his arms, resting his chin on her head. Perfect. She fit perfectly. Too bad, though. The pleasant picture they made wouldn't last for long.

She leaned back and frowned. "Then what?"

"Let's sit down. Would you like another fire?"

He hated how she went from comfortable to reacting like a deer about to bolt, her eyes wide and pulse jumping at the base of her neck.

"No."

Fatigue etched lines on her fine features as she sat in the easy chair, alone. Even her perky button nose seemed tired. His preference was to pace, but it didn't feel right for this conversation.

Settling in the nearby futon, he turned toward her, dread weighing him down.

"I need to share some things with you."

Fear sparked across her face.

He cleared his throat and mentally forced himself to stop fidgeting. He literally never got nervous. Why now?

Because what she thought mattered to him. A lot. More than he wanted to admit.

He couldn't meet her expression, which was both terrified and hopeful, like an animal about to be abandoned, but he'd be damned if this conversation would remain unfinished. Where to start?

"About your time in Philadelphia…"

She froze. Her brown stare held him in place as surely as chains. "What about it?"

"Raymond Jackson."

The damn knife pulsed to life, insisting on blood. *Jävla skit.* God damn it. Horrible timing. The cursed blade wanted to be fed. Now. And he was in no position to answer its call. He'd have to fight the urge until he was in a position to hunt and kill a criminal. But not now.

Dante dragged his gaze back to Hannah with iron will.

"You told me he's dead," she said.

"That's true."

"But?" she whispered.

"I killed him."

Her skin bleached to a deathly white. He wanted to hold her, but she bent her legs up in front of her and wrapped her arms around them in a protective barrier.

"What?"

"It's complicated."

"Try me. I bet I can keep up."

He rubbed his temple. He'd never fully revealed himself to a mortal, not even Marguerite. "I'm sort of like a hit man."

"What the heck? 'Sort of like a hit man'?" She pushed herself into the corner of the chair, shoulders rigid, not moving her wide stare away from him.

"Okay, I *am* a hit man, in a manner of speaking. But really, it is complicated. Listen, I need to tell you—"

"Are you here to kill me? Oh God, out here, in the middle of nowhere—"

Her horrified expression gutted him.

"No!" he growled, too angry, too loud.

He cursed at her response as she curled up even more and watched him. Wary, like a cornered animal. Accusing him. He deserved it.

"So what, then?"

"I was sent to kill Raymond Jackson several weeks ago."

"What? Why?"

"Because along the line, he did very bad things to… some people. And my job is to get rid of monsters like that."

She unwrapped her hands from her knees and clamped them onto the arms of the chair until her knuckles blanched.

He bowed his head. "I didn't get all the details of his crimes, but I believe the information was true. What do you think?"

A choked sob erupted from her, and she covered her mouth.

"What did he do to you?" His hands curled into fists as he struggled to rein in his fury.

"How—"

"Does it have anything to do with that?"

He pointed toward her lower leg, and he didn't need to hear her response—she moved her hand over the denim at her ankle.

"Yes."

"Was I right to kill him?"

"I don't know. Probably. That was a while ago."

Her fingertips shook as she pulled a strand of hair out from under the earpiece of her glasses. He had to strain to hear her trembling voice.

"My aunt was dying, you see. I loved her, but I couldn't heal her. I tried. But it would've killed me."

"What happened?"

"He wanted me to heal Aunt Linda of her terminal cancer."

He held his breath. This part of the story, he hadn't known.

"So I tried. I mean, what else could I do? She was so sick, so thin. Except for that huge belly full of tumors." She folded an arm over her midsection. "My power went kind of crazy with that much sickness. Sucked every bit of my soul into Aunt Linda's body. It tried to consume me, move those hard lumps of cancer into my body, push all that fluid into my lungs. It was like breathing underwater with a body that had stretched to its limits and was about to burst. The worst thing I've ever experienced in a healing."

"The worst?"

"Even worse than with you."

He flinched.

She focused on the cabin walls as she rubbed her upper arms. "Ray loved his sister. Who wouldn't? Aunt Linda was so sweet. When I couldn't save her, he kind of went... crazy. I mean, he'd been having anger issues before then, but we didn't realize how nuts he'd become. He kind of snapped."

"How?"

"Snapped. Like threw me down the basement stairs, beat me up." She motioned to her foot with a shaking hand. "He threatened to kill me if I wouldn't heal his sister."

Dante shoved his hands beneath his upper arms to keep from ripping apart the futon. He wanted to kill Raymond all over again at the idea of Hannah being beaten like an animal. His body temperature increased as base compulsion warred with rational sense.

"He got so mad. Mad about Aunt Linda. Mad at me. He just took it all out on me."

"Took it out how?" He pitched his voice low and soft, suppressing the steaming rage that threatened to explode.

Tears streamed down her cheeks. She stared at nothing in front of her. Her dull, flat voice shredded his heart. "He was drunk. When he threw me down the stairs, that's when I broke..." She rubbed the fabric covering her ankle.

Dante leaned toward her. He didn't realize it had been this bad. He had figured Raymond had hit his kids and yelled at them. Dante had no clue what she'd truly been through.

"I tried... I mean, I couldn't get away. But I did try," she whispered. "Then he did... he put his hands on me... It hurt. It was awful. Afterward, there was blood everywhere." She covered her pale face with her hands.

"*Herrejåvlar.*"

He crossed the short distance, scooped her up, and sat in the easy chair with her curled in his arms. Those noiseless, shaking sobs ripped a hole in his chest. Her small hands fisted the fabric of his shirt with a tenacious strength.

"*Älskling*, you're safe now. I have you. No one will hurt you."

Powerful as he was, he couldn't wrestle her pain away. He couldn't fight those demons or undo the damage. This crime had been worse than he'd presumed when he took on the assignment to kill Raymond. Far worse.

She would've been no match for the burly Raymond. Dante might be an arrogant playboy and a cold-blooded killer, but he'd never harmed a helpless human being.

Taking off her glasses, she pulled away from him and dabbed at the dampness staining the T-shirt.

"Sorry. Your shirt. I'm—"

"Never apologize to me. Ever. This evil was not your fault. It was Raymond's." Gently he took her glasses and placed them on the arm of the couch. He smoothed back her hair and cupped her head in his hand. "How did you get away?"

Hannah sniffed. "The first time he went nuts, he locked me in the basement for a few days. Ray had only beaten me that time. Scott had been away for the weekend, and when he came back, we called the cops. Ray went to jail, and I saw the doctor. Things were better. But before Scott and I could leave, Ray posted bail and came back, madder than ever. He rebroke my ankle. And that was when…"

She tucked her face in his chest for a few more minutes before continuing. "That last night, Scott slipped something in Ray's drink so he'd pass out. Then Scott drove us to Portland. We got new identities, everything. He was really helpful, going to urgent care clinics and pretending to have a sinus infection so they'd give him antibiotics, which he gave me. For the infection." She gestured toward her leg.

"How bad was it?"

"Not good. I ran fevers and hallucinated for most of the trip. I guess it could've been much worse than just a broken leg and ankle. But now I still can't feel part of my foot. It never mended correctly after it broke that second time."

"*Herre Gud.*"

As she leaned back in the crook of his arm, her red-rimmed eyes glistened. "What I don't understand is why you killed Ray. Or how did you decide to kill *him*?"

"It's a strange story. I'm… under contract to kill… certain people. Criminals."

"Under contract by whom?" She wiped her cheeks.

"By someone powerful. I'm forced to kill. But I am no threat to ordinary people."

"What the hell?"

"It's true. I made a deal… years ago." Before he registered the action, he'd tucked a strand of her strawberry blonde hair behind an ear. She flinched again. Damn.

"A deal?"

He hesitated. Damn it. In for a penny. "With the Devil."

"You mean as a figure of speech, right?"

"No, for real."

"I don't understand."

"My brother was dying. I made a commotion, yelling up at the heavens, promising my soul, anything, as long as he would live. Someone heard me—the wrong someone. Satan."

"You're joking."

"I couldn't create a wilder fiction if I tried."

"How many people have you killed?" She blinked and pushed away from him.

He hated her response. Hated himself.

"More than I can count," he said. "I get an… urge… to kill when my boss, Jerahmeel, needs to feed on evil again. The knife compels me."

"Knife?"

"It's a part of me."

He motioned toward the lump on his lower leg, visible beneath his jeans.

"Oh. Do you have the urge now?"

"Truthfully, *ja*, I've been fighting it for the past several days. But if I use the knife to kill, it will reveal our location."

"Reveal to whom?"

"Ultimately, Brandon."

The silent pause made his ears ring.

She finally cleared her throat. "Then Brandon would come for us?"

He wanted to remove the stark terror from her face. "Probably."

"And he wants to hurt you? Or me?"

"Both." He shoved a hand through his hair. "You."

"And you want to kill someone because of the knife."

"Yes."

"That's bad. Every last bit of it."

"Keeping you safe has kept me focused. I can resist the knife."

"For how long?"

"For now."

"And then what? You search around for easy prey?" She opened her hands in invitation. They were shaking.

"Absolutely not you, Hannah. Never."

"How long can you fight the urge to kill?"

"I don't know."

"At some point, will the knife care if you pick a criminal or not?"

Jåvlar. "No."

The damn knife throbbed in sick reminder. Of its own volition, his hand slid down the denim toward his lower leg.

Hannah cried out and jumped off the chair, her foot buckling. In a split second, Dante grabbed her before she hit the floor. After setting her on her feet, he stepped back.

"How'd you move so quickly?"

"Extra good reflexes?"

She crossed her arms. "I don't buy it. You're too fast. And the attack yesterday and how you ran? No one moves like that. It's not normal."

"You're right. It's all part of my condition from the contract. I'm not exactly... human."

"So what are you? Dead?"

"In between."

"In between what? God. Just move away from me for a minute."

He did as she asked, and she backed up until her legs hit the futon. Sitting down hard, she scooted to the end farthest from him; little would the distance help against an Indebted. Damn, but her fear eviscerated him. Suave confidence wouldn't salvage this disaster.

"So, meeting you at the bookstore? It wasn't an accident?" She squinted until he handed her the glasses and moved back several paces.

"Not an accident, no. Right before I killed Raymond, he asked me to find Jessica Miller and tell her that he was sorry."

"Jessica no longer exists." Her monotone voice sent chills down his arms.

"I understand. Nevertheless, Raymond sent me to apologize to you."

"Oh. Well, that makes everything all right, doesn't it?"

"No. It doesn't."

"So why didn't you just tell me and leave?"

"I couldn't. My interest in you goes beyond Ray's request."

"Should I be grateful? Relieved? Or maybe you're just waiting for a good time to kill me. Easy picking, huh?"

Tears coursed down her face as she trembled. She stared down at her hands resting in her lap and didn't look up.

Dante struggled to be patient.

He'd held out sick hope that she'd still accept him. Somehow. If he'd lived for hundreds of years, he could give this woman more time, right?

Dåre. Idiot.

"Well," she began.

He hung on the syllable. Needed her to understand. Needed… much more. But he deserved nothing. He studied the floor while she sat in silence.

"Okay."

His head snapped up. "Pardon?"

Her gaze was steady. "Look, do you think you can keep me safe tonight from whoever it is coming after us?"

"Of course, yes." He stood up straighter. "You're safe here."

"Under the same roof as a known killer?"

Touché. "Yes."

"Who has been fighting the growing urge to kill again?"

He descended into abject misery. "Yes."

"Who, at a point down the road, won't be able to control it, no matter how nice of a killer he is?"

"Maybe. Yes."

"Well, that's good news."

"Hannah, I would never—"

She cut him off with a shaky chop of her hand. "I'm glad you had a chance to deliver your sick message from the great beyond and then tell me about your career choice. I will have wonderful dreams tonight, waiting for you to lose control and kill me. Unless the crappy memories we've dug up of my own hell don't ruin the night first."

When she stood up, he took a step forward. She crossed her arms, and he paused.

Despite being one of the most powerful creatures walking this Earth, he didn't have the strength to handle this rejection. He dipped his head, hands planted at his side.

She had destroyed him more surely than a knife ever could. And damn it, he had no solution, no recourse. No promise of hope to give.

"We're quite the pair, if you think about it." She laughed until a sob cut off her voice. "Freak of nature compulsive killer and bizarre healer who's damaged goods."

At his protest, she held up her hand. "I don't want to hear it. That's just how it is."

"Hannah, please."

"Is there anything else we need to work on tonight?" With her jaw set, her expression was both grim and matter-of-fact. "I'm done with messed up revelations for now. Done with worrying about people who want to kill me. Done with this ridiculous excuse for a life. If it's all the same with you, I quit."

"You quit?"

"Done. As in, not dealing with this stupidity for now. It's too much."

"All right…" *Where is she going with this train of thought?*

"So my quota has run out. I can't handle anything else tonight. No more killer stuff. No more of my baggage. No more bad thoughts for a while."

He could gladly live with that request.

But she was right about one thing: At some point, he wouldn't be able to control the knife's call. He only hoped to override the instinct if the urge hit when he was with her, but there were no guarantees.

"Can you do one thing for me?"

"Yes, anything. Name it."

"Don't kill me tonight."

Chapter 13

"Did you take care of the Blackstone situation?" Jerahmeel growled into the cell phone.

He hated loose ends but hated not being kept up to date even more. His energy had been waning of late. He could no longer leave his den and easily walk in the mortal world without burning a great deal of reserve strength. Couldn't check in as frequently on his favorite employee.

Since he needed to be judicious with his energy, he had to rely on minions to do his work. *Merde*, he hated how his power had become limited.

"Um, no, my lord, you see, that asshole Dante—"

"Excuses?"

"But Blackstone, my lord. I tried to… dissuade him like you ordered, make him stay away from the woman so he'd focus on your needs. But it didn't work."

Rumbles transmitted through Jerahmeel's receiver. That idiot minion must be driving.

"What happened?"

"Raymond Jackson's daughter. She healed Dante."

"She. Did. What?" he screamed into the phone.

The scent of hot rotten eggs rose from his clothing. *Merde*, he'd have to throw this outfit away.

"I had him down, out cold, so I could get rid of her. But the police were coming. Then she jumped on top of Dante, grabbed him, and boom, he woke up like nothing had happened. And then she went down for the count."

"She healed one of *us*? How is that possible?"

"Hell if I know. But don't worry, boss, I'll find her and destroy her, like you want."

"*Attente sur!* Hold on now." Jerahmeel tugged at a black curl of his hair. "This has intriguing possibilities. Find the human."

"And kill her?"

"No. Her ability to heal might be of use to me. *Très intéressant.*" His hunger hollowed out his soul. She could help fill the emptiness.

"So I need to track her down but not kill her?"

"Exactly."

"And get her away from your strongest employee?"

"I prefer to say, 'most valued.'"

"So how do I do that?"

"I don't care, moron. However, you were unable to complete a simple job before, and I am sore displeased. Don't disappoint me now."

"Ok, I'll—"

Jerahmeel hung up on him and began fantasizing about how an unlimited stock of perpetually healed beings would keep him supplied and well fed. Renewable energy *was* all the rage nowadays.

• • •

Hannah grabbed the blanket and huddled on the mattress, shivering, miserable. She left the light on in the bedroom, but it didn't matter. The light didn't keep away the bad thoughts.

Exhausted, she finally slept, and the dreams came again.

Horror. Death. Scott. Ray.

The pain returned. Pain from being broken, from healing.

She relived the frantic trip across the country, her pajamas crusted with blood. Ghost pain seared her foot again, and her skin, wrinkled and soft from soaking in the basement puddles, throbbed in agony. Phantom fevers racked her body. Her pulse pounded in the ankle, pounded in her brain, pounded in her damaged core all over again.

The boundaries of reality began to smear. Dante. Killing Ray. Killing her. Dante loving her, blood coating his hands. Her blood. From Ray. On them, between them, between them all.

Sweating, she thrashed on the bed. This misery was all karma for not trying harder to cure her aunt's illness. Aunt Linda's gaunt face floated in Hannah's memory. Her aunt's kind expression morphed first into disapproval, then into a rictus of horror. Shame froze all of Hannah's muscles, paralyzed in grisly stasis, indicted by Linda's sad smile.

On and on her dreams played. At one point during the night, her hip and shoulder became superheated, waking her briefly.

Dante's forehead pressed against the mattress as he knelt on the floor, his large hands resting on her. He sat still, breathing slow and steady, at her side. Her heart actually went out to this guy, even after everything she'd learned about him.

She had tender feelings for a murderer? What kind of twisted world did she live in?

Falling asleep again, she returned to more hours of endless, miserable dreams.

When she woke for good the next morning, her eyes still burned from last night's tears. Her chest still ached from sobbing.

The extra blankets remained folded on the floor across the room. No one had slept in this room except her. But the indention in her own mattress near the edge told her that she hadn't dreamt it. Dante *had* been there during the night. He hadn't killed her. Hadn't done anything improper. He had watched over her and kept her safe, like he promised.

Maybe they could at least figure out a way to escape from this mess before he had to attend to whatever other obligations he must have. Before he decided she'd be an easy mark for his knife. Even now, she couldn't imagine that Dante would try to kill her. For all his muscles and swagger, his every action had centered around her safety and comfort. This whole situation played like a hallucination, like when she had the flu as a child. Being here, in this cabin in the middle of nowhere, with Dante's knife issues, felt like a disconnected dream.

Did she want to try to evaluate the dream? No way. What good would it do? No good. Time for some good old-fashioned avoidance.

With muscles protesting, she rolled out of the bed, donned jeans and white T-shirt, and washed up in the bathroom. Throwing on a light green hoodie to ward off the morning chill, she entered the main cabin.

Dante sat with elbows propped on the table, his golden head resting on his fists, his massive shoulders slumped. Defeated. Wounded. Hurting. Her heart ached.

As she approached, he lifted his head and his icy, pain-filled gaze locked on to her. She rested her hand on his warm shoulder. After a moment's hesitation, he covered it with his hand.

"Breakfast?" she asked, breaking the tension.

"What?" His voiced cracked on the single word.

"Do you want breakfast? I'll fix something for us."

He scrubbed at his face. The slash of his mouth softened a tiny bit. "Uh, sure. I picked up granola and milk in Caldwell. Will that work?"

"Perfect." Trying to ignore the tension remaining in the room, she heated two bowls and set them on the table.

He smiled halfheartedly as they ate in silence.

After breakfast, he said, "We should get out of the cabin."

"What did you have in mind?"

"There's a nature trail here. It doesn't look fancy, but it might be nice to get some fresh air."

"You sure it's okay for us to be outside where people can see us?"

"There aren't many people here. Just retirees in RVs, mostly. I think we're safe."

She took a deep breath. "Sounds good to me."

They exited the cabin into clean morning air and walked along the John Day River on a graveled path. With her damaged foot, she couldn't move quickly on uneven surfaces. Her steps were roll-y, and she had to concentrate to keep her balance. He slowed his steps to match her slow pace.

The crisp fall day yielded blue skies and a breeze that moved Dante's hair over his forehead. A gray thermal shirt stretched over his large frame. With each step, his thigh muscles bunched beneath denim. She shivered, recalling those thighs locked on to her hips as he kissed her in the Hummer.

The shallow river rushed by, swift and clear. Small cataracts, combined with the rustling gold-tipped leaves, created relaxing background noise.

They plodded along at her geriatric pace until they arrived at a logging pond. Circling the pond, they sat on a rough dock with their legs dangling over the edge and let the sun warm their backs. A few ducks paddled amiably around the far side. The bright sun made the water glitter.

She hated to interrupt the serene moment.

"I have more questions," she said without preamble.

The sun behind him created a halo that turned him into a beefy, avenging angel. She shook her head to rid herself of the image. *He's a murderer, remember?*

"Of course. I'll tell you anything."

His voice, subdued this morning, rolled through the wood of the dock and into her bones. That crystal-blue gaze was still wary.

For a moment, a pang of guilt gave her pause.

"This situation is a mess, right?" she asked.

"Yes."

"How do Brandon and your friends, Peter and Allie, figure into it?"

"Valid question. I don't think I explained everything properly."
He took a deep breath. "But first let me start at another place.
You're might not believe what I have to say, but please try."

"More unbelievable than being a hit man who made a deal
with the Devil?"

"Yes, even more unreal."

"Sounds interesting. Go ahead."

He raked his hair off his forehead. "So, remember I told you
why I made this deal?"

"Yes."

"Well, that occurred in 1718. In the Great Northern War."

"1718? Not possible."

"Yes, I'm that old." He grimaced. "Please hear me out."

She went cold. Even the leaves stopped rustling. He didn't look
old.

"You're serious?"

"Dead serious."

"Great Northern War? Never heard of it."

"Not many Americans have. It was an ambitious military
campaign to expand the Swedish Empire. A nice idea, promising
in the beginning, but poorly executed in the end. And obviously
not well received by those who were conquered. Some would say
a failure."

"You're serious? So you're telling me you're 300 years old?"

"Closer to 320."

"But who's counting, right?"

Her laugh sounded hollow, even to her own ears.

He at least had the sense to look embarrassed.

She threw a few twigs into the calm water, watching the ripples
spread out. "Go on."

"So, we campaigned during one miserable winter. As several
companies traveled back over the mountains from a failed siege
in Norway, men were dying of frostbite and starvation. The death

toll was horrific. If it had been only me, I wouldn't have cared. I'd have just tried to save myself.

"But my brother had been conscripted from our *rote*, a group of farms, in *Varmland* to represent us in the military. We weren't rich and couldn't bribe the selectors, so he got picked to go to war. My *moder*, mother, was frantic for his safety. At that time, we all knew the war wasn't going well anymore, and I agreed to enlist with him in the infantry and serve alongside him. I promised *Moder* that I'd keep Lars safe."

His face lit up when talking about these so-called family members. Hannah searched for deception but saw no visible evidence of lies in his damnable, sincere, blue eyes.

Dante inhaled and continued. "That failed campaign in Norway became part of what history later termed the 'Carolean Death March.' We called it frozen hell on Earth. About 10 percent of the soldiers survived the blizzard that caught us in the mountains between Norway and Sweden. Lars had collapsed, frostbitten, dying. I loved my brother. My *moder* would never forgive me if he didn't return. I had given him my food, my clothes, my last tinder, and yet he still lay dying. So I called out to the sky for someone to help me. I would do anything if Lars could live."

He scrubbed at his forehead and took a big breath.

"And?" she said. He might be making up this fascinating story, but he appeared to believe it himself.

"Jerahmeel, the manifestation of Satan in human form, arrived. He said he'd save my brother if I agreed to his terms. I had nothing to lose. I signed on the dotted line right away, no questions asked. *Loven Gud*, praise God, Lars got up and walked home. Out of thousands of men, he and I were two of only a handful in my regiment who survived. *Moder's* prayers came true. Lars survived.

"But I could never go home again. Jerahmeel had me bound to his eternal contract. I now have to kill a certain number of criminals each year to maintain the possibility of ending the contract. To avoid eternal servitude."

"I don't understand." She tucked a piece of hair back behind an ear.

"We have to kill with the knife in a strike through the heart. That's the only way the kill works. Normally, we use our judgment to find our victims. For example, I could stalk a criminal myself—I know what to look for nowadays—and kill the scumbag. That counts as part of my regular quota. But at other times, Jerahmeel discovers a particularly disgusting, evil specimen and instructs me to kill, like with Raymond. As long as I keep up the regular quota and take care of the special orders along the way, there's still a chance."

"A chance for what?"

"That I might break the contract one day."

"How likely would it be to get out of your contract?"

"Not very, in my opinion. Jerahmeel needs nasty souls to feed upon. It gives him his strength. The meaner the criminal, the more nutritious the meal. We sustain him. He's not interested in any of us retiring."

"If you can't retire, why couldn't you just stop? In protest?"

He held out his big hand, palm up. "Good question. For a while, I can resist the mandate to kill, but then the urge becomes overwhelming. It takes over my mind, my body. The need burns like a fire worse than anything you've ever known, and I kind of… go crazy to put out that fire. With blood."

"Good grief."

"The lifestyle kind of sucks."

"Fair enough." All of a sudden, a million pounds weighted her shoulders. "So how are your friends involved? How are they in danger?"

"They're only involved in an indirect way now. Technically, Jerahmeel can't touch them anymore. But he's got other ways of hurting people, and that's what worries me."

"I don't understand." Did she truly want to know more about the world in which Dante operated? Only a crazy person would sit here and continue asking questions.

When Dante shifted to face her, the regret that creased his brow made her chest ache. A lump formed in her throat when that regret turned to cold, blank resignation.

"It's very rare for one of us to complete our contract. You need something called a Meaningful Kill, but I'm not convinced it's always possible. I've performed all sorts of quality kills, getting rid of some of the most horrible people in society, but still I'm not released from the contract."

He rubbed his lower leg that dangled over the edge of the dock, fingering the knife beneath the denim. Hannah watched him, her nerves tightening. What if he couldn't stop himself? She inched away from him.

"But have others succeeded?" She hoped to distract him from his interest in the knife.

"*Ja*. My friend Barnaby apparently did it many years ago. Then Peter got released last year. Exactly how, I don't know."

"Why not?"

"They can't tell me. Rules. But suffice it to say, Jerahmeel wants as many people as possible working for him, feeding his power. To lose an employee weakens him, reduces his energy supply, and frankly, it pisses him off. He needs to retain those of us who are left, now more than ever. Needs each of the remaining killers to supply more souls to make up the deficit."

"There are more like you?" The back of her neck prickled as she sensed imaginary fingers reaching for her.

"*Ja*."

She looked over a shoulder. "How many?"

"Not sure, maybe a hundred across the world. Barnaby thinks our numbers are decreasing."

"How? You all live forever, right?"

"Like I said, maybe a few get out with the Meaningful Kill. And it's possible for our kind to die. It's difficult but not impossible."

She rubbed the back of her neck where the muscles ratcheted into a tension headache. "I don't understand. How does all of this eternal Meaningful Kill stuff tie in with Ray?"

"I killed one of Jerahmeel's minions last year, which piqued my boss's interest. Then, right before I killed Raymond, your stepfather asked me to find you and apologize. That act attracted Jerahmeel's attention—in a bad way. The way he sees it, any mission other than collecting souls is counterproductive."

"What can he do about it?"

"Jerahmeel hates to get his hands dirty, so he inserts bad beings—minions—into situations to carry out his wishes and to ensure that employees stay employees. He uses the minions to stop us from trying to attain the Meaningful Kill."

"So, a minion tried to stop Peter?"

"Yes, and in the process, it almost tortured Allie to death."

"Oh no." She rubbed the goose flesh on her arms, unable to imagine anyone wanting to hurt Peter's sweet wife.

He ground a fist into the palm of his other hand. "Oh, yes. I may be an *oåkting*, a bastard, but I won't stand by while innocents get hurt. I killed the minion, Peter saved Allie, and well, the rest of it, as you can see, is history."

"So where does Brandon come in? How—"

At a sudden rustling in the trees at the water's edge nearby, Dante tensed.

"Don't move."

With one arm, he slid her back behind him, and he leapt to a crouch on the edge of the dock. Keeping one hand back on her shoulder, he peered into the foliage across the pond. Waves of heat flowed from his hand into her skin.

Hannah's heart tattooed her ribcage. Had someone found them? Was Brandon here? Oh God, what he had done to Dante before…

The rustling noise increased. Sweat beaded her upper lip.

The leaves quivered until two chattering birds erupted from the foliage. She gasped and put a hand over her mouth. After her heart slowed to a normal pace, she smirked at her silly fears.

But as Dante's posture, still in a crouch, attested, danger awaited them.

His shoulder muscles bunched as he smoothed his hand over his pants leg near the ankle. Over and over. Caressing the knife, as if he were in a trance. The danger was long gone, but he looked off into space, rubbing his leg.

Tentatively, she touched his back. "Dante?"

He whipped around, knocking her back. Her head bounced off the wood planks. When he crouched over her, she shuddered. His eyes had turned onyx. He didn't act like he saw her, but instead looked right *through* her.

With a feral grunt, he pinned her shoulder to the dock with one heavy hand as he reached for his knife with the other.

Her heart thudded in her chest.

Dante blocked out the sun.

Her world narrowed down to the black stare inches away from her face. Death. He had become death, hungry and desperate for a soul to feed the knife.

And any lifeblood—including hers—would do right about now.

She had often wondered what emotion lay beyond fear. With a glance at Dante's dark, possessed expression, a brand new feeling encompassing terror, horror, and betrayal reared back, about to strike at her heart.

Chapter 14

"Dante?" She tried, without success, to rise.

His harsh breaths burned furnace-hot air over her skin. When she struggled, he stilled her, his massive weight pinning her in place.

She saw a glint of light on metal.

Oh God, he had the knife.

Even in the bright autumn sunlight, the foot-long blade glowed with an eerie green intensity. Like a man in a trance, he drew sinuous patterns in the air with the tip of the knife, his blank stare focused on the green metal.

"Oh, yes," he said, his voice a singsong croon. "You're hungry."

He'd told her there would be a time when he couldn't control the knife. Flat out, mind-sucking panic took away her ability to think. Like when Ray had taken her into the basement and destroyed everything.

But maybe Ray hadn't annihilated all of her spirit. She still wanted to live. Even after all that she'd been through.

Ray. Dante. The knife. The hand holding her down.

Damn it.

She wrestled for a grip on her eroding sanity.

Fight for her life or accept her fate?

We all have to die sometime. Damn it, though, she didn't think it would be now, like this.

"Dante!"

She grabbed his hard jaw with her free hand. He didn't react.

"Stop it!" she screamed.

Despite his blank expression, the knife drifted lower, over her neck.

She slapped him, the sound sharp in the still air. He blinked, and blinked again, but the knife continued toward her heart. The metal threatened to blister her skin.

Closer.

She strained her head away but continued to track the weapon's inexorable path.

When the heated blade brushed her skin, a scream burst from her lips.

"*Herre Gud!*"

Dante flung himself off of her as he vaulted in one fluid movement over her and onto the grassy bank. He knelt, holding the knife toward her in two hands, like a dowsing rod. The tip of the blade shook as it pointed at her. Sweat rolled down his face as muscles bulged under his sleeves, like he fought in a tug of war with an imaginary opponent. He tilted forward and then shook as he pulled the knife back toward his body.

"Hannah," he rasped. Sweat now stained the neckline of his thermal shirt.

She knelt on the end of the dock, the water behind her and a crazed giant wielding a knife before her. Did he truly see her now? Would he stop?

This is what he meant by the urge to kill. She shuddered.

"Please stop. Please." She pitched her voice low.

Don't make a movement. Hold perfectly still. Maybe he'll wake up.

"Dante. You don't want to do this."

"Oh yes, I do."

She stopped breathing.

The knife tip quivered as if magnetized, pulling his arms toward her. With a guttural yell, he heaved forward and plunged the knife into the dock.

"But I don't want to do it to you, *älskling.*"

The knife continued to glow as it remained embedded in a wooden plank.

Silence wrapped steely fingers around her ribcage.

When he moved toward her, she lurched backward, nearly falling off the dock. He grabbed her hoodie and pulled her up toward him, wrapping her in his arms.

She fought against him, not sure which Dante held her, the struggles futile against his iron grip.

This man determined whether she lived or died.

"Please don't kill me."

"I will not." He bit out the words.

With a curse, he stepped back, holding her wrist but giving her space as he balanced on the balls of his feet. That black stare made him appear lost.

"What the—"

"Forgive me. Please. *Kristus*, I almost—"

She glanced at her body—all there. Her heart—beating closer to a normal rate. Air—moving in and out of raw lungs.

She'd survived. Again. Giddiness, like a bubbling fountain, burbled up into her chest. She was still alive. Hadn't thrown in the towel.

All right, then. Now what?

Time to check on Dante.

His lost expression cut a jagged hole in her heart. Every muscle remained in bunched tension as he stood, frozen.

She spoke first. "Are you okay?"

"Am *I* okay? I tried to kill you." He yanked her back into his inferno of an embrace.

While nausea roiled through her gut, she held still as he ran his hands over her face, her arms. When he reached the notch above her sternum where the knife had been aimed, he paused and rubbed it, his rough fingers gentle on her quivering skin. His jaw clenched with so much tension, she thought the muscles would burst.

His mouth formed into a hard slash of fury, and his brows drew together, hooding his gaze.

After another minute, he took a deep breath and touched the skin of her neck once more, as if to reassure himself that it was unmarred.

He blinked, and the black color reverted to blue.

Dante had returned.

The angry corners of his mouth curved downward. "There are no words."

"That's an understatement." She stepped back, cold despite the streaming sunlight all around. "You're better now, but for how long?"

"As long as it takes. I am so sorry. This will never happen again, I swear."

"Can you guarantee that?"

His muscled chest heaved once. "No."

"So then I should feel... reassured?"

He jammed his hand into a pocket. "I respect your skepticism, but understand that I would kill myself first."

She crossed her arms and stared him down.

He reached toward her, his rock-solid hand uncharacteristically shaking. When he smoothed her hair off her forehead, his lost, intent expression nearly undid her. She struggled to reconcile the earnest shame with the black-eyed killer from a few moments ago.

If this was the regular Dante, how long would he hold the cold-blooded murderer at bay?

Should she trust this man? Probably not, if she was completely honest with herself.

She had two choices: certain death from Brandon or a little less certain death if Dante lost control. At least Dante appeared sincere when he tried not to inflict bodily harm. But how long could he fight that hard-wired need to kill?

It kept getting better and better, her life. Karma raised its ugly head once again.

What could she do? Not a hell of a lot right now. Whether she trusted this guy or not, he wasn't going to let her leave. Not alone. Not right now.

His mission to keep her away from Brandon overrode his base need to kill. Barely. Well then, she would simply have to work with the situation she'd been given, crazy as it appeared.

What about Scott? What had Brandon done to him? Maybe he'd left her brother alone in his desire to get to Hannah. She still wanted to try to help Scott.

But there was nothing she could do to help him, other than stay alive. Maybe an opportunity to get him out of Brandon's influence would emerge later. For right now, her only recourse was to wait.

She exhaled and tried to relax the muscles in her shoulders. Time to try to manage the parts of the situation she could.

"Um, could we walk some more, please?"

He blinked, like a sleepwalking man waking up. "What?"

"A walk. Let's go for another walk. Do something normal."

"But I just—"

"I know. But I need to feel normal. I can't deal with what just happened."

He rocked back on his heels with a stunned expression. His outstretched hand enveloped hers as he led her up the grassy bank.

"Hold on a moment. Stay here," he said.

Dante stepped back onto the dock and bent down to pick up the knife.

Hannah froze.

Its green glow was still visible, lurid, hungry. Her neck itched, but she refused to move an inch.

As if in slow motion, he tugged up his jeans leg and sheathed the blade with an emphatic snick. When he stood up again, he had the expression of a man who could move mountains by force of will.

He stopped right in front of Hannah. His lips pressed into a grim line.

"Perhaps we can continue the conversation we were having before I became... distracted?"

Unbidden, the corner of her mouth twitched upward. Even in this surreal situation, she could take a hint.

Okay, I can do this. He's not trying to kill me. Right now.

Consciously relaxing her neck and shoulders, she tried to calm down. Maybe if she stayed casual, he'd play along. She lobbed him a normal topic.

"All right, then. Where were we before the interruption?"

He cleared his throat, but focused over her head. "I was about to tell you how Brandon fits into our situation."

"Scott's friend," she said.

He grimaced and restarted the story as they returned to the gravel path along the river. "He's a minion."

"Like the kind who tried to kill Allie?" The blood froze in her veins. "He's what's after me?"

"Yes."

"That's bad."

"Yes, that's bad."

"But you can beat him, right? You killed one before."

The sun warmed her back as their footsteps crunched leaves and gravel. Dante kept to the slow pace next to her.

"The minion I killed had been weakened from an earlier fight. Even so, he was challenging to destroy."

Dante discussed murder so casually. Hannah rubbed her arms, chilled despite the bright day.

"And there's no Peter to help you anymore."

He nodded. "Peter would be killed immediately if he tried to intervene."

"Allie?"

"The minion would go after her, too."

"Even with the baby?"

"Yes."

"So your friend got out of his contract, which pissed off this Jerahmeel guy. Then you killed his minion, which pissed him off even more. Then you went on an unsanctioned mission from Ray. So Jerahmeel's now extra mad at you. And anyone you hang out with is likely to die, because he holds a grudge. That's it in a nutshell, isn't it?"

"Uh huh."

"And what about Scott? Is the minion going to kill him, too?" Panic welled up. As weird as Scott had been acting, he was still her brother.

"I don't think so. It appears the minion is manipulating Scott to get him to push us apart, mostly so I'll leave you alone and stay committed to my job. But keeping you away from me might not be enough. As a matter of fact, it might be desirable for Jerahmeel to have you dead. Or worse, alive, if he sees you as leverage to keep me working."

"How?"

"Your nifty healing trick. It's a liability."

As she stumbled on her numb foot, he cupped her elbow to steady her.

"Why?"

"For two reasons. First, you can potentially undo any kill, thus depriving Jerahmeel of his tasty soul. Second, it's possible that he might force you to heal a criminal over and over so he can keep feeding off of one person. It wouldn't satisfy Jerahmeel completely, but might sustain him nevertheless."

Her legs wobbled. "That sounds awful."

"You'd be worse than a slave."

"Oh, God."

He grabbed her arms, stopping her in the path. His grip was the only thing keeping her upright. A ringing in her ears accompanied blackness on the edge of her vision.

He gave her a light shake, anchoring her back in reality.

"I'm not going to let those scenarios happen," he said.

"Peter and Allie and their baby may die because of me. And Scott, too." As fear and anger took over, her knees trembled.

"No, that will not happen."

"Do you have a plan?" Because Hannah sure as heck didn't see a way out of this mess without someone dying, and it might just be her.

"Not yet. Peter and Barnaby are discussing options. There's also another undead working with Barnaby. She might be helpful."

"She?"

"Ruth. Apparently she had been a Civil War nurse. She could probably kill people with her glare."

"Well, that's helpful." Hannah backed away from him and continued walking along the path. "So what about your super speed and strength and ability to heal yourself?"

"All part of the contract with Jerahmeel. It's inconvenient for us to get old and die of disease or injury."

"So when Brandon saw me heal you, that was bad?"

"He already knew you could heal."

"How?"

"Scott told him."

"What?" She stopped again, sick at her stomach. "No way. He wouldn't tell."

"He would if he was drunk."

Oh, geez, Dante was right. Scott's loose lips could've wagged any night when he and Brandon hung out. Her brother had marked her and some very good people for death. Or worse.

What would be worse than death? Not having Dante around. Being forced to heal criminals for the Devil's consumption. Pain every single time she touched someone with an injury or illness. Without an end in sight.

She wouldn't do it, then. She'd just die.

But this Jerahmeel guy would make her do it, wouldn't he? Anyone she knew remained at risk. Anyone she cared for became leverage over her will.

As for Brandon tracking her? She'd never be able to run far enough or keep everyone safe.

Just a matter of time.

All the air, all her energy, deserted her.

She sat down on the gravel, hard. The edges of the rocks jabbed into her palms as she leaned forward.

"Hannah?" Dante knelt next to her, his warm hand on her back.

"Everyone'll be hurt because of me."

"No. We'll find a way out of this situation."

"There are no options. You said so yourself. Even though Peter and Barnaby are out of their contracts, they're still vulnerable. So are Allie and Scott. Just because this Jerahmeel guy can't touch them doesn't mean one of his cronies can't attack them. People are going to get hurt. You're going to get hurt."

"You needn't worry about me. I've managed for 300 years; I'll be fine."

That was the problem, wasn't it? He'd be alive for hundreds more years. Longer than she fathomed. Longer than she would live, that's for sure. A shiver crawled up her spine.

When he rubbed her shoulder, she startled. Then, unbidden quivers of desire flowed up her spine. She shook her head to clear it of the growing interest in his touch.

"This situation is not good," she said.

His caress flooded her entire body with warmth. She briefly closed her eyes until he cleared his throat.

"No, it's not great. But then again, it's all relative. I've lived through far worse. You, too. When it all boils down to it, we're both survivors."

He pulled her to her feet, the river murmuring next to them. The contact with his hand flowed like a warm wave through her chest. For a split second, she saw him as a constant companion, a loving partner, someone to grow old with. As a breeze moved the hair above his eerie blue eyes, he blinked, and the image shattered into a thousand pieces.

She tried to swallow, but the movement stuck halfway down.

What a stupid dream. She wasn't normal. Dante wasn't normal. Hundreds of years after she was long dead, he'd still be roaming this Earth. Time to deal with reality.

She tilted her head upward to meet his gaze, framed by an upraised eyebrow and tilted corners to his sensual mouth.

"So, what do you recommend we do now?"

He squeezed her hand, which still rested in his big paw. "You know what I like when the going gets tough?"

His wry grin lit up even the dark shadows of her mind, and she found herself smiling in spite of everything.

"No, what?"

"Lunch! Let's eat."

He held out his arm to support her as they walked back to the cabin.

• • •

Although he acted calm, Dante was panicking inside. He had tried to distract her from the near disaster earlier today. If one could understate nearly killing an innocent as a mere disaster.

Since when had he been unable to escape a predicament? Since never.

Until now. At the rate things were going, they were screwed.

How were they going to escape this mess without someone dying?

They weren't.

Allie's death visions always came true, and she'd seen one of Hannah when the two women had briefly shaken hands.

Kristus.

Hell, he'd almost fulfilled Allie's prediction himself, trying to gut Hannah with his damn knife. What a pathetic protector. What a *dåre*, idiot. *Jävlar*, the knife still throbbed, reminding him he remained overdue for a kill.

Peter and Barnaby were working on options, but when Dante slipped into the backroom to turn on his cell phone, there were no messages. He threw the phone back in his bag. For right now, he and Hannah were on their own. He paused at the doorway of the bedroom and watched her cleaning the plates from lunch. The sweet, domestic image pinched inside his chest until it hurt to breathe.

He didn't care how much he had to fight his killer instinct. He had to keep her safe. Or destroy himself trying.

The urge to kill had started to consume his thoughts. What if he could sneak away and kill a human, slake the killing instinct? But not in this area. To be safe, he'd have to go hundreds of miles away, and he refused to leave her unprotected for that long.

If he killed anyone in this town, the minute he sank his blade into a human, that cursed unhuman radar would alert Jerahmeel of his location. Brandon would soon follow.

Oddly, Dante hadn't gotten so much as a whiff of the minion yet. Not detecting the minion was either neutral or very bad. It wasn't good. Brandon wouldn't stop until he got hold of Hannah. Either the minion still searched for them, or he'd stopped looking and was formulating a new plan. Neither option boded well.

Damn, another wave of hunger fired up again. It wasn't completely knife lust this time, though. He had no right giving into any base instincts where she was concerned. The seesawing killing desire versus male desire wrecked his ability to think.

His fingers involuntarily stretched toward the knife. He wanted to sink the damned blade into a human more than he'd wanted any prior kill. Dante shook his head, trying to concentrate. No one ever fought the pull of the knife for long. But he had to try harder, be stronger. For Hannah. For everything she'd already been through. For what she might yet have to endure.

The thought of her in the basement, beaten and raped by Raymond, sharpened his focus, temporarily replacing the urge to kill. Well, kill anyone new, at least. He'd prefer to gut Raymond again and again, but even that act could never exact adequate justice.

Fury and protectiveness boiled in his gut until raw emotion cleared his mind of the knife lust.

Cleared his mind of everything.

Except Hannah.

With sudden clarity, he watched her small hands move through the water and grasp a towel to dry the plates. Such a simple task she performed. But he needed those hands on his damp skin, moving over his body. Raw desire drilled a spine-wrecking shudder through him, and the wood of the bedroom doorframe creaked beneath the pressure of his fingers. How much longer could he fight this other battle?

Long enough.

Right?

Damn her delicate fingers, flitting over the countertop.

His jeans strained against his inappropriate interest. He had no right to respond in this way. Not with Hannah.

Not after he'd lost control and tried to bury the goddamned knife in her earlier today. A monster who would do such a thing— he had no right to ask her for anything.

But he could only stay in this cabin, so close—enjoying her sweet smile, her scent of flowers and fresh air, listening to her low voice—for so long without breaking.

He had suppressed the killing urge. Maybe he could suppress his other urges.

When she raked back her strawberry blonde hair, she exposed her creamy neck. His groin tightened as if a vice had been placed on his balls. How had she made it so difficult for him to maintain control? Perhaps his mind was addled. Maybe every one of her actions, no matter how innocent, turned him on because he'd become a giant, horny mess. How did she weave such a spell? He had no idea, but she'd done it ever since he had first seen her. At least her allure was consistent. Or his active libido was consistent.

Damn it, where was a book to read when he needed it?

Maybe sunshine and nature would divert him.

He cleared his throat so as not to startle her as he walked into the kitchen. "Want to sit on the porch?"

When she glanced up, those inquisitive brown eyes, framed by the glasses, pinned him.

He indulged in a sudden fantasy of her lying beneath him, naked. Except for those glasses. She should leave those on; they were cute.

Kristus, he needed to get out of this cabin before his mind and balls exploded.

She wiped her hands on the towel.

He groaned.

"Sure." Her stiff frame belied her light tone. Probably worried he'd try to stab her again. He was an idiot. Here she tried to hide her terror of him, and all he could think of was his own carnal needs.

Praying that he wasn't making a foolish choice, he motioned for her to precede him out the door. He scanned the area and inhaled. No sign of danger. For now.

She perched in the double porch swing and scooted over to make room, but her jaw remained set.

Her lack of trust hurt, but he deserved her doubt. Somehow, though, he'd try to prove that he would never hurt her.

After dubiously assessing the s-hooks suspending the swing from the rafters, he shrugged.

Hannah had the temerity to giggle when the wood creaked as he eased into the swing. When Dante growled at her, she laughed even more. The tense line of her shoulders relaxed, and she rested her hand on the arm.

He didn't care that her lack of fear came at the cost to his pride.

Satisfied the seat wouldn't drop out from beneath him, he, too, relaxed, dropping an arm behind her on the back of the swing. Strands of her silky hair slid over his hand, sending sparks of sensation up his entire arm. But he didn't move a muscle.

She fingered the supporting chain at the end of the armrest. "So you're really Swedish?"

"*Ja, definitivt.* Definitely."

"Not a strong accent." Gold glints like effervescent bubbles swirled in her brown irises.

His heart thumped. Nerves? What happened to the great Dante, waylaid by this slip of a women? Ridiculous.

He swallowed. "Depends on the mood and location. Don't need the accent in this country. Also, it's been a long time since I visited Sweden. Too many memories. Doesn't matter. No one is left."

"Three hundred years ago. For real?"

"I would not lie."

She pursed her lips. "So, what was your home like?"

Leaning back on the wooden slats, he sighed. "Ahh, my province was called *Värmland*. I lived in a small village, really more a collection of small farms. The village doesn't even exist now. A beautiful, lush region with thousands of streams and creeks.

Like western Oregon near Portland, only the hills are softer, more rolling. Lots of lakes."

"Was it cold? Did it snow a lot?"

"I was young then and didn't know any different, but yes, there was a tremendous amount of snow. But when spring came with the flowers, it was spectacular. And the summer days lasted forever."

"Family?"

The chair creaked as he pushed the swing. The gentle rocking combined with a cool fall breeze to calm his strained nerves.

"My *fader* died early on in the Great Northern War, doing his duty for the Swedish Empire. *Moder* carried on with my help and that of my brother, Lars. He and I were near inseparable. Even in war."

"Sounds like a good family."

When she rested her head against his arm, he swallowed a lump in his throat.

"Yes. Our family had love, happiness, and… lots of hard work." He laughed. "And sometimes the switch when Lars and I did wrong."

"How often did you get in trouble?"

"Often enough. But I always ran faster than Lars."

The river rushed along in the background. Leaves rustled. Light wind moved pieces of her strawberry blonde hair over his arm. He'd love nothing more than to sit here with her forever.

She pressed her cheek to his shoulder. That simple act twisted something both sweet and terrible in his chest.

Hold still. Don't mess anything up. Keep rocking the swing.

Damn it, this perfect moment would never last.

When she rolled her head to look up at him, a sick dread dropped like a rock into his gut.

"So what were you and Allie talking about before we left? She and Peter gave me strange looks, and you seemed really upset. Did I do something wrong?"

Dante cupped her shoulder reassuringly while struggling to formulate an answer. Could he answer honestly? He might be an oaf, but he generally told the truth.

"Absolutely not. It's nothing to worry about."

She blinked. "I don't believe you."

Did she need the truth? She was already a marked woman. Maybe she deserved to know. He rubbed his neck with his free hand.

"Ah, Allie has a… gift, too."

"Can she heal people?"

When Hannah gazed up at him like that, all hopeful and trusting, he wanted to kiss the tip of her nose, wrap her in his arms, and keep everything bad in this world far, far away.

Damn it.

"No, Allie's ability is different. She sees death when she touches some people."

"Wow." Then her expression changed. "Oh. She saw mine?"

His silence answered her.

Damn those earnest, gold-glinting eyes. "Is she ever wrong?"

"Once she had a vision of her niece's death, and she prevented it from occurring."

"But it would've happened if she hadn't intervened?"

"Yes."

"So she's never wrong."

"No."

She leaned forward, elbows on knees, and pressed her face into her hands. "Oh. Well, that's that, isn't it? You don't think I have a way to survive this mess… intact. Allie's never-wrong death-seeking ability agrees with you. Done."

"No."

She laughed sadly. "You're a contract killer who is semi-immortal, and I'm about to be dead."

"No."

When she planted her feet on the porch, the swing stopped. "I'm a marked woman. Brandon isn't going to stop. Your friends' lives are at risk because of me. Oh no, Allie's baby—"

"It's not your fault." He dropped a hand onto her thin shoulder.

"Answer me. If I hadn't met you, if I weren't... the way I am... none of this mess would be occurring, right?"

"It's not that simple."

"Seems pretty cut and dried to me." She stared off in the distance. "Actually, it sounds like it's not healthy for anyone to be around me. Who'd want to take the risk?"

"Hannah. No."

She was wrong.

He needed to prove it.

Giving in, he pulled her back into his shoulder and tilted her chin toward him. When he touched his mouth to hers, she tasted like hope and light. Her lips were the sweetest ambrosia, and he could sip at them forever.

Damn that word again, forever. *Jävlar.* There was no forever.

But he did have right now. And right now, he wanted to erase her fear, to keep her safe.

For once in his unnatural existence, his base sexual needs took a back seat to something more, an emotion he refused to name.

He would give her comfort, however small a kindness it might be in this insane situation. Wrapping his arm around her shoulders, he tucked her deeper into his embrace and bent his head to take the kiss deeper.

As she pressed up toward him, a tiny cry escaped her lips. He kissed her forehead, her chin, her cheeks, and then back to her soft mouth. The taste of salty moisture stopped him cold, and he lifted his head.

"*Älskling?*" He pulled a strand of hair off of her damp cheek.

She fisted his shirt and pressed her forehead to his chest. "Don't ask me anything. Please." Her hoarse entreaty ripped him to the core.

More. He needed more contact, to envelop her more, protect her more. Reassure her.

Of what? That nothing bad would happen? He might be unnaturally strong, but he couldn't keep that promise of total safety.

So what did he have to offer?

Himself. Such as he was.

Jävlar.

He drew her over onto his lap and settled her legs on either side of his thighs. The slight weight of her frame barely registered. Snaking his arms around her waist, he tucked her tightly to his chest. She fit perfectly in every way. He'd do anything to protect her. Do anything to have her forever.

What was he thinking?

Burying a hand in her hair, he let the silky strands slip through his fingers. When those cinnamon-brown eyes drifted closed, he pulled her head to rest next to his neck. As he massaged her soft scalp, the gold hair glinted with coppery sparks in the sunshine.

With her lips resting on his neck, he lost the ability to think straight. And when she brushed her mouth beneath his jaw, the movement sent a lightning bolt of desire straight into the part of his body trapped beneath her hips. He ground his teeth together, employing sheer willpower to keep his hands from traveling over her body. Sweat prickled his forehead.

She drew back and tipped her chin up, the movement exposing the hollow between her collarbones. Where he'd almost lost control. He froze. Guilt gripped his stomach and squeezed.

It took a superhuman act of strength to meet her gaze. But the expression on her face didn't condemn him, didn't blame him.

Instead, those warm eyes studied him. She blinked. Her tongue darted out to wet her lips.

The thuds of his heart reverberated in his head until he lost all coherent thought. Fixated on the sweet hollow at the base of her neck, he swallowed.

Unable to resist, he dipped his head and brushed his mouth over her neck. When he tasted her skin, she shuddered. The wave of satisfaction from her reaction stunned him and whetted his need for more. Even still, he kept one arm around her waist and a hand resting lightly on the back of her neck.

With a shy smile, she rose up on her knees, trailing her soft lips over his jaw, up to his ear. A sensual electrical charge shot through him at the warm breath at his sensitive earlobe. He clenched his hand in her hair, and she squeaked.

"Sorry." Basic language skills had become a challenge for him.

"Not okay?" she said.

Her moist lips were swollen, parted and ripe for the taking. But he wouldn't take, not from her. And that restraint went against every fiber of his being.

However, he'd become a different man—a better man—for her, if that was what she needed.

"What you're doing is very okay. You are a dangerous woman."

When she kissed his mouth, he struggled to hold still.

"If you keep it up, I will lose what's left of my mind," he groaned.

He gently took her lower lip in his teeth until she gasped.

Tightening his grip on her neck, he grinned. "But losing my mind is okay."

She bent back to his ear, her light nips making his groin tighten. She made him crazy. Forget the knife compulsion. Right now, his desire for her trumped the hungry blade times ten.

Sliding his hand from her neck down her back, he kept a loose grip around her tiny waist.

When she leaned back, she trailed her fingers over his chest and abdomen, making his muscles jump. What would those hands feel like on other areas of his anatomy? His mouth went dry.

He shifted his legs wider, trying something, anything, to relieve the pressure in his jeans. All that maneuver accomplished was planting her cute derriere more firmly onto the one mutinous area of his body that was about to detonate. Amazing what this slip of a woman did to him. He wanted her. Badly.

When her hands drifted lower on his belly, he caught her wrists in his hand.

"Hannah, I need you." He nodded toward the cabin. "In there. Now."

Swallowing convulsively when she sat down firmly on his lap, Dante struggled to concentrate. His nether region had ideas of its own, and it was becoming more insistent by the minute.

"I want you," he repeated.

She didn't move. Air stirred her hair around her shoulders.

He let go of her hands and rested his palms on her hips.

Her brow furrowed as she opened her mouth and closed it.

Trying again, he said, "I need you. But not if you don't want, if you can't—"

Who the hell can form a sentence with a woman sitting on his kryssbåge?

"I will do whatever you want. Or not." He mentally slapped his palm to his forehead. How had the eloquent Dante been reduced to a few sputtered words?

He hoped he could keep his promise. At some point you couldn't unexplode a grenade. But he'd stop for her. It might render him a permanent eunuch when his balls burst into flames, but he would do whatever she needed him to do. However she needed him to do it.

For a torturously long time, he held her loosely at the waist as she sat on his groin, blithely unaware of the devastating effect her butt had on him. He suffered, but what beautiful torture.

After what seemed like centuries, she pinned him with a questioning expression. "You truly want me?"

"Like I've never wanted any woman in over 300 years."

Please believe me, älskling.

Tears shimmered. "Even knowing… all that's happened to me? That I'm damaged?"

"I want you. The good and the not so good. All of you. For me. Only for me."

He traced his fingers over the small of her back, pleased when she arched into his hands. "Truly, I care that you have suffered horrible things, and I would do anything to take those away. But you are not defined by another person's cowardly act. You are Hannah, beautiful and strong. You seduce me like no woman has since the beginning of my entire existence."

She studied him with soulful eyes. He fought to hold her gaze and also remain still. Give her time. Be patient. His gut clenched.

She finally answered him. "Yes."

"Yes?" He had to consciously close his gaping mouth.

Glancing toward the cabin door, she said, "Please, Dante."

When she laced her fingers around the back of his neck to kiss him again, her whole body trembled.

He wrapped his arms around her shoulders and waist, trying to surround her as much as possible. With her legs locked around his waist, he stood and walked into the cabin, kissing her, murmuring reassurances. She weighed next to nothing, which only made him want to protect her more.

When he closed the door, she twisted her head around.

"Lock, please."

"Anything you want."

Chapter 15

When he drew the bolt with a firm twist of his wrist, the feeling of safety relaxed her limbs. She entwined her limbs around him and relished in the warmth of his frame as he carried her to the bedroom, where he stopped and locked that door as well.

Dante kept her in his arms as he stooped and spread out the blankets on the low bed. When he deposited her on the side of the bed, she instantly missed the contact.

Uncertain of what to do next, she took in the grim set of his mouth. After a big breath, he knelt on the floor in front of her, not taking his ice-blue eyes off her face. The intensity of his stare set her heart pounding.

He dipped his head and laced his fingers in hers, drawing her hands to the bottom of his shirt. Curious, interested, and wanting more, she worked her hands under the fabric and pulled it up.

Surprisingly soft skin covered the hard heat of his torso. She paused and reveled in the lines of his bare back and belly. When he groaned, she snatched her hands away until he captured them and brushed his lips over the backs of them.

He grabbed the hem of his shirt. "May I?" His hoarse voice made her nerves tingle.

At her nod, he ripped off his thermal shirt and threw it to the floor.

With a hunger that surprised her, she studied the muscled ridges and planes. As if he sensed her perusal, his muscles twitched. But he didn't move.

Even when she leaned forward to trail fingers over his bare chest, he held utterly still. The knuckles of his fisted hands whitened when she brushed a finger over his hard, flat nipple. He paused mid-breath. She could get used to watching him respond to her touch.

Fine hair covered his chest, and she wanted to know how her cheek would feel against him. "You're amazing," she whispered, as she traced the hard lines of his shoulders.

"I was thinking the same thing about you. May I?"

At her nod, he grasped the hem of her T-shirt and hoodie and slid them up and away. His hands skimmed her ribs and arms in an amazing trail of warmth. She shivered in the cooler air. For a split second, she fought the urge to cover herself, but one look at his darkening eyes bolstered her confidence.

The electricity when he brushed his fingers over her bra sent a delicious quiver straight into her belly and then lower. He licked his lips, unclasped the bra, and peeled it off of her.

"*Kristus*, you're beautiful."

When he sucked one tip into his mouth and flicked his tongue over it, she gasped and grabbed his shoulders. His groan echoed her own as he moved to the other breast, driving her to clench the hair at the nape of his neck. Arching toward his mouth, she realized what she wanted.

More.

More of his mouth, his hands, his intensity.

More connection. More Dante.

Wanting his mouth on hers, she caressed his jaw and tilted his strong face up to hers. When she pressed her mouth to his, she no longer hesitated. He responded by kissing her deeply, opening her mouth wide as his tongue probed and tangled with her tongue. So delicious, his scent, his taste, how his hands cupped her breasts and rolled the nipples until she gasped into his mouth.

Half standing now, Dante eased her back onto the bed. Instead of hovering over her, he lay on his side next to her and continued to trace patterns of pleasure over her face and chest. With a shock, she realized that the panting sound came from her, and she rolled toward him, kissing him again.

Popping the button of her jeans, he slid a hand over the soft skin of her lower belly.

"Is this ok?"

She nodded. When she lifted her hips, he smoothed the fabric down her legs and away, leaving her in cotton underwear. As he trailed his hands down her leg, she froze and made a noise of protest when he approached her ankle. The damned panic rose again as she shifted to hide her foot.

"Don't. Please. No, it's not—"

"Shh. You're perfect."

He murmured reassurances as he trailed kisses down her leg. When he reached the puckered pink line of scar that she hated, the deformed bones that represented everything evil done to her, he paused. As the recipient of that onyx black stare, she couldn't breathe.

What did he think of her damaged foot? Did it disgust him? Did the acts surrounding the injury repulse him? Oh God, this was a mistake. She shouldn't be here, doing this, with him.

She tried to crawl backward and pull her offensive leg away from him.

"Stop." He laid his big hand on her calf.

She froze.

"Do you trust me?" He ground out the words between clenched teeth.

She couldn't breathe. Couldn't run.

"Watch me." His gentle but firm command calmed her nerves.

No part of his expression suggested displeasure. There was no indication that he was going to reject her. In fact, he looked like a man who wanted to ravish her but was using every ounce of strength to hold back. The hard slash of his mouth curled upward into a rakish grin.

He pressed his mouth to her leg and down onto her ankle along the scar, all the while keeping his eyes locked on to hers. Gently, he lifted her damaged foot, and devoured her with his avid gaze as he kissed all the way around her ankle. He flicked his tongue over the bones that jutted beneath the skin of her foot. Even the numb underside of her foot benefited from the warmth of his mouth.

As he caressed her leg, she finally let her head loll back with a deep sigh. From her ankle to her spine and neck, all of the muscles gradually relaxed. When he worked his way up the opposite leg, she shivered.

He paused on her upper thigh and nipped the sensitive skin, startling her. His chuckle sent ripples of pleasure through her entire body. As he licked her flat belly, she quivered beneath his touch, unable to control the moan of pleasure escaping her mouth.

"You're beautiful." He laved her belly button, sending a bolt of desire into her groin. "Soft." He punctuated his words with a nip or a lick. "Sexy. Perfect."

He ran a hand low, over the cotton-clad skin, and rubbed. The heat centered near her core spread out to her limbs.

"I want to pleasure you, *älskling*. Make you crazy." He hooked a finger beneath her panties. And paused. "*Älskling?*"

Tension cranked deep in her pelvis as his hand drifted lower. "Yes," she panted.

He tugged her panties down and away. The cool air over her sensitive skin was replaced by the warmth of his palm. He cupped and stroked her until she couldn't hold her hips still. Tiny gasps escaped her lips.

Her heart thudded, and not from fear.

He slid a finger over her entrance, then along her folds. The rhythm pushed the delicious tightness in her pelvis higher and higher.

"God, Dante. You're torturing me."

When she reached for him, he dodged her arms and continued the relentless movement of his fingers. His jet-black eyes managed to twinkle.

"Good. It's about time you experience a fraction of the torture you've put me through these past few days. I've wanted you so badly."

His words unlocked a piece of her soul that had been buried for years. Her heart wanted to soar out of her chest.

"Please." She shifted her hips, wanting more of his finger, more of his warmth. She groaned in frustration when he retreated.

"Soon."

Nudging her legs apart, he glided his fingers along the inner and outer folds, brushing against her entrance. With each upward motion, he briefly circled sensitive flesh, increasing the pressure with each pass until she couldn't think.

"Dante," she gasped.

"Yes, *älskling?*"

"I need…" She shook her head and reached for him.

"More?"

When he pressed a finger deeper into her opening, the sensation ricocheted pleasure through every pore of her body. He leaned forward and absorbed her gasps with his mouth, but when she dug her nails into his shoulders, his breath became ragged.

"More?" he said next to her ear. His low voice rumbled through her body, setting nerve endings on edge.

As he advanced his finger, her muscles clenched.

"Yes," she whispered.

He shifted to kneel next to her side, slid an arm under her neck and slanted his mouth over hers. He explored her mouth, filling her. His finger built a slow, relentless rhythm. Bumping her leg with his, he nudged her wider until she lay open to him.

Open. Vulnerable. For an instant every muscle tensed.

In any situation other than this one, she should be terrified.

Should be, but no more. Not with Dante.

He had healed those invisible scars from years ago. Or maybe they'd healed them together.

Didn't matter.

All that mattered was this moment, in his arms, safe. Cherished.

When she fisted a hand in the hair at the nape of his neck, he pressed his finger into her and palmed her sensitive skin as her hips shook. He continued to devour her mouth with his own until she couldn't tell where she ended and he began. The tension in her hips mounted until the pleasure exploded in her body and in her mind.

With a hard arch toward him, she came apart in his hand, her inner muscles clenching. He continued the relentless rhythm, drawing out more spasms from her core. A few aftershocks later, she finally lay on the bed. Her limbs refused to move. Her entire body buzzed with happiness. Her defenses now laid to waste, the transfer sensation flowed freely between them, dancing up her limbs in warm connection.

With an expression that managed to combine swagger, sexual hunger, and a boyish grin, Dante withdrew his finger and smoothed his hands over her hips and waist until she shivered again.

He trailed his mouth down the center of her body. Chin, neck, breastbone, navel. He was going to drive her to the brink of insanity.

Time for payback.

When she touched the band of his jeans, the shudder that ripped through him shook the bed.

Good. She had something to contribute as well. Confidence growing, she ran her finger over his lower belly, the intense heat flowing from him into her fingertips.

"Dante. More."

"Anything you want." He grinned. "Especially if it's me."

He removed his pants, his member standing out, obvious and hard. When he knelt over her, she fought another wave of terror and froze. Damn it.

"Dante, please, I—"

He had stopped moving as well, and the tenderness in the big man's face almost brought her to tears. Silently, he rolled onto his back and lifted her to kneel above him.

"You're in charge," he said.

She hesitated, and then sat down on his groin.

His gut-wrenching groan was followed by a strangled cough. "But with you sitting there, you will kill this undead man if you don't move that lovely ass away. You have no idea what you do to me."

"No mercy." She smiled.

Imitating his actions earlier, she eased forward to nip lightly along his torso. With every lick, she tasted his male essence, smelled the light cologne. His hands clenched her hips every few seconds, but he made no move to do more. His growls shot delicious vibrations through her mouth and pelvis, turning her insides to goo.

When she leaned forward, she brushed against his erection, and both of them groaned.

"You're driving me out of my mind, *älskling*," he ground out beneath a tight jaw.

"I'd like to drive more."

His black eyes glinted. "You're in charge. I might go insane, but God help me, you're in charge."

She eased away and stroked his hard erection, uncertain in her actions but enjoying the thickness sheathed by silky skin. Stroking down the length and back up to the tip, she looked up sharply at his grunt.

"Okay?"

"Please continue. What you're doing is—"

His ribbed belly muscles clenched when she ran her finger over a particularly interesting ridge. Sweat trickled down his temple.

Emotions she hadn't experienced before rolled through her: appreciation for the man on the bed, satisfaction that she could bring him such pleasure. She hadn't been in control of much of her life for the past four years. Here this giant of a man ceded all control to do what she wanted. Amazing.

She pushed up, balanced on her palms on his chest, and stared at him.

"You've got to stop looking at me like that," he said.

"Like how?"

"Like the best sexy-librarian fantasy I could ever imagine."

Darting a glance around, self-conscious, she reached for her glasses.

He manacled her wrist in his hand. "Keep them on. A naked beauty in glasses sitting on top of me? Delicious." He drew her arm to his mouth and pressed a kiss to the inside of her wrist. Shivers shot through to her core, and she shifted her hips, trying to relieve the need for him there.

"Do you want more, *ålskling*?"

"I want to… but it'll hurt." She bowed her head.

He brushed her hair back and framed her face with his hands. "It won't hurt if you're making the choice. I promise."

"Help me," she whispered.

"With pleasure."

He sat partway up and guided her hips forward and down onto his erection. She eased down his shaft, gasping as her muscles stretched to accept him. His hard and silky length filled her completely. Pulling her hips up and down, the friction made her want more. Her palms moved quickly on his chest as his breathing rate increased.

"Oh wow."

"Try sitting up, *ålskling*." He panted.

In doing so, the movement shifted him even deeper inside, and she bit her lip. "Dante."

"*Kristus*, you're perfect."

She shifted, rubbing against him until he grasped her hips. When he moved one hand to pinch her swollen nub, she couldn't contain a cry of pleasure. He slid his other hand to her breast and stroked her until she couldn't think coherently.

Their moans and gasps filled the room as she rocked faster against him. It wasn't enough. She needed more. She needed him.

"More," she whispered and gave herself into his hands.

He grasped her hips. When he pressed her onto him, he met her with thrusts of his own, hot, hard strokes consuming her, marking her. She relaxed her hips and gave into the mounting rhythm, grabbing his forearms for support.

God, this is like flying through heaven.

He moved faster than she could register, blending sound and pressure into a swirl of pleasure. When she leaned back to hold on to his bent knees, he rubbed her exposed flesh, making her inner muscles clench in delicious response.

The orgasm hit like a tidal wave. Every inch of her body contracted and expanded in ecstasy. When she squeezed around him, his release came at the same time. On and on the rolling pleasure consumed her. She couldn't think, couldn't hear. Her vision had reduced the room around them to sparkles of light.

Unable to control her body or mind, all barriers dropped and transfer flowed between them, amplifying the orgasm. They were linked body and mind as her healing ability pulled his essence into her skin. The texture of his blood, his thoughts, his soul linked with hers and intertwined across the connection. Even her heart began to beat in time with his.

After what seemed like forever, she collapsed forward onto his chest, still joined to him. Their damp skin connected them from neck to hip. As his breathing slowed, Dante pulled the blanket over her and wrapped his arms around her. She never wanted him to let go.

• • •

Contentment, such as he'd never experienced before, oozed through Dante's entire body, pressed as he was against Hannah's soft frame. He throbbed, still lodged inside of her. If his kind could die, he'd gladly expire in this manner, here, beneath this woman.

He stroked her back until quivers rippled over her skin. Her tiny body fit within his arms as if by perfect design. And she fit him elsewhere just as perfectly.

As if on cue, his cock hardened. Hell, every part of his body knew exactly what it wanted.

Hannah.

With her glasses since discarded, she rose up on her arms and pinned him with a golden-flecked stare. He wanted to drown in those soulful eyes. Forever.

Forever. *Kristus.*

Skimming his hands over her subtle curves, her shivers gave him satisfaction no other woman could match.

She snuggled into his broad chest and kissed and licked until he growled. In turn, he tightened his arms until she squeaked.

"I won't hurt you," he whispered.

"I know."

He caught a flicker of her smile as she lowered her mouth back to his neck and chest.

He promised to keep her safe. But truly, could he?

Safe. A nice illusion for now, but one he couldn't sustain. At some point, evil would catch up to them. Then what?

Then he'd do whatever was required to save her.

Would it be enough?

A nip with her teeth distracted him from black thoughts, and he gladly buried his hands in her silky hair.

"You have to stop."

She froze. "Or what?"

"Or I'll retaliate," he growled.

To demonstrate, he thrust his hips upward.

"Oh." She gasped. Then smiled.

Dodging his hands, she dipped her head and worked on his nipple. How did this small woman turn him into a pile of mush with only her mouth? At another flick with her tongue, his breath hissed out.

"Now you've done it." He pressed his mouth to hers as if he needed to consume her.

She panted. "Done what?"

"You're addicting. Like a drug," he said.

"Do you want a cure?" she asked, breathless.

He flipped her over on her back. "You're the cure for me, *ålskling*." He entered her again in one smooth thrust. "It's my turn."

Hooking his arms under her knees, he pulled her legs up and outward as he rocked into her. She was open completely to him. Trusting. Beautiful. And he wanted even more.

With her legs still draped over his arms, he gripped her shoulders, pulling her into him hard with each thrust. He wanted to surround her, wanted to give her unimaginable pleasure. Wanted to erase hell and replace it with heaven.

He paused and studied her face. No pain, only ecstasy. No hesitation. "Are you all right?" he asked.

"You have no idea." She opened her legs wider to welcome him.

With a harsh growl, he locked his hands on her shoulders and drove into her. Waves of desire, of hunger, consumed him until his entire existence narrowed down to the woman in his arms.

When they broke at the same time, the orgasm exploded even greater than the first one. He never wanted to let her go. He leaned back to watch the shudders roll through her frame, felt the tightness around his cock as her muscles contracted. In hundreds of years of existence, he'd never seen anyone as perfect as this woman.

• • •

Day had flowed into early evening. They'd been in bed for hours, talking about their lives and dreams, drifting along in each other's arms. They woke to make love and floated back to sleep again.

If her entire existence boiled down to this room in this cabin with this man, she would be satisfied. She didn't care that her life might end soon. Didn't care that he was a 300-year-old undead Swede.

She'd made her decision earlier in the day. She would not live in terror; she'd open herself up emotionally and not allow the act that had wrecked her life to dictate the rules of her existence. No longer a victim, she had taken control of her life, decided to be with Dante completely, and was rewarded in ways she hadn't imagined.

Damn it, if she was a marked woman, she might as well make up for the years of her life that would be taken from her. God, it was so worth it.

Stretching, she winced at new sore spots on her body.

He rolled partway over her and kissed her on the nose. Pulling her firmly to his solid chest, his warmth conducted right through her body, the heat welcome in the cool evening air.

"I'm getting up," she said.

She pushed against his massive frame, and he flopped back on the bed, acting weak and docile. His interested electric-blue glint spoke of anything but weakness.

"Well, I'm staying here. And if you know what's good for you, you'll come right back." He reached for her.

She laughed and danced out of the way. "Sounds delicious." She popped on her glasses. "I'm going to the bathhouse, so I'll be a little while."

"I'll be waiting."

He rolled over, and soon, light snores emerged from the bedroom. Funny, she thought his kind didn't need sleep and didn't get tired. Maybe it'd been a long couple of days even for a being like him.

She quickly donned jeans and the T-shirt and hoodie, grabbed her purse containing toiletry items and slung a towel over her shoulder. Out of the cabin, on a whim, she turned on her cell phone. The light blinked for voicemail. The message time indicated a few hours prior.

Scott's number.

Her stomach pitched.

The voice on the recording stopped her cold. With a trembling hand, she pressed the phone to her ear.

The cool air froze the sweat on her brow.

It wasn't Scott.

Chapter 16

"Brandon here, using your beloved brother's phone." Hannah visualized his thin mouth pinching as he talked.

A horrific, ear-splitting male scream overloaded the phone speakers. She collapsed to her knees on the gravel, barely able to hang on to the phone. Air whooshed out in harsh gasps.

"As you can tell, Scott's unavailable right now, but if you get your skanky ass back here before midnight, I might let your idiot brother live. If you cooperate, we might let Scott go. I've texted you the address. Come alone, or I'll quarter your brother alive. Don't be late."

Scott's tortured wail of pain cut off abruptly as the call ended.

Glancing back at the dark cabin, she thought of Dante, sleeping within. What should she do?

If Dante went with her, Scott would die. Brandon had made that perfectly clear.

If Dante went with her, this man she cared for might die. And if she didn't follow Brandon's rules, Peter and Allie might die.

Panic squeezed her lungs until she saw stars. Making a conscious effort to take slow breaths, she calmed down and cleared her thoughts. She needed a plan.

If she went to Scott on her own, at least Dante might be safe. Allie and Peter might be safe. Maybe she could get Scott out of this situation.

In every scenario, Hannah would probably die. Or, as Dante had alluded, maybe worse. She might not die.

Trapped. A different prison but trapped all the same.

Bile burned her throat. She couldn't tell Dante what she needed to do. He wouldn't listen. He'd come with her and be destroyed trying to protect her. And if she didn't come alone, Scott would die.

Oh no, no, no.

With shaking hands, she used her cell phone light to scribble a note on a piece of scrap paper from her purse. Slinking back to the cabin porch, she stuffed the paper between slats on the swing. Dante would find it later. And then what?

Well, he would have to guess where she was going. He could run pretty fast but surely not for 200 miles or however far it was to Portland.

Shivering in the evening air, she picked up her purse and towel and crept down the path to the parking area. Dante had mentioned that he kept a spare key under the front mat of the Hummer for emergencies. This situation qualified. Shame heated her face. Like a criminal, she was stealing Dante's car. What a way to repay his kindness.

What a response to his tenderness and trust.

Opening the heavy car door, she left it slightly ajar. It would make too much noise if she closed it. She scrabbled with her hands under the mat; sweat pricked her forehead. No key. Where was it?

Her heart leapt at the muffled jingle. Jumping into the driver's seat, she scooted it forward, inserted the key, and turned it one click. The dashboard lights came on, but the engine remained silent.

When she glanced back up the path, she half expected Dante to come running out of the cabin. If he followed her, it would seal his destruction and that of his friends.

Come on, come on. Think.

She had to do this without alerting him.

Putting the vehicle in neutral, she kept the lights off and rolled down the slight incline from the parking lot onto the park road. She was probably only doing three or four miles per hour, but revving the engine this close to the cabin would draw immediate attention. So she coasted, incredibly slow but somewhat silently. Each individual crunch of rock on the rough road sounded like huge explosions to her hypersensitive ears.

The Hummer crawled toward the park exit.

She let gravity take over; the Hummer got up to ten miles per hour. Another glance in the rearview mirror. No pursuit yet. She gripped the wheel with sweaty hands.

Keeping her foot off the brake, Hannah let the momentum carry her up the slight rise to the highway. She spotted no oncoming traffic and kept on with the maddening, lethargic coast, inching west, away from the town of John Day. The highway paralleled the state park, so she kept the engine off and vehicle coasting until she spotted headlights behind her.

Shutting the front door, she engaged the motor and floored it up the highway. She pushed the vehicle up to seventy, putting as much distance between herself and the state park as possible. Tears streamed down her face.

After every mile passed, she relaxed a tiny bit. Dante would live.

After every mile passed, her heart clenched with stabbing pain. She wouldn't see him again.

Her vision blurred, so she rubbed at her cheeks, dabbing under her glasses to wipe away the wetness. The headlights she'd spotted in the rearview mirror were long gone, and Hannah eased off the accelerator to a more appropriate speed.

She'd stolen a car and left Dante.

Scott, what have you gotten yourself into?

The console clock read just after seven o'clock. Five hours to get to Portland and make the deadline.

A sign pointing north toward the Fossil Beds National Park also listed Portland. She had no map. This way must be as good as any. She chanced a final glance in the rearview mirror: no cars; no giant, sprinting, undead killers.

The green sign on the right read 234 miles to Portland. She hoped to hell this would be a straight road, or she might not get to Scott in time.

Three hours and a million hairpin turns later, Hannah's hands and arms burned with effort to maintain speed without coming off the road in the top-heavy Hummer. Highway 19 had followed a river closely for miles, twisting with speeds listed far below what she needed to maintain to reach Portland before the deadline.

She was running out of time. She had to keep pushing. Get to Scott.

The highway climbed into a forest where, instead of a river, she traveled up and over gullies and hills.

For the love of God, would it be too much to ask for a straight patch of road?

Stopping at a crossroads gas station, she filled up the vehicle and used the restroom. As she washed her hands at the sink, she didn't recognize the person in the mirror with swollen, red eyes. She didn't think it was possible to cry for three hours, but apparently overcoming the impossible had become her mission.

Thinking about Dante made the tears flow again. Her chest ached like someone had ripped her heart out, leaving an empty cavity of black nothingness.

Exhaustion dug bony, phantom fingers into her shoulders and threatened to drag her down.

She would never see Dante again. Even if he forgave her for running away and stealing his car, it didn't matter. She was a marked woman. Her freak of nature ability had attracted all the wrong attention from the very start. Now she paid for her bizarre gift.

If she didn't show up in Portland, her brother would die. And by arriving alone, at least Dante would be safe. Wiping away tears and fatigue, she shrugged out of the hoodie, hurried back out to the Hummer, and headed north and west toward Portland.

Toward death.

Or worse.

. . .

Dante rolled over in the quiet cabin. The blanket where Hannah had laid was cool to the touch.

Hannah.

That sweet, trusting face. Her body—*herre Gud*, just thinking about their lovemaking made him harden with lust. He needed to be inside of her yet again. He shook his head, amazed at what she did to him.

An oddly familiar motor revved in the distance. Turning his head toward the bedroom window, he tried to place the sound.

The Hummer.

The Hummer?

Blood running cold, Dante exploded out of the cabin, still naked. Sure enough, down the highway heading west, moving at speed, his Hummer's taillights disappeared into the night. He reached the parking area in a millisecond. Where was Hannah?

Sprinting to the bathhouse, he quickly established that she hadn't been there. The shower stalls were bone-dry.

Herrejävlar.

Gone. Had someone taken her? Maybe Brandon had found her.

Or had Dante scared her off? What had he done?

Hurt, deep hurt, choked him like a noose. Had she truly rejected him?

As he walked back to the cabin, a slight flutter in the breeze caught his attention. Pulling a folded piece of paper from between pieces of wood, he flipped on the porch light to read. His stomach dropped at Hannah's flowing script.

Dante, I have to leave. You're safer if you stay here. I'm sorry. I love you.

Hannah

What would be safer for someone like him? There wasn't much that could hurt him. Except finishing a contract and pissing off Jerahmeel to the point where his boss lashed out at anyone: Peter, Allie, Barnaby. And Dante had told Hannah all of this information and more.

But would that make her leave? Now?

He dialed her cell number, but it went straight to voicemail. *Kristus.* When he called Peter, his friend answered on the second ring.

"Peter, I've got a problem. Hannah left."

"What do you mean, left?"

He sat down on the porch, ignoring the wood digging into his bare ass. "She took the Hummer and left. I think something's wrong."

"You think?"

"I think she's trying to protect me. Maybe all of us."

"Hell."

"Exactly. Bro, any chance you can use Allie's police chief brother-in-law to break into Hannah's cell phone but not ask too many questions?"

"Maybe. It might take a little while. You have her number?"

"Yeah, got it three days ago when we were walking home from work."

Had it been only three days? It felt like so much longer.

"Can you still track the Hummer?" Peter asked.

"*Ja,* but I'd like to know what I'm getting into. If there were any texts or voicemails I can access, that'd be helpful. Something's going down. I feel it in my bones."

"I agree." Peter murmured to Allie. "I'll talk with Bryce and see what he can do. No guarantees."

"You two safe?"

"For now."

Peter's voice came through strained, hesitant. Who would blame him? As mortals, Peter and Allie were helpless if Jerahmeel unleashed his power or his minions on them. Damn. Dante couldn't be everywhere. Damn.

"Lay low, Petey. I'll call if I find out anything else."

Clicking off the phone, he sprinted toward his laptop still on the kitchen table and fired up the wireless hotspot. He pulled up the tracking program, something he figured he'd only need if someone stole the Hummer. It *was* stolen, technically speaking. A blip on the map showed that Hannah traveled up a highway west of town. The road appeared to be pretty windy on the map, and he shuddered to think of her going off the road in the darkness. She possibly traveled toward Portland or maybe would catch I-84 and go east back toward La Grande.

Hannah, what are you doing, ålskling? *Why are you running away? Tell me where you're going.*

He pulled on a thermal shirt and jeans and threw his remaining personal items into a bag. Closing the laptop and stowing it on top of his clothes, he slung the bag over his shoulder and jogged through the campground section of the park. There weren't a lot of people around this time of year, but enough for his purposes. He wasted precious minutes searching for the right vehicle. He excelled at most things, but carjacking wasn't his best skill. He'd rather not break in and hardwire a car. Better to try it the easy way first, then go to plan B if that didn't work.

Several of the people staying in the campground lingered outside, sitting by crackling fires. Low voices drifted back to him near some of the RVs. Dante had to stick to shadows and move silently, a challenge for a person his size.

As he crept to the back of each vehicle, he searched for the magnetic extra key owners occasionally hid there. Finding nothing on the back bumper, he checked the front wheel wells, where folks sometimes stashed their keys. On the fifth vehicle, the metal jingle when he reached over the driver's side wheel sounded like beautiful music to his ears.

Throwing his bag into the hatchback, he crammed himself into the driver's seat, turned the key, and cringed as loud country music blared from the radio. Cursing, he threw the car into reverse as the panicked owners ran around the side of their RV.

Jävlar. The cops would be looking for him in a heartbeat.

His vision blurring, he almost ran off the park road as the knife pulsated. It wanted him to kill someone, this very minute. He reached for his lower leg, his hand pulled against his will.

Not now, helvete, I can't do this now.

With a guttural yell, he yanked his hand back and forced it to the steering wheel. His thoughts shifted to Hannah. *No. Ignore the pain; ignore the knife.*

Instead of traveling west on the highway toward Portland, he drove back a few miles to John Day. Pulling off behind a local repair shop, he hid the car from view of the highway. He broke into the shop's key box, fished out as many keys as he could hold, ran over to a Jeep and tried out each one until, thankfully, he found a match. Sirens blared as Dante ducked down. Police cruisers raced east on the highway, probably searching for the stolen hatchback.

Turning the Jeep's lights off, he confirmed that the vehicle started. He spied thick paper on the floorboard; a good sign the car had been serviced.

With the Jeep purring, Dante flipped open his computer again and checked Hannah's position. The Hummer moved north on Highway 19 toward a crossroads. He had to make an educated guess: follow her route or assume that she traveled back to Portland. If he guessed correctly, he could take a more direct route on

Highway 26, which cut straight through the mountains. Closing the computer, he decided to go the direct route. Unfortunately, with the police out in force, he couldn't speed as much as he'd prefer until he had passed well out of the area.

He pulled out of the repair shop lot and drove east, fighting against the instinct to stomp on the accelerator. As he passed the state park, flashing blue and red lights winked in the campground.

He kept going.

In the monotony of the dark night, as mile markers and small animal eyes flashed by, his thoughts remained in constant motion. What the hell had happened with Hannah? Why did she leave? Was it all to do with Brandon? Or had Dante really scared her off?

Didn't matter. He needed her. Needed her to be safe. He'd kneel and beg for her to stay with him if it would help. Nothing mattered without Hannah in his unnatural existence. He would figure out how to make her a part of his life or die trying.

An hour west of John Day, he pushed the speed up to fifteen miles per hour over the speed limit. Really, the big danger out here was deer, not cops. Of course, hitting wildlife wouldn't kill him, but it'd slow him down tonight.

The moonlit high desert flew by as he raced west. When he stopped to fill up in the crossroad town of Madras, he rechecked Hannah's position. Just as he thought, she traveled on I-84, passing through Hood River, heading straight to Portland. But where?

He tried her cell number again but went straight to voicemail again. *Kristus.*

His phone rang. Peter.

"What've you found out, bro?"

"We tapped into the voicemail on Hannah's phone. Brandon left her a message. It sounded like he was torturing a guy he identified as Scott—"

"*Jävla skit!*"

"Yeah, I hear you. He said if she doesn't get there by midnight, he'll kill Scott."

Dante glanced at the clock. Ten thirty. Not enough time to intercept her. *Herrejävlar.*

"Where, bro? Where's she going?"

He'd kill the minion if he so much as looked at her. Damn Jerahmeel's wrath and retribution. She was an innocent who didn't deserve to get mixed up in the Indebted mess.

"I'm sending you the directions. Brandon texted them to her phone. Be careful. This feels like a huge trap. For both of you."

"I'll take precautions. Thanks, bro. Keep Allie safe."

The text came through with the address. Dante swore, threw the car into gear and sped into the night through the Cascade Mountains to Portland.

Chapter 17

Hannah steered the Hummer down a deserted street to the address on North Rivergate Boulevard, an industrial area north of downtown Portland. Streetlights cast cruel halogen shadows against her destination, a complex of stark metal warehouses at the road's end.

Yes, she had truly reached the end of the road.

Across the broad Willamette River, traffic hummed in the distance, drivers blissfully traveling home, or to work, or wherever they were going. Probably not to their deaths.

Lucky people.

When she opened the SUV door, the cool air off the river raised goose bumps on her arms, and she rubbed her skin, trying to warm up. No trucks rumbled down this road tonight. The parking lot was empty. No lights on in the buildings. Not a soul in sight.

She expected evil to jump out of the shadows and grab her. What did it matter? What more could happen?

Lots more, unfortunately.

A boat horn boomed from the nearby Port of Portland, plaintive in the night. Half a million people in this town, and she stood in the middle of the city, completely alone.

She missed Dante's warmth. His strength. His assurance that he would protect her from any and all bogeymen out there.

Dante.

A sob lodged in her throat, but she pushed it back down. She wouldn't think about his big, muscled arms. His hot kisses. The hope of much more for their relationship—if this were a normal relationship. However, nothing about their connection was normal, thus why she stood next to a stolen vehicle while the sexiest and sweetest man in the world cooled his heels hundreds of miles away.

At least he'd be safe. That was her main goal where Dante was concerned.

Shivering in the evening air, she considered grabbing her hoodie—but why bother? She wouldn't survive long enough for it to make any difference.

It was 11:54. *Got to get moving. Help Scott.*

She grabbed a Leatherman multitool from the console. Pitiful protection, but it made her feel a bit braver, gave her strength.

She refused to think about Dante's confident, broad smile and that intense blue gaze. As she closed the solid Hummer door with a thud, the sadness swamping her didn't originate solely from her dread of what awaited in the warehouse.

Tonight would ice the cake on her crappy life.

She tiptoed around the second warehouse building to the loading bays, per the texted instructions. Every creak of metal and crunch of leaves made her jump. All of the truck bays were dark, except for the last one where a sick, yellow glow spilled out from the door onto the pavement. Sneaking beneath the bays so anyone looking across the loading area wouldn't see her, she strained to catch any sound.

Only light traffic across the river and faint maritime sounds at the port a mile away.

Then a gut-wrenching scream pierced the darkness, like the one on the phone. The hairs stood up on the back of her neck.

Scott.

Hannah took off at a clumsy, crouched run, stumbling on her bad foot. Dodging under the truck loading pads, she flew up the stairs to the loading dock and peeked through the window on a metal door. She blinked twice, unbelieving, her palms sweaty when she pressed her hands against the glass. Turning the cold metal knob slowly, she slid open the door and slunk inside, still keeping to the shadows.

Row upon row of heavy metal racks stretched from the closed loading bay doors far into the warehouse darkness. The racks rose a good fifteen feet high. A figure paced between the nearest two racks, only about twenty feet away. Even with his back to her, she recognized the shock of red hair. In one hand, he held a short whip. The tips had a metallic glint in the dim light.

Brandon walked away from the garish light into the aisle, out of her line of sight. He chuckled, the sound both grating and nauseating. Then a whoosh and a snap split the still air. Another soul-shattering howl sprinted up her spine. Scott. She had to do something.

With shaking hands, she eased the door closed and slipped deeper into the warehouse, the rough sound of her shuffling steps masked by Scott's screams. Inching around the first huge set of shelves, near the wall of the warehouse, she hid behind a stack of pallets. Brandon's footfalls receded. When she peeked around, her vision went dim at the edges.

Scott's wrists were bound to the metal shelving so tightly that his hands were a lilac color. He dangled, his toes not quite reaching the ground. There were stains on his torn clothing, and on the floor below him, dark liquid pooled. His guttural moans echoed through the huge warehouse.

She had to get him out of here.

Her heart beating its way out of her ribcage, she crouched on the floor and scrabbled for something, anything, that might help. On the bottom shelf, she found a box of small metal bolts. She grabbed a fistful and hurled them down the back aisle into the darkness as forcefully as possible. Brandon never saw her, crouched on the bottom shelf in the shadow of a large bin, when he ran past. He disappeared into the depths of the warehouse.

Scott opened his mouth to speak when she reached him, but she shushed him. One of his eyes had swollen shut. Linear slices in his clothes revealed oozing wounds. His good eye rolled back, and he sagged against the shelving. Each of his breaths rasped too loudly in the concrete and metal building.

Climbing up one shelf, Hannah pulled at the leather binding Scott's wrists.

Too tight to untie.

She had to hurry. Brandon wouldn't stay away forever.

Clumsily opening the multitool, she sawed at the straps. The knife slipped in her sweaty hands every few passes.

Brandon's footsteps became louder, but he walked up the outside aisle. He couldn't see them yet, hidden as they were between the first two rows of shelves. But he sure as heck would spot them when he turned the corner.

Go faster.

She sawed desperately on the straps.

Sweat beaded her forehead.

Please.

Free of the restraints, Scott crumpled to the floor with a sickening thud. Scrambling down, she tugged at her brother's inert body. *Get up!*

Footsteps approached.

If she could get Scott into the next aisle, they might be able to lose Brandon in the maze of shelves.

Scott moaned when she draped his arm over her shoulder; his shoulder creaked and popped, the sounds turning her stomach. Somehow she hefted him to his feet. Urging him to move, she half dragged him to the end of the racks.

Just get around the corner and we'll have a chance.

Almost there.

Come on, Scott, walk.

Scott's weight disappeared.

She staggered backward, landing hard on her butt.

Brandon's sneering upside-down face entered her field of vision. "Hey, skank, nice of you to join the party."

He grabbed a fistful of her T-shirt and yanked her to her feet.

Scott lay in a semiconscious bloody ball on the floor, wheezing and gurgling.

"Well, this is perfect. Big hero Hannah trying to save her brother. Which is funny because we wouldn't even be in this situation if your drunk brother hadn't blabbed all over creation about your abilities. No one cared about you until this moron opened his mouth. Now you're the most interesting girl at the ball."

"What are you talking about?"

He lifted her until the T-shirt fabric cut into her armpits.

"I had to make sure that idiot Blackstone stayed focused on his job and not on a crusade to deliver your stepfather's apology from the great beyond. Keeping Blackstone away from you would have been enough, but then Judas here sold you out big time."

Brandon poked Scott with his boot and shrugged. "Moron can't hold his drink. It was much too easy."

"Let him go. He's not part of this."

"That's true. But he's only step one: get you to come here."

"What?"

"Step two is to get him out of here. Then it'll be just you and me. Oh, and you'll need to heal him."

"Then he can go?"

"Of course. We don't want this worthless mess. He was just bait, and he almost couldn't complete that one simple task."

"Who's we?"

He laughed, a nasty, razor-sharp sound slicing through her ears. "Blackstone's and my boss, our lord Jerahmeel."

Hannah held her breath. Dante had thought Jerahmeel might be interested in her abilities. Disastrous. Things had just gone from bad to worse.

"My boss wants you for sure. My job is to deliver you. What the lord of evil does to you, I can only guess."

When Brandon grinned, his tiny pig eyes disappeared in his pinched face. He sneered at her brother, who still lay crumpled on his side on the concrete floor.

"Enough chitty-chat. You need to heal him soon, or he won't get out of here alive. He looks pretty bad off."

"You're a jerk."

Brandon dropped her, and she staggered forward, her knees barking on the concrete. She crawled over to Scott.

"I'm sorry, sis," he rasped over cracked and swollen lips. Blood trickled down his cheek as he lay curled on his side.

"At least let me get you out of here." She reached out her hands.

"No. Healing me will kill you"—he wheezed—"or they'll kill you."

Brandon's nasally voice cut through her concentration. "Actually, no, we won't kill her. We'll do worse than kill her. Right, babe?"

She refused to meet his twisted expression. Swallowing a lump in her throat, she focused on the one thing she could do before her existence became a living hell of unimaginable proportions. Hannah pressed her hands against Scott's forearm. The transfer was like hitting a brick wall at full speed. She couldn't move beneath the force of his pain.

Get it all out of him. At least one of us can have a normal life after tonight.

Burning agony flowed through her hands and into her veins. All of Scott's whip slashes appeared on her body and sluiced fire over her raw skin. The torn ligaments in Scott's shoulders from where he'd hung by his arms crackled and shifted in her joints. Tears coursed down her cheeks as she struggled to inhale against bruised rib muscles—even the smallest effort stabbed poker-hot pain into her chest.

Every place where Scott had been kicked or punched, she absorbed it. The pain sucked. Badly.

Scott, healthier now, pushed her off him as he rolled away. She shuddered as she curled in a ball on the cold concrete. The open wounds burned. Her shoulders throbbed.

"Hannah," he whispered.

"You're free. Go have a good life."

Her brother scrambled to his feet. "Brandon, you asshole. Leave her alone. Let me take her for medical care."

"Get out of here, douchebag, or I'll mess you up so bad, even your little sister can't fix you. Be thankful I didn't hurt you more. You're a loser piece of shit. I only hung out with you to get to your sister and her thick-headed boyfriend."

"Damn it."

"Get out of here, idiot." Brandon lunged at him with the whip.

Scott jumped back. "I'm sorry, sis."

He shot away; the slam of the metal door echoed in the vacuous warehouse. So much for her brother sticking up for her, although she didn't blame him. There wasn't much anyone could do against a deranged, inhumanly strong monster like Brandon.

"Speaking of idiots, Miss Thing, where is the ass clown you've been hanging out with? I thought he'd be on your ugly tail."

"Left him behind," she choked out. "He has no idea where I am."

"We'll see."

When he pulled her by her arm, her transfer-torn shoulder threatened to dislocate. She screamed.

"Shut it, bitch."

He trailed the metal tips of the whip over her neck, scoring fire across her damaged skin.

"Part of the problem is that you're more delicate than we'd like. We'll have to toughen you up so you can be more useful to us."

"Go to hell." Her jaw ached with the act of speaking.

He hauled her to the opposite shelf, lashed her leg to the thick metal column, and tied her hands behind her back. Throwing her glasses far into the darkness, he shoved down a black toboggan over her entire head and neck.

Trapped in the dark again, she had only pain and her endless screams for company.

• • •

Slamming the Jeep into a gear-grinding stop next to his abandoned Hummer, Dante sprinted across the parking lot.

A figure wove in and out of the shadows of the warehouse floodlights.

Dante froze, went into a stalk, and waited next to the building.

Blood darkened most of the person's face and clothing, and the hunched shoulders made it impossible to identify the figure. Heart in his throat, Dante reached out of his hiding area to grab the person.

The male yell cut short as Dante identified the man midswing and pushed Scott into the wall. Dante blinked as he studied the guy. Although his shirt was torn, there were no cuts on his skin. A few small bruises on his face, but no major injuries. Only some dried blood.

"Where is Hannah?" Dante growled, fighting the knife's call to kill someone evil. This *oåkting*, Hannah's brother, would suit just fine.

"Hey, meathead, you're too late. Brandon forced her to heal me after that sick fuck tried to torture me to death." Scott tried to kick, but Dante sidestepped him.

Dante saw red. "You didn't stay and help her?" He shoved the man harder against the warehouse wall. Scott gurgled until Dante let up the pressure enough for him to talk again.

"And do what? He's going to kill someone tonight, and I got the golden ticket to escape, so I took it."

"And abandoned your sister?"

"Nothing else I could do," he whined. "Look, man, I love her. She's my sister. But there's nothing but death back there. We've gotten mixed up in a ton of messed up shit. I'm just glad to be free of it."

"So you did nothing to help her? Your own flesh and blood?"

He looked at the ground and mumbled. "I told her not to heal me."

"That's it? You're not a man. You're an embarrassment."

He flung Scott away like toxic waste.

"Run away like the scum you are. Trust me, you don't want me to ever see you again, understand?"

"Won't matter. Dude, you're dead too if you go in there. Brandon wants you to show up. That's exactly what he's hoping for."

"So?"

"So at least sneak in any other way than the obvious approach. Maybe you'll have a snowball's chance."

"You disgust me."

"At least I'm alive. More'n I can say about you if you decide to play hero again."

Scott disappeared into the darkness.

Staring at the massive building before him, Dante fought the hard-wired instinct to rush headfirst to the loading dock, exactly where Brandon's text instructed Hannah to go. So Dante quickly circled the large building. On the side of the warehouse nearest the river, he spotted a window. It was ajar.

He easily leapt up six feet to grab the casing with one hand and hung on while he carefully opened the window. A rusty creak froze him for a minute until, hearing no answering sound from within, he continued.

With barely enough room for him to squeeze through the gap, he balanced his torso on the sill, ignoring how the casing cut into his belly. He gauged the contents of the room. Someone's office.

Careful of the knickknacks and pens, he descended onto a bare area of the desk and silently dropped onto the floor. Unlocking the door, he stepped into the main warehouse. A small amount of light filtered down from the end of the warehouse. He held still, listening. Dante heard scratches of boots on dusty concrete at the far end of the structure and an occasional soft feminine groan and whimper. *Jävlar.* Hannah.

Control the stalk. Do not rush in there.

Row after row of shipping boxes and materials filled the warehouse shelves. Using breaks in the shelves, Dante traveled through the aisles until the outer warehouse wall was at his back. He crawled into a space between boxes and pushed his head out until he could scan the area lit by a flashlight on the floor.

Brandon paced the aisle, muttering to himself as if he were having a conversation with an imaginary friend. Every few steps, he knocked the handle of a whip against his leg.

Laying on the cement floor, a small figure rocked back and forth, working her hands behind her back.

Kristus.

One of Hannah's legs had been bound to the rack, her hands were tied with straps, and her head covered by a kind of hood. An occasional cry emanated from beneath the cloth as her arms kept twisting. At her whimper, Brandon knelt down and lifted her a few inches off the floor by her shirt collar. Dante nearly burst out of his hiding place at her strangled cough, but he fought for patience.

"Shut up, bitch." Brandon dropped her onto the concrete with a stomach-turning thud.

When she didn't move, Dante's heart stopped. His hands curled into deadly fists.

After Brandon continued on his shuffling circuit, those hands behind her back twisted again. Pride welled in Dante's heart at her determination.

Good girl. Keep fighting.

He crept down the back row until he positioned himself on the opposite side of the shelf as Hannah. A few boxes were missing, creating space to hide. If only he could move more boxes aside, then he could pull her through the shelf. Depending on the timing, maybe he had a chance to get her out of this hell.

He waited for Brandon to turn and walk back to the end of the row. Hearing the bastard's footsteps fade away, Dante grasped a heavy box and scooted it over, inch by agonizingly slow inch, until it rested on the concrete floor. Now he had a clear view of Hannah's back and shoulders as she continued to wiggle against the bonds.

Dante squeezed himself through the open shelf space and froze. Brandon stopped in front of a now-still Hannah.

Dante was trapped in the tight darkness of the bottom shelf. He stared at the minion's booted feet, planted two feet away.

"Where's your boyfriend? He should've been here by now," Brandon muttered.

When she didn't answer, he prodded her stomach with his foot. Her entire body jumped as air whooshed out. Dante almost exploded from the shelf. Suppressing the natural urge to annihilate the minion who was hurting Hannah, he relaxed his entire body and cleared his mind. He slowed his breathing and remained motionless. If he drew the minion's attention, everything would be lost, including Hannah's life.

"Hmm. Where the hell is Blackstone?" Brandon walked away again.

Dante reached out and gently touched Hannah's arm.

She jumped again, but he squeezed her arm and stroked the skin with his thumb. Although she stopped moving, tiny gasps escaped from under the hood. Her body quivered.

Please don't move, ålskling.

He'd have to pull her across quickly and then get them the hell out of here. A long shot, but there was still a chance he might save her. Grasping the leather strap on her leg, he quietly tore it, the superhuman strength in his fingers serving him well.

What would they do to her if they had him, too? *Herre Gud,* he didn't want to even think about it. All he wanted to do was remove the woman he loved from the nightmare in which she was trapped. An immortal nightmare he'd brought down on her tiny, human shoulders.

Brandon's footsteps had grown faint but hadn't stopped yet in a pivot at the end of the aisle.

Dante tightened his grip on her bound upper arms, cursing as she whimpered faintly.

The steps slowed.

Now.

He slid Hannah's limp body over the metal pallet, hating her little squeak as she bumped on the shelf. In one motion, he ripped through the bonds holding her arms, hauled her to his chest, and tugged off the knit cap. He kissed her sweaty lips so desperately that their teeth scraped.

Helvete, he'd never wanted someone in his arms more than Hannah right this minute. Cradling her thin frame, he sprinted down the row.

A figure appeared out of the darkness.

Lurid, red light flared from the palm of a spidery hand.

"Going somewhere?"

Chapter 18

The thin voice of evil cut through the darkness like a lazily drawn blade. Not good. Dante lowered Hannah to her feet and tucked her into his side, holding on to her as she wobbled. How could Dante keep her safe when *he* had shown up?

"My lord Jerahmeel." Dante dipped his head in expected deference, trying to hide his panic. Surely the Lord Most Vile could hear the drumroll of Dante's heart right now. "Uh, we were just leaving."

"Of course you weren't," purred Jerahmeel.

In the dim shadows, the evil man flicked his nonilluminated hand, indicating the end of the warehouse, toward the dock area.

Deep, sickening dread dropped like lead into his gut, and Dante supported Hannah as they walked down the aisle. Her shaky legs gave out from under her after only a few steps.

Dante glared at the seething, sulfurous figure behind him and swept her into his arms. Damn it, she was beyond vulnerable. Watching her squint into the dark surroundings, Dante groaned. She couldn't see her way out of this warehouse, much less stand a snowball's chance against Jerahmeel and Brandon.

He considered his options to get her out of here. Nothing came to mind. This situation had no good ending.

Brandon met them at the end of the aisle. The blow the minion landed on Dante's jaw rocked him back so violently, he nearly dropped Hannah. Dante spit out blood.

"You can't take my bait." Brandon snickered. "Well, actually you did!"

"Shut up, minion," Jerahmeel growled.

They rounded the end of the aisle and stopped between the two racks. Dante stood still, trying not to see Hannah's unspoken question as she peered up at him. He had no answers, only horrible options.

Jerahmeel and Brandon flanked them.

Waiting. Circling.

Jerahmeel brushed a piece of lint from his tailored silk shirt; a tiny finger of smoke rose from the fabric.

Kristus.

"You'll want to set your human down for our little demonstration," Jerahmeel said. He maintained only the thinnest veneer of decorum now.

How would Dante get her out of here?

Helvete. He wouldn't.

Neither he nor Hannah would leave here alive. Or worse yet, they might leave here alive. Only it wouldn't be on anyone's terms but Jerahmeel's.

Dante lowered her to stand again, but her knees buckled. His rage flared as lines of blood seeped through her clothes. She hung on to Dante's arm but remained stooped over. Bruises purpled her delicate skin. She squinted up at him. Damn. She still believed he'd get her out of here. Unfortunately, he had nothing to offer but disappointment and pain.

The only sound in the cool warehouse was the minion snickering softly to himself. His red hair glowed eerily in the yellow rays of the flashlight.

"She's an innocent, Jerahmeel. Let her go," Dante said.

"This human is anything but innocent, my dear Dante, as you well know. Besides, she's interesting. I want her."

Dante's hand curled into a hard fist.

"Ah, ah, ah. You can't touch me." Jerahmeel's voice oozed like slime over Dante's ears.

"And you can't touch her." Dante prayed for leverage.

A dark frown creased Jerahmeel's normally unlined countenance, and he seethed, the smell of burnt eggs emanating from his fastidiously groomed appearance.

"But I sure can." Brandon ogled Hannah.

"And I can compel her to do my bidding any way I see fit as long as I don't touch her," Jerahmeel rumbled. "I find this human's... abilities fascinating and would like to learn more. Just like Peter's woman—her delicious blood was refreshing, unusual. Reminded me of someone else." He stared into space for a minute until he blinked his coal-black eyes and focused on Hannah. "Perhaps a bit of experimentation is in order."

"No," Dante growled.

Hannah held her ground, keeping close by his side, but she swayed where she stood. Stark fear suffused her features.

"Let's get started," Jerahmeel said.

Brandon smirked, his thin lips disappearing.

Herre Gud, this would be bad.

Hannah straightened up and squared her shoulders. Unfortunately, even at full height, her tiny frame intimidated no one in this room. Dante's heart swelled with pride at the effort.

"What exactly are you going to do?" She squinted in the general direction of Jerahmeel.

The Lord of Evil's black, groomed eyebrows rose as he sketched a slight bow.

"Why, we're going to find out what skills you have, my dear. We'll determine exactly what your limits are and how your talents can benefit me. And, as added incentive, if you cooperate, I might not destroy your lover."

"What?" Paling, she looked up at Dante. "What?"

"Don't listen to him. Listen to me. Just try to survive. Please."

"Dante?" Tears welled in her soft, brown eyes—eyes he might not see again after tonight.

"Let's begin." Jerahmeel motioned to Brandon.

Dante tensed as he stepped in front of Hannah. If they were going to do her harm, they'd have to come through him first.

Brandon struck without warning.

Dante, intent on protecting Hannah from the minion, didn't react fast enough when the ginger asshole's fist shattered his cheekbone. Stars burst in his field of vision, but he had no time to regroup as Brandon pounded him in quick succession, splintering his ribs, rupturing God-knew-what else.

Finally recovering enough to respond, Dante fought back with bone-crushing blows, driving the minion back. One satisfying crunch of bone told him he'd destroyed the minion's weasely nose. *Utmarkt.* Excellent.

Hannah's terrified cry drew his attention. Jerahmeel had backed her up to the shelves, effectively trapping her. He didn't touch her. He couldn't. But she didn't know that. At least Jerahmeel stuck with the rules.

Brandon's violent punch blindsided Dante enough to drive him to the floor. Then there was silence. Why didn't the minion finish it?

The swish caught his attention a split second before the whip dragged fingers of jagged metal through the skin of his back. *Jävla skit.*

The minion grinned, brandishing the nasty weapon. Another strike and Dante's arm opened up, bleeding in eight fiery tracks.

"Dante!" Hannah cried out.

Jerahmeel stepped aside with a magnanimous smile and a negligent wave of his arm.

"No, Hannah, stay back!" Dante yelled.

She ran to him right when Brandon struck again. The metal-tipped weapon shredded the skin of her upper chest. The horrible cry wrenched from her lips flayed Dante's heart, and he caught her as she collapsed.

"Oh my, unanticipated collateral damage," Jerahmeel said sarcastically. "Too bad. But, since you're there, my dear, would you please heal Dante's wounds, too?"

"No!" Dante wheezed, pressing his hand against the knitting bones of his chest. With a sick pop, his cheekbone repaired itself. "She just healed her brother. You'll kill her."

"I think not. Besides, I want to discover her limits. Know what she can do for me."

Jerahmeel licked his blood-red lips and steepled long, manicured fingers in a contemplative gesture. Dante didn't buy the relaxed pose for a minute.

The top of Hannah's T-shirt hung in bloody tatters.

Dante needed to kill someone. Now. Screaming fury filled his head as the knife vibrated against his leg, making its desires known.

Fists ready, he rose and spun around.

"Ah, ah, ah, Dante. Let her try to heal you, or we'll flay her alive while you watch." Jerahmeel's avid grin never reached his eyes.

Brandon tapped the whip handle on his leg. Dante took grim satisfaction that the minion's grin was missing a few teeth.

But not satisfying enough. Problem not solved.

Dante knelt back down over Hannah's shaking body. He tried to move her but was unable to touch any part of her without causing pain.

She reached bloody hands up to him.

"Don't. Don't do this. Please," he said.

Hannah suffered because of him. And this? This hell was what he had to offer a woman?

"If you're okay, then it's worth it," she said.

Shame burned his face. He deserved none of her willingness to help him. Zero.

Kristus.

"No. Healing me will destroy you, *älskling*. It's not worth it."

"If I don't try, then they'll destroy you. This may be your only chance to get out of here," she whispered.

Her skin glistened with blood. Tears rolled over freshly bruised and swollen skin, the injuries she'd taken from her brother. How much could one human absorb and survive? Apparently, Jerahmeel wanted to find out.

Hugging him close, she put her mouth to his ear. Even in this hellish situation, her warm, low voice sent a frisson of desire into his groin. Always thinking with his cock; how sick could a man get? He focused on the words she whispered.

"Act like the healing doesn't work. Might buy you time."

He stiffened and she shushed him.

"It's your last chance," she breathed.

With her fine hands pressing his jaw, she transferred quickly, sucking his pain away like a candle that had been snuffed out. She made a show of trying to heal him for another minute, finally collapsing on the ground, acting defeated.

"I can't make it work, there's nothing there."

She curled in a ball, hiding her extra-battered face and broken torso, full of Dante's injuries.

To do his part, Dante wearily moaned and continued to act wounded. Truth be told, his condition couldn't be better. He felt like he could go another ten rounds. Ready to launch into action, his muscles quivered in adrenaline-fueled anticipation. Hopefully, with the blood staining everything, Jerahmeel wouldn't notice that Dante had been completely healed.

She had given him one chance to save her.

One chance to save them both.

"It's too much," she said to Jerahmeel, holding her head in her hands. Somehow she got back to her feet and stood up straight with what had to be an immense force of will. "I'm so sorry, Dante; I can't heal you," she said.

At a nod from his boss, Brandon snickered and approached Hannah.

"Then Dante won't be able to stop me from doing my job." He waited in front of her, tapping the wicked crop on his leg. "Your turn."

She flinched away, but the metal-tipped whip still caught her arm. Screaming, she tried to protect herself.

Jerahmeel's eyes glowed like embers. "She'll learn the price of disobedience. If I'm going to keep her, there can be no dissent." He gestured to Brandon, who brandished the weapon again, stepping closer to Hannah huddled next to the rack.

"Finish it," Jerahmeel said, throwing his arms up in the air. "She's useless, too weak. This human can't help us. I'd hoped for much more." He rolled a glossy curl between two thin fingers and inspected his nails.

Dante consolidated his rage into one colossal burst of fury. He slammed into Brandon, sending him crashing against the metal shelves.

Hannah's bruised body distracted him again. When Dante turned to check on her, Brandon hit him at a dead run. Dante hurtled backward in the air twenty feet down the aisle and dented the sliding freight door at the end of the building. His vision dimmed.

Fight, damn it. Stay conscious. For Hannah.

Off to the left, he spied a movement. *Vad i helvete?* He squinted into the shadows. A khaki-clad form emerged, severe bun and all. Nurse Ratched. And… Barnaby?

A slight smile lifted the corners of Ruth's lips, and she nodded at Dante.

He might just pull this off.

Shaking his head to clear it, he peeled himself off the metal freight door. His world was still off balance, but it would have to be enough. At least he had reinforcements. Or witnesses.

Down the aisle, lit by the eerie yellow flashlight glow, Jerahmeel stepped aside to avoid the pool of Hannah's rapidly spreading blood. Murmuring to Brandon, Jerahmeel tugged at his oiled curls thoughtfully with a bored, bemused expression.

Brandon had thrown down the crop and now gripped Hannah by the neck, pushing her into the metal shelves. She didn't make a sound as she stared at Brandon.

Jerahmeel chuckled. "A little deception from this human? Mumming as though you couldn't do the job, my dear? No matter. Paltry as your powers are, no one else will have use of them. And she only serves as a distraction to you, sir." He tipped his pointed chin at Brandon. "Minion, destroy the human."

Dante's world narrowed to the horrific scene before him. The minion dropped Hannah to her feet, pinning her upright by the neck as she sagged.

Dante flew off the sliding door at a blazing sprint.

Brandon drew back his hand and aimed it at Hannah.

She glanced toward Dante, a sad, sweet smile on her battered lips.

Brandon sneered at Dante. And then he drove his fist into Hannah's chest, collapsing bones and ligaments.

She crumpled to the floor, her head cracking against the concrete.

Chapter 19

Dante smashed into Brandon with every ounce of strength in his body and his soul. Knocking Brandon into a shelf, he indented the minion's skull, but even semiconscious, Brandon still fought.

With an iron-fisted blow, Dante stunned the minion. Pulling Brandon's head around 180 degrees with a grinding crunch, Dante slammed the minion's neck against his bent knee.

He dropped Brandon, now truly dead, to the floor with a satisfying thump.

Ruth skidded to a halt next to him.

"Need help?" Not a hair was out of place. She wore an impassive expression across her smooth, sculpted features. Even her functional khakis were pristine and wrinkle free. Nurse Ratched indeed.

"You're a little late, aren't you?"

"Ah, Dante, your woman." Ruth indicated toward the floor.

Hannah's face was purple. Curled in a ball, she convulsed violently, her entire body spasming. Veins stood out starkly against her thin neck. Her eyes rolled back, unseeing, as she gurgled. Blood flowed from her mouth.

No, ålskling, no! Not after everything we've overcome.

He sunk to the floor, cradling her in his lap as she suffocated in his arms.

Barnaby knelt next to him.

"What, old man? Can you help me?"

"No." The bald man smiled and winked.

Dante struggled to understand what Barnaby was trying to convey. *Tell me.*

Jerahmeel called out to Barnaby, "You can't intervene, my friend."

Barnaby replied, "And you can no longer interfere. Your minion failed. Rules are rules, my lord." He looked straight at Dante and repeated, "Rules are rules, got it?"

Barnaby winked again.

What the hell?

With sudden clarity, the pieces of a puzzle came together: the Meaningful Kill, Hannah's healing power, Dante's inherent ability to heal himself. There was a connection.

On instinct, Dante stripped off Hannah's tattered shirt, wincing at the damage. Her sternum had caved in from the strike, purple and crushed, her ribs moving out of sync around the breastbone. Sharp bone edges jutted up against the skin of her chest. He quickly removed his shirt as well. He lay flat on the cold, concrete floor and pulled her on top of him and into his arms.

Please don't let her be too far gone.

"*Älskling*, my love. Let me in."

She wheezed a horrible, tortured gasp and stopped breathing. There was nothing he could do, except maybe one thing.

"Please, Hannah, let me in."

She now lay deathly still on his chest.

Kristus, no. Not this woman. He chafed her cooling arms and her blue-tinged skin, trying to revive her.

She was gone.

Pulling her into his body, he put a leg over her thighs, trying to surround her with his body heat, to revive her. He wanted to give her what was his—his immortality, his strength.

His love.

Nothing.

No breath.

Just her still, tiny frame draped over him.

Tears seared the sides of his face. He hadn't shed tears since Lars lay frostbitten and near death on that fateful night. The night that put everything in motion and led Dante to this moment.

Their chest walls pressed tightly together, Dante detected a tiny flicker of sensation. Then sluggishly, as if the dying cells sensed the great effort it would take, the transfer began. One drop at a time.

Too slow.

Please, keep going, he begged silently.

She lay limp, hanging over his body.

"Come back to me," he said to the warehouse ceiling.

Coldness surrounded him, the frigid floor beneath him, the ice-cold body on top of him. He opened his soul, his heart, his being, to the little connection that remained between their skin. He visualized pushing his will and his soul into her and pulling the damage away from her. A trade. Within the connection between them, her damaged body tentatively probed back. Within the transfer, her skin clung to him, as if they were magnetized.

More. He wasn't sure which one of them had that thought, linked as they were.

The knife. This had something to do with the knife.

He bent his knee and released the starving blade. Pressing it flat against his own bleeding chest, he took care to avoid Hannah's body. The knife glowed hungry and green, pulsing in time with Dante's heart. *Ja*, he'd give the knife what it desired tonight. Slake the blade's relentless urge to drink its fill of a soul.

The transfer now flowed more briskly between them; the remnants of her essence moved into his body, trading with his Indebted healing ability. Agony sliced through him as her pain rushed in like a tornado, sucking his life force out. Wounds bled anew. His chest ached as his own sternum cracked and collapsed as he absorbed her suffering. He couldn't breathe.

Take it. Take all of me for you, älskling.

He found his purpose. A reason to live all these years.

He would trade his life for hers.

Fire-laced cuts, snapped bones, ripped muscle. He wanted it all. Every ounce of pain he absorbed reduced her torture. But would it be enough? Would she make it back to him?

An odd sensation grew against his chest until he realized her ribs had pushed back into proper position. The strange creak of her sternum expanding against his chest sent an empathetic shudder through his spine. Then his own breastbone caved in.

Had she warmed up or was that just his own body heat radiating back toward him?

One thump. Did he imagine it? Then two. Doubt. Elation.

Her heart beat once, twice, against his shattered ribs. The knife pulsed in time to the slow, stuttering rhythm. Dante's blood flowed over the greedy knife, coating it, feeding it what it most desired.

Please, take more, ålskling. *I give you everything.*

He concentrated on opening his body and soul. Visualized propelling his essence into her small body. Icy death coursed through his veins. He let it stream into him, let it consume him. He didn't care as long as it helped her.

He took all of her pain. Exchanged it. Welcomed it.

Eternal release, his soul for hers. Anything it took to get the destruction away from Hannah.

Above him floated three faces. One wrinkled and worried, one nonplussed, one fashionably furious.

"This is unacceptable." Jerahmeel scowled. "I have to keep my employees working to feed me."

"Looks like your plan to get rid of the distraction may have failed. Remember, you cannot interfere," Barnaby said.

"Well, you'd best recall your end of the bargain, old man. No help," Jerahmeel growled. "Let it run its course. If Blackstone survives, he should never again bring attention to himself or I'll find him and destroy him myself."

It sounded like the two men were talking in a bowl; their voices were separated from Dante by miles of empty space.

Barnaby dipped his bald pate. "Of course, my lord."

"Hell. I've lost another minion and one of my sources of power. I will not soon forget your meddling, old man. Your days are numbered." Jerahmeel tipped his dark head to the ceiling and howled, "*C'est vraiment des conneries!*"

Barnaby smiled. "Yes, I know you think this is bullshit, but you're powerless in this situation, my *lord*."

Ruth's disembodied head displayed a satisfied smirk. Funny, Dante didn't picture her the jocular type.

"I haven't forgotten your presence, as well, madam." Jerahmeel stared at Ruth. "You look particularly lovely this evening. Perhaps we can spend more time together."

Her upper lip curled as she cringed away.

The fury on his countenance darkened. "Well, then *mademoiselle*, you'd better perform exceptional work now that I've lost another employee. If you don't, anyone you care for will suffer. That's a promise."

Her neat eyebrows rose as she melted away into the shadows, out of Dante's line of sight. His field of vision dimmed around the edges. The knife glowed brightly now, and Dante couldn't hold it anymore. He dropped it to the concrete floor, but it continued to consume his pooling blood.

"I should simply finish him myself. Put all of us out of our misery. This theater of suffering is ridiculous," Jerahmeel said with a glare.

Dante struggled to keep his weakening arms locked around Hannah.

Barnaby cleared his throat. "You shall do nothing, my lord. If he's alive at the end of this ordeal, then he's alive. If not, he'll be dead. Either way, it's no longer your concern. He won't be part of your cadre of soul-takers anymore."

A howl of fury echoed off the concrete and metal of the warehouse. Jerahmeel leaned down and snatched the knife away from Dante. The evil one gazed longingly at the sated, glowing knife and licked his ruby-red lips. He stroked Hannah's bruised shoulder with an expression of desire mixed with anger. Then, with a rumble from deep in the Earth that shook the entire warehouse, Jerahmeel disappeared.

Footsteps on the concrete grew louder. Dante twisted his head to see Ruth grab a bloodied Scott, stopping his headlong rush.

"Going somewhere?" she said, her eyes turning the Indebted's characteristic black of heightened emotion.

"Hannah, oh God." Scott panted, sweat and blood mixing on his face. "I left this building, but then all of a sudden, there was no Brandon here—" He pointed to his head. "What the fuck happened? I remember bits and pieces. It's like the last few weeks were a big fog. Hannah? Jesus, is she dead?"

"Yes, thanks to you." Dante wheezed against his broken ribcage. "Get him the hell out of here."

"My son, reconsider," Barnaby said. "I daresay this boy was under the minion's thrall."

"That's no excuse. If you really loved her, you would have fought it." Dante clamped his teeth together at a wave of pain. Hannah's pain.

"I tried to fight him, damn it, but nothing worked. Even when he let me go, I tried to stay here, but the need to leave was too much. I had to get out of this place. Christ, I'm a bastard."

Scott knelt and laid his hand on a less-bloody area of her back. She didn't move.

"Is she dead?" he whispered.

"Barnaby?" Dante stared up at his elderly friend.

With his limbs becoming icy and lifeless, Dante couldn't hold her any longer and his arms dropped to the floor. Hannah lay motionless on his chest, her skin warming him. Normally he would love to have her body against his, but not like this.

Still unconscious, she gave a paroxysmal, shuddering gasp and fell limp again, her repaired ribs rising slowly now.

"Barnaby, help her. I can't," he whispered.

The man nodded solemnly. "We will take care of both of you."

Scott sniffed. The wetness on his face was from more than sweat and blood now.

Dante took a deep, painful breath and exhaled completely, one long whoosh emptying his body of air, of life, of 300 years of meaningless existence.

Dante Blackstone finally died.

Chapter 20

Hannah burned.

She swam through a surreal watery expanse. When she tried to inhale, she clawed at the frigid liquid lodged in her throat.

So cold. Her bones froze, cracked. Was this real?

As she tried to surface, she bumped up against solid ice, smooth and hard beneath her fingers. Not air. She skimmed beneath it, searching for an opening as she held her breath for an infinite amount of time. She should desperately need air. She should panic.

There, a break in the suffocating frigid depths.

Through that opening in the ice, odd sounds washed over her, indistinct, murmuring. Maybe a whale? Or bull seals chatting somewhere above her? How had she gotten to the Arctic?

So cold. It was becoming difficult to fight the downward pull. Blackness beckoned with the promise of succor, luring her into the depths to sleep forever. Why try to push through the ice above when she could simply drift into the open arms of the deep?

Aching legs propelled her upward once more. Where was that opening? She pressed against the hopelessly endless ice that stretched far into the distance. Why try to find a way out?

She couldn't come up with a single good reason within the mind-numbing, cold watery expanse.

Too much effort.

Couldn't move.

Rippling sound rolled over her suspended body once more. She couldn't discern individual tones. Piqued curiosity motivated her to push against the enticing blackness below.

Move, legs, move. Up.

Too tired.

I'll rest in this deep. Drift lower, away from the unyielding surface. It will be so much easier.

She had no reason to push through the ice.

As she sank back into the depths, the water sounds flowed over her once more, forming into words she could not quite hear. Interested, she struggled again toward the barrier, listening.

A soothing, familiar voice, warmth coursing over her in the frigid darkness. Out of reach.

She skimmed below the surface, not caring to breathe. Her heavy legs barely moved for all the exhaustion.

"'... for most men are unaware...'"

Kicking the water a few extra times, she strained upward to press a cold ear against the smooth ice.

"'... that what is in the power of magicians to accomplish...'"

Where was that opening in the ice?

"'... that the heart can also accomplish...'"

She raised a hand against the glacial smoothness and propelled herself along, looking for release from the watery tomb. Pressing harder on the ice, she began to panic. Her lungs burned, craving oxygen.

"'... by dint of love and bravery.'"

Don't stop.

She had to get to the voice. A line of warmth flowed from an opening in the frigid, watery abyss. When she held up her arms, the warmth tugged at her.

She floated in air, not water. A crisp flapping sounded familiar, like a page being turned.

A throat cleared.

As she rose once more, she squinted against the brilliant glow. Abused lungs ached with futile effort.

The rumble next to her felt familiar.

She wanted to reach out. Couldn't. Too tired.

Lying on a fluffy cloud in the heated air, she let the words roll over her as she left the cold depths far behind.

"Fold your arms 'round me close and strain me so that our hearts may break and our souls go free at last."

The low, vibrating tone resonated through her bones.

Tristan and Iseult?

"'Take me to that happy place of which you told me long ago.'"

His smooth bass voice broke. Squinting against the painfully bright light, she saw his golden head bowed over the book as he sat in a chair next to her.

Dante? What was he doing here? Where in the world were they? Without her glasses, she could only make out a bright area nearby, probably a window.

"'The fields whence none return, but where great singers sing their songs forever.'"

The book closed with a comfortable, thick thud. He lifted his head slowly, as though it weighed too much. She squinted and saw dark circles under his eyes. Pale skin. Pain. Fear. His clear, blue gaze locked on to her.

Sadness and hope flickered there.

"Hannah?" The chair clattered to the floor as he leapt to his feet.

It took so much effort to push the corners of her mouth up. Exhausted by the movement, she drifted back down toward the water for a moment.

"Hannah, are you here with me now? *Älskling?*"

A large wave moved her. He'd sat on the bed.

When she cracked open her eyelids again, his broad face hovered above her.

"Dante?" she whispered, throat raw.

"*Herre Gud*, I thought you were gone. It's been days since…"

"Tired."

"*Ja*, me too."

She tried to move her hand toward him and failed. Gently, he picked it up and guided her palm to his warm lips. Not as warm as she remembered, but his touch sent tendrils of happiness through her all the same.

"How do you feel?" he asked.

"Like I've been taken apart and put back together all wrong." She stretched her legs and wiggled her toes.

"My foot, I can feel it again! What happened?"

"A miracle."

"How long has it been since…"

"You've been gone for nearly a week."

"So how am I still alive?"

"I know a very good doctor and nurse."

He twirled the IV tubing in front of her, tracing it to a bright yellow solution that infused into her arm.

"It was a team effort. Allie scrounged supplies. Peter drove everything we needed up here, and Ruth hooked you up."

"So what's that?"

She pointed toward the tubing.

"Nutrition. We weren't sure if it would work, but I wasn't going to give up. I had no idea if any of my Hannah would come back." He sandwiched her hand between his. "Can you heal?"

Opening herself to unwrap the imaginary barrier, she released all resistance to let the connection flow.

Nothing happened. Her hand remained in his firm grip, but all she sensed was warmth from his skin, no prickle of an essence for essence exchange.

"No transfer."

"Interesting. I wondered whether or not you'd still have your gift." He rested his forehead on hers. "Truthfully, I'm not sorry. Every time you used your ability, it hurt you."

She relaxed back into the pillows. "I'm mixed about it. On one hand, I liked knowing I had something to give to others. But you're right, whenever I'd absorb an injury, it hurt like heck."

"You have plenty to give just by being here." His voice rumbled through her skull and into her chest.

"What about Brandon? And Scott?" She tried to sit up and failed, sinking back into soft cotton bedding. "And you?" Where were the injuries he'd endured for her? The bruises on his face?

"Brandon... well, he wasn't really alive to begin with, but I suppose calling him dead is the easiest explanation. He'll never bother you again."

"Gone?"

When he cupped his hands around her face, she drowned in those clear blue eyes.

"He tried to take away the one thing precious to me in this world. He nearly succeeded. So I destroyed him."

"Scott?"

"Once Brandon died, his control over Scott stopped. Your brother came back to try to help. He wanted to be here with you but wouldn't stick around."

"I don't understand."

"He cleaned out the house and left. Said he'd try to return when he was able. Said he was sorry, but he needed to go away for a while."

"Explains why he'd been acting so out of character the last few weeks."

She sighed. Scott had moved on. She wasn't sad or empty. Just adequately informed. Strange. She licked her lips.

With a groan, Dante brushed his mouth over hers tenderly. Waves of warm happiness flowed through her body.

Finally, he pulled back. "Also, I was dead for a few days there."

"What?"

"Right before your heart stopped, I got you to open up enough to do one more transfer and exchange my unhuman healing abilities for your injuries."

"What happened to you?"

"I took on all of your damage and died."

"Dante!"

He scooted back, leaned against the headboard and pulled her into his lap. Nestled between his muscled legs, his body emitted less heat than she remembered. He held her securely, and her head tucked into the hollow between his shoulder and neck. If he didn't support her, she'd slide back down onto the bed, so poor was her strength. Reaching over to the nightstand, he retrieved her glasses and gently slid them on her face.

He kissed the top of her head. "I got better."

"How much better?" She craned her neck to study his expression.

"Mostly better."

Although he smiled down at her, fatigue etched new lines on his handsome features.

"I'm human now."

"Is that good?"

"It's wonderful. Killing myself to save you counts as a Meaningful Kill by the twisted rules of the Indebted."

"So?"

"So I'm officially unemployed. I had to see if my efforts paid off, if you would come back to me. If you didn't survive, I wouldn't have continued on much longer."

"What?" Would he have truly killed himself?

"Shush, I'm here now. And so are you."

Dante caressed her cheek as he cradled her in his massive arms. His strong but gentle fingers were like heaven as they slid through her hair.

"Are you totally healed now?" she asked.

"A few aches and pains I didn't have before, but I'm okay."

"But you're human?"

"*Ja.*" His smile lit up his entire handsome face.

"What will you do now as a human?"

Her heart thudded.

"Well, I was thinking about settling down."

"Sounds boring, especially after the wild life you've lived for centuries."

"That wasn't living."

"Won't you miss living forever?"

"Being human sounds fantastic right about now. Maybe I'll get a nine-to-five job. Become schlumpy and bald. Grow old with someone special. Yup, a perfect life."

She lifted her hand to stroke the arm that supported her. It took so much effort.

"Got a lucky lady picked out?" When she looked up at him, he grasped her hand and pressed it to his lips, closing his eyes for a moment.

"I wasn't sure if she'd come back to me."

"You pulled me back. Your voice. You, Dante."

His strong features shone with a new light. He scrambled out of the bed and stuffed several pillows around her legs and hips to keep her from sliding back down. The motion unbalanced her, and it took a moment to focus again.

He knelt next to the bed.

"Hannah, I am ancient and unworthy. I've done so many bad things that I have lost count. But with you, I'm a better man. And I want to be an even better man. Would you please put me out of my eternal misery and do me the honor of becoming my wife?"

"When you say it like that, it sounds so tempting." She chuckled. "So you want me to marry a criminal so he won't hate himself anymore?"

"Um, well, I guess it didn't come out right. Can I try again?"

"No."

"Oh." His expression was crestfallen.

"Dante?"

"Yes?"

"Of course I'll marry you. I don't want anyone else. I'll never want anyone else. It's only been you from the moment we met."

The bear hug that pulled her away from the pillows hurt her joints, but she didn't care. She'd been right.

She was his.

He was hers.

About the Author

Jillian David lives near the end of the Earth with her nut of a husband and two bossy cats. To escape the sometimes-stressful world of the rural physician, she writes while on call and in her free time. She enjoys taking realistic settings and adding a twist of "what if." Running or hiking on local trails often promotes plot development.

She would love for readers to connect on Twitter @ jilliandavid13 or on her blog at *http://jilliandavid.net*. Readers are always welcome to email her at jilliandavid13@yahoo.com.

More from This Author
(From *Immortal Flame* by Jillian David)

Old things weren't always useless. Take the Swiss watch Peter Blackstone wore. Tired leather strap, scratched face, older than most mortals. He had taken it off the wrist of an enemy, a dying *Wehrmacht* captain, in the icy forest of northern France in retaliation for the captain shooting Peter in the arm. Call it a souvenir turned taunting, old, reliable companion.

Not that the damned watch helped the traffic. A cold mist slowed the cars on I-84 outside La Grande, Oregon. Steep, pine-rich mountains rose on either side, funneling bumper-to-bumper vehicles into the narrow canyon. No gritting of Peter's teeth or clenching of the steering wheel could stop that interminable timepiece from tick, tick, ticking down like a demolition bomb timer, reminding him how late he would be and the likely outcome of his tardiness.

His final assignment. He hoped.

Damn endless existence. He needed to complete this last assignment, the Meaningful Kill. Finally put an end to the monster he'd become.

His gut knotted. Being late for his assignment created too much attention. Better to stay inconspicuous. Hell, he wore a seat belt only so police wouldn't have a reason to ticket him. Too much to explain.

The semi ten inches from his front bumper flashed its brakes. Peter slowed and negotiated one of the curves on the stretch of road. He rubbed his jaw and glanced again at the watch.

Hell, even now, he could smell the sweet-sharp scent of snow and blood and hear the moans from the not-yet-dead as bodies littered the forest that ugly night in the Ardennes. Men crying out for their mothers in English and German, the sounds blending into a nightmare of suffering, as they were frozen alive.

He glanced in the rearview mirror out of habit. Even after all these years, his dark brown hair would never turn gray, no matter how much he wished to age. It was the curse of the Indebted.

Screeching tires jolted him back to reality. *Hell.* He swerved and barely missed the braking semi. The driver behind him wasn't as quick, and the pickup plowed into the back of Peter's SUV, propelling it into the concrete barrier. Air whooshed out of his lungs as he jerked against the seat belt. His neck snapped forward as a ripping sensation seared pain into the base of his skull.

His SUV ramped the barrier, the undercarriage screaming against wet concrete. Peter's entire world inverted, sky beneath him and rocks above, with only a thin casing of metal standing between his head and the scraping rocks. *Not good.* He threw his hands over his head and pushed against the charcoal upholstery in time for the airbag to erupt from the steering wheel. His ribcage exploded in sharp, hot agony that sent fireworks of light bursting in his vision.

After that, it was as if his own car waged a personal assault on him. But the blade would be no match against the airborne missiles of glass piercing his face. To make things even more interesting, the SUV righted itself but then jolted halfway down the mountain slope.

Peter's head snapped forward and back, and a loud crack reverberated from his lower back, out of tune with the groans and screeches emanating from the nearly obliterated vehicle.

An eternity later—he didn't use the term lightly—the crumpled metal death trap came to rest at the bottom of a muddy embankment, the yellow hazard lights flashing, horn blaring... and upside down.

Stunned, Peter dangled from the seat belt. His ears rang. His skull throbbed. His left arm had bent into an unnatural angle against the door handle. *Not good at all.* A normal human would be dead by now. Unfortunately, he still lived.

Hell. He was most definitely going to be late for that appointment.

The knife strapped to his lower leg pulsed, warming up in hungry anticipation for the assignment. That damned, cursed weapon tied to his damned, cursed existence.

The sky and ground continued to spin in his vision. Over the hum of his ringing ears, liquid drizzled onto the fabric ceiling, a constant tapping sound in the sudden silence. One touch to his head revealed a chunk of skin partially detached from his skull.

Steam hissed from the engine as the tangy-sweet scent of antifreeze mixed with burnt oil. Taking a deep breath, he dragged fumes into his burning lungs. From far away, voices drifted down to him.

Pain lanced through his neck when he tried to see out the window. He had to fix that broken arm.

Damn, this is going to hurt.

With his right hand, he grabbed his left wrist and pulled. His guttural howl echoed in the destroyed car as he forced arm bones back into place, grinding the broken ends against each other. He squeezed his hand over the injury. The arm had started to knit, but he needed the bones to heal even faster. His body would repair the life-threatening injuries first and his head and broken bones second, but it would take way too much time.

The whine of his car's smoking engine and drone of the horn muffled the shouts of bystanders scrambling down the hill.

Have to get out of here.

He attempted to exit the car, leaning against the mangled door, but his numb legs wouldn't move. They'd lodged between the pedals pushed in by the crumpled engine block and the steering column. Instinctive fear rose up. Trapped again. He forced himself to relax while suspended upside down. In the distance sirens wailed.

So much for being inconspicuous.

Damn it. He needed to stash the knife before anyone saw it.

Reaching his unbroken arm down—no, up—to the pinned, insensate leg, Peter unclasped the top strap of the holster. One more strap. As he strained against the seat belt, pain erupted in his lower back, but now he could touch the lower clasp.

The voices of his rescuers drew closer, urging him to work faster. Frantic, he brushed the buckle with this fingertips and opened the clasp. Fresh sweat beaded his brow, and his jaw ached from clenching.

The strap slid free of the buckle, and the knife fell to the roof with a dull *thunk*, landing in pooled blood. The physical agony of separation from the weapon hit him like a punch to his gut. The yearning to connect with the blade burned with a searing inferno in his chest.

Focus.

Stretching, he grabbed the knife and shoved it into the seam of the passenger seat.

He gritted his teeth as another wave of pain swamped him.

• • •

It had been one month and twelve days since her last vision.

Allison La Croix pulled her hair from the jacket collar, straightened her scrubs, and closed the car door. Hefting her overnight bag onto her shoulder, she paused and inhaled the cold, early spring air. Could she do it today? Could she walk through the doors of Grande Ronde Hospital's emergency department?

Every day when she passed through those sliding glass doors, apprehension mounted like a needle tip poised just above her skin. Her right hand still throbbed with residual echoes of electrical fire on her fingertips from her last connection. How long could she avoid touching anyone skin to skin? How long could she avoid triggering her twisted gift? The intervals between her visions were growing shorter, but she had no idea why. How many more could she handle?

With a determined breath, she entered the ER at 7:55 a.m., right on time. Ambulance bays vacant? Check. No screaming family members outside the ER door? Check. No *whump, whump* of chopper blades coming in for a landing? Double check.

Maybe today will be a good day.

She twisted her long hair into a clip as the familiar flowery scent of chemical disinfectant wafted over her. As Allison reached the registration desk, she waved at a plump, smiling, older woman.

"Morning, Doctor Al," the woman said.

"Hi, Marcie. How's it been so far?"

The receptionist held up the latest bestselling medical thriller. "Real calm. I've had time to catch up on some reading."

Allison smiled at her choice of words. Doctors and staff *never* said the "Q" word when they came onto shift. Merely thinking the word "quiet" seemed to magically attract multi-victim traumas, drug-seekers, and large quantities of cardiac arrests.

"You think it's going to rain today?" Allison asked.

She averted her gaze as Marcie changed the computer screen from a shopping website to the hospital registration system.

"Hope so. Maybe light rain later. The Wallowas look good. Might get more snow next weekend."

To the east, powdery snow covered the 9,000-foot peaks of the Wallowa Mountains. She'd give anything to be up there right now, surrounded by the mellow scent of pine, serenaded by the burble of clear water running down the valleys. Hiking or snowshoeing, it didn't matter; either was like aloe on a burn to Allison's soul.

Walking to the back of the ER, she dropped her overnight bag on an empty chair in the doctor's work area. She waited until her graying counterpart, Dr. Buddy Clark, finished a dictation, his voice gravelly. His shoulders sagged from the twenty-four-hour shift, which had also deepened the circles beneath his kind eyes. She thanked her thirty-two-year-old body for its youth; at least she recovered much faster than her sixty-something colleague.

"Anything I can take care of for you?" she asked.

"Not this morning. Last night was pretty tame, long may it last." He made the sign of a cross, merrily kissed his fingers, and raised them as his eyes twinkled. Buddy, cheerful even when tired, was nothing if not consistent with his superstitions.

"Don't jinx me." She patted him on the back, careful not to touch his skin.

"Hey, Al, did you consider my offer to set you up with that physical therapist?" He leaned back in his chair and rubbed his stubbled jowls. "He'd be a perfect match. Educated, outdoorsy, probably a good family guy. Cute, but not too metrosexual. Ruggedly handsome."

She cringed. A family guy? God, no. Too many risks. The possibility of another vision of a loved one filled her with cold terror. She couldn't trust herself to invest in a relationship when all she would think about was when that next vision of death would arrive. No, thank you. She wasn't putting herself through that pain ever again.

At least working in the hospital allowed some semblance of purpose, an opportunity to perform penance. Here she could make a difference, atone for the devastating knowledge her ability yielded. If she had the power to randomly see the death of people she touched, at least the medical training gave her the ability to save other peoples' lives. Saving someone—anyone—made up for the inevitable deaths she predicted. Her gift might have been easier to manage if she got images when she touched every person, or if she knew which people would trigger her visions, but no, she received sudden, random pain instead. The nasty surprises never got easier, even after years of avoiding hugs, declining to brush her niece's hair, and refusing to kiss her own sister's cheek at her wedding. Allison only risked direct touch when she had no other choice. She only risked touch when she felt emotionally braced, and that wasn't often.

"Aw, thanks for thinking of me, Buddy, but I've got enough on my plate right now. Why don't you get on home? Enjoy your day off."

• • •

A few hours later, an ambulance pulled up to the entrance of the Grande Ronde ER, lights flashing and sirens blaring. Allison raced out of the warm ER into the crisp air, her body heated by zips of adrenaline. Already gloved up, she met the patient as the EMTs called for help to unload his gurney from the ambulance. The patient moaned and strained against the backboard straps, then lapsed into unconsciousness. Her five-second assessment as they rolled him into the ER was grim: facial trauma, bleeding flap of scalp that was thankfully still attached, loss of consciousness.

"Are there more victims?" she asked an EMT.

The EMT maneuvered the gurney into the small trauma room. "No, just this lucky guy. His car launched over the interstate barrier and down the embankment. He almost went into the creek."

She breathed a sigh of relief. At least she could focus on one patient. "Do we know anything about this guy? Name? Age? Any medical problems?"

The EMT shrugged. "State troopers told us to get him to the hospital and they'd look for ID later."

Then she'd have to work blind. "Let's get a cross-table C-spine stat. And a trauma panel."

Nurses and EMTs carefully transferred the patient, who lay still and silent, secured on the backboard, to the ER bed. The staff unstrapped the man and quickly cut away his bloodstained T-shirt and faded jeans. An empty knife holster on his lower leg gave her pause, but her curiosity disappeared with the rest of his clothing. At last, they had him draped in a hospital gown and covered with a starched hospital sheet.

Allison placed the bell of her stethoscope over the man's broad chest. Normal heart rate. Lungs clear. Pressing on his ribcage dusted with dark hair and his flat abdomen, she found no crepitus or rigidity. She inhaled deeply.

A nurse raised an eyebrow. "Anything?"

"No trace of alcohol or drugs." All she smelled was the metallic scent of blood and a typical male essence like almonds and very faint cologne.

With the Velcro straps off, the staff carefully logrolled him to one side, a maneuver that kept his neck, spine, and hips in safe alignment so she could evaluate his back for injuries. Once the staff rolled him back onto the backboard and re-secured the wide straps, radiology personnel shot a quick neck x-ray.

A final assessment of his muscled extremities completed the exam. She felt oddly flushed, like his skin radiated too much heat. Strange.

When she touched him, a vibration flowed through her gloved hands. She had never gotten a vision through gloves. Then again, she'd never gotten a warning signal, either. What the hell was going on here? The vibration jolted up her arms.

Oh God, not now. Please wait until I finish treating this man. Please.

"Do we have a set of vitals?" she asked.

Her patient breathed on his own, unlabored. An old, scratched watch with a dried leather band was fastened around his thick, tanned wrist. Despite the horrific bruises over his body, only his head injury needed intervention. Damn it, she had to examine his wound. She shook her hand, hesitated, then took a deep breath and braced herself. When she lifted the palm-sized flap of scalp, it bled into his dark hair until she taped the gauze back down. She could repair the wound after the CT scan. Jerking her hand away from the buzzing sensation, she pulled off her gloves and replaced them with a clean pair.

She stepped away from her patient and relaxed. Maybe this man's injuries weren't as life threatening as she had initially thought.

The EMT frowned. "Blood pressure is one thirty over ninety, pulse eighty, respiration sixteen, temperature…107?"

"Okay." She stared at the EMT. "Wait. What? Could you retake that temperature, please? That can't be right."

"Ma'am, I already rechecked it with a different machine. It's 107.3 to be exact."

With her heart thudding, she searched the unconscious man for obvious signs of infection or malignant hyperthermia from drug use, anything to explain the temperature reading.

"Start him on IV fluids and get a cooling blanket hooked up."

Screw those visions, she had to touch him again. She needed to figure out what was wrong with this patient before his brain fried.

She eased his eyes open and flashed her penlight. Normal pupillary responses. The deep brown, almost black color of his eyes surprised her with their darkness. His open eye locked onto hers and focused, at the same time a blast of vibration drilled from his face through her hand.

The depth of that gaze pulled her like a particle into a black hole. Her heart expanded then contracted, and her breath caught. Vertigo washed over her. She grabbed the IV pole for balance. The rush of vision took hold, blocking out all sound, like voices obscured by a stiff wind. Faces swam too quickly to make out details. Far in the distance of her mind's eye, the focus sharpened onto a man. She could see—

A radiology tech tapped her on the arm. "Doc? Doc?"

Allison moved her hand away. The patient's eye fell closed, and the vortex sensation ebbed.

For the space of two breaths, she felt like a woman surfacing from under water. "Yes?"

"C-spine x-ray is here for your review, and CT is warmed up and ready if this guy's okay to go." The tech passed her a plastic film.

The nurses turned on the water-cooling blanket now draped over the man. Allison could run him through the scanner with the blanket on top of him. But damn it, why was his temperature so high? Broken neck? Head injury?

She lifted the film to the light. No obvious vertebral fracture, so it was safe to move the patient. "Sure thing. I'll go with you."

Once they arrived in the CT room, the staff transferred the man's backboard into the scanner, handling the man with ease, though to look at him, he must have been 200 pounds of solid muscle. This guy gave Captain America a run for his money.

The machine whirred and hummed. Images of his head, thorax, and abdomen slowly downloaded onto the computer screen. Allison leaned forward. No obvious internal bleeding or spinal injuries. No chest or abdomen damage. The overview scan revealed callus formation on his skull, forearm, and ribs, no doubt from old, healed fractures. A few minutes later, the standard scan images appeared. Where she'd noted callus formations before, now there were none. These new scans belonged to a man with no previous fractures. But how?

She glanced between the crash victim and his inconsistent scans. How did a man crash at fifty-five miles per hour and destroy his vehicle without so much as a hairline fracture? And what would explain the hyperthermia?

Allison rubbed her tight neck muscles. "What do you think? I'm not a radiologist, but it looks good to me."

The tech gave the okay sign and put a finger to his lips. "I'll have the radiologist call in a few minutes with the official word. This guy was lucky."

"Yeah, lucky." She stared at the screen and then back to the enigma on the other side of the lead glass window.

When the staff moved him back to the trauma room, his feet hung over the end of the gurney. He had to be well over six feet tall, maybe mid-thirties, probably a healthy guy. So why the temperature? Why the ghosts on the CT scan?

She reviewed the labs. White cell count was normal. Okay, so no infection. Drug screen negative. And the CT was negative, so the hyperthermia wasn't due to brain damage. Her pulse sped up as she called for the nurse to start cooled IV fluids. She had to try something to help this man, but damned if she knew what the hell she was treating. Shivers skittered up and down her neck, part frustration and part fear for this man's life.

When things don't add up in the ER, people end up dead.

Marcie poked her head into the doctor's work area. "Teleradiology's on the phone." Allison picked up the line, ready for her colleague to shed light on the mystery of this patient.

"Hi, Al, it's Becca Lawson in Baker City."

"What do you see?"

"Nothing much. What was the mechanism of injury?"

"Car went down the bank off the interstate, rolled a couple times. Restrained passenger, stable in the ER, with a head lac that I'll sew up in a few." She paused. "Oh, and a temperature reading of 107. I can't find any reason for that. He should at least be sweating and seizing by now, with markers of muscle breakdown. Yet there's nothing on lab. You see anything to explain it on your side?"

"No, his head is fine. There's some swelling near the head wound and some facial bruises. I presume he's black and blue?"

"Uh-huh."

261

"His neck and spine are clear, no swelling, no fracture. Abdomen and chest are clear." She whistled low. "Are you sure you've got the right patient? I'd say this guy cheated death."

"It's the right guy. Anything to explain the hyperthermia? Maybe something in the midbrain?"

"Hmm." Taps and mouse clicks transmitted through the phone. "Nothing. No blood, no swelling. Did you check your thermometer?"

Allison blew an exasperated breath. "Yes, it's reading correctly."

"Don't know." Dr. Lawson chuckled. "This is why I have the computer screen and not a stethoscope."

"Ugh. Thanks, Becca." She set down the phone and pressed her fingers to the bridge of her nose.

A nurse's scream shattered the silence.

In the mood for more Crimson Romance?
Check out *Cravings by Lynn Crandall* at *CrimsonRomance.com*.

Printed in the United States
By Bookmasters